THE Gift AND THE Crown

The Gift and the Crown

Jerry Kuttler

Copyright © 2021 by Jerry Kuttler.

All rights reserved. No part of this book may be reproduced in any form or by any electronic or mechanical means, including information storage and retrieval systems, without permission in writing from the publisher, except by reviewers, who may quote brief passages in a review.

ISBN: 978-1-63821-635-3 (Paperback Edition)
ISBN: 978-1-63821-636-0 (Hardcover Edition)
ISBN: 978-1-63821-634-6 (E-book Edition)

Some characters and events in this book are fictitious. Any similarity to real persons, living or dead, is coincidental and not intended by the author.

Book Ordering Information

Phone Number: 315 288-7939 ext. 1000 or 347-901-4920
Email: info@globalsummithouse.com
Global Summit House
www.globalsummithouse.com

Printed in the United States of America

Chapter 1

It was a damp early spring day mid-May. The year was 1865. The trees hadn't yet budded. Esmira looked around. She couldn't get her thoughts off of the burial of a great friend and foreman of her E & J Stud Farm that she had known for thirty years. Not only was he a great friend and companion but he was greatly respected for his craft. He was the last horse whisperer that she knew. He died in his mid-sixties and was at peace. Esmira was twenty years younger than Jim and he was her deceased husband's best friend. After the loss of her husband seven years ago Jim became a friend that she could consult with, not only about the stud farm but about personal stuff as well. Whenever she was teary eyed and lonely his words would settle her down. She could always count on his friendship and he became her companion through the many trials since her husband's death. That was one of the reasons she missed him so much, not only was he the best horse whisperer in the state, he was also her one and only true friend.

She looked outside the kitchen window and noticed the stallions all seventeen of them gathered up to the east fence. There the funeral procession was driving up to the place where they would bury Jim. Even the stallions looked teary eyed and sad, maybe this was their way of saying good bye to him as well.

She had to hurry and get out to the funeral area. The trail leading up to the small cemetery was beginning to fill up, with the people that admired Jim for his friendship and horse whispering talent. They knew Jim had a special quality that brought and to kept people close to him, not only in life but in death as well. Jim was a type of person that would give his shirt off his own back if he thought it would help another human being. Esmira went over to the east fence and instructed the funeral people that she was ready for the service to begin. It seemed like everything was in a rush and moving way to fast. It was only nine o'clock am and soon Jim would be buried and the life that she had known would be gone forever. Soon she would be looking for a new foreman for the E&J Stud farm and the try outs for this position were to begin after Jim's service today at 1:00 this afternoon. She knew what she was looking for a man that could handle himself as well as the horses. Esmira hoped the men who were trying out were better than the last bunch of cowboys that had shown up demonstrating their skills. The last lot looked like they had just been introduced to horses and what Esmira was looking for was a man that could read horses as well as people. Surely there was a man out there with better talent then what she had recently seen. Her mind was racing with everything she had to accomplish with Jim's death and the future of her farm and her horses. She had to clear her head long enough to get through Jim's service and burial procession. As they lowered Jim into the ground and everybody tossed either flowers or dirt in a friendly manner onto the casket, Esmira noticed the line was coming to an end and the last gentlemen carried a silver bucket with coarse dark dirt inside, he emptied the bucket and made the sign of the cross and said a heartfelt good bye. Esmira noticed that he was teary eyed. She noticed that he appeared to be feeling as distraught as she was and came over and introduced herself. She stated "I don't believe we met". He stated in a low masculine voice that his name was Jeremy. She asked him "Are you from around these Wyoming hills" and he said "No", that he was from Colorado. Esmira thought to herself, there was something special about this gentleman.

Esmira had her curiosity peaked. It had been a long time since someone or something had peaked her interest. This gentleman held himself with poise and confidence. Time was just flying by! Before this man got away, she had to find out who he was! It was 12:45 and almost time to make her way over to the Gymkhana for the foreman try outs. She viewed the cowboys ready with their saddles. She noticed that most of the cowboys looked like they had their eyes wide open. She couldn't tell if they were gawking at her or her stallions. Esmira was a well-built lady and very attractive and not more than a mere five foot one, her build was vivacious and curvy, her measurements caught everyone's eye. But that wasn't the kicker. She always wore blouses or dresses all the way up to the neckline. Esmira knew she was picturesque to look at and had to be careful around men she didn't know especially now that Jim was gone. That was a blessing in disguise. No one ever thought of her as the rugged and determined woman she was.

"**Well,** let's go" said Esmira, as one after another of the copious rugged looking cowboys tried their skills with her black and Roan stallions. Many were thrown off within seconds of putting their saddle on the horse's back. The next cowboy, number fourteen got up and chose an appaloosa to demonstrate his and horse sense, sort to speak. This appaloosa was Esmira's one and only and was known to be high strung and rough to ride. To Esmira's shock and surprise this cowboy made it past the eight seconds required for a successful ride. Esmira thought to herself, there must be a better way to make a living, fourteen cowboys and only one successful ride, where have all the good cowboys gone? Number fifteen got up and made it six seconds and was thrown into the fence. There was only one more rider. As the last cowboy got up to show off his skills there was something about him that caught Esmira's eye she looked at him again. She noticed his chiseled firm body and his muscular build. He didn't look over five foot ten but his chest muscles were huge and defined as well as his biceps that made him appear strong enough to handle the horses as well as other things that she had not thought about in a very long time. Esmira noticed this man taking his time and wondered what he was doing when he should have been getting the horse ready to ride. "What are you waiting for" Esmira shouted out? Jeremy grabbed the Palomino, put his saddle on his back and lead him around the gymkhana. He then put a gunny sack over his head and led him around some more. For what seemed like eternity he was saying something to the horse. This was very similar to what Jim used to do. Esmira watched Jeremy slowly take the gunny sack off the horse's head as he was stroking his neck. Jeremy got on the horse. The horse bucked twice but then settled down.

Esmira was shocked! No handler had ever paraded around the arena like that before and especially with the palomino. "Hey" she yelled," in excitement, "you've got the job". As her emerald green eyes looked into his sky blue eyes, she continued to say "Be able to start tomorrow and put Blondie up in the barn." As the other cowboys went grumbling away, Jeremy introduced himself to Esmira and she recognized him for the funeral procession earlier in the day. Jeremy finally made his way to the stall and found a curry brush and started to curry the stallion down. Esmira came around the corner and asked "what are you doing?" Jeremy replied "The most important part about riding an animal is taking care of it afterwards. When you show respect to the animal, you will always know that the animal will take care of you." Jeremy tried hard not to stare at Esmira's beauty as she patted and firmly stroked the animal. It surprised him that he noticed this. It had been awhile since a women had caught his interest. Esmira said "I like your style" and thought to herself I must be dreaming, I wonder if he can handle the bedroom like he handles the horses, then blushed at her own thoughts. Jeremy humbly said "Thank you". Esmira said "I'll see you at six o'clock sharp. Don't keep me waiting" as she looks at his behind and thinks what a nice butt!

The next morning Jeremy arrived at five-thirty and greeted all seventeen of the stallions by six o'clock. One could say that he was in the right place because the stallions were not stirring at all. Esmira walked thru the barn door wearing an orange and green dress with her riding boots on. Only she knows that what she's wearing underneath the dress and there is nothing... She selects the cloth saddle and saddles a roan. Jeremy takes out Blondie again and follows Esmira as she says "let's ride."

They head up to the apple orchard, where Esmira has a spot picked out amongst the trees. Since Esmira is but five one she can't reach the apples she asks Jeremy if he wouldn't mind picking the apple. Within seconds Jeremy puts his hand under her bottom and lifts her to the apple. Esmira is shocked. She had no idea of this kind of strength, as she is literally in the palm of his hand, if he only knew how excited and emotional she was feeling. Jeremy innocently asks " can I help you" referring to the picnic, as he sets her down his arm accidently brushes across her full breast and he says "Oh, I'm sorry" and Esmira reply's in a breathless gasp "don't worry about it".

So Esmira asks "where did you learn your gift"? Referring to his magnificent build, however Jeremy thinks she is talking about his whispering to horses so he replies "from Jim." "No" Esmira says" the gift of body building." "Oh" Jeremy says "that comes naturally by just working out on the farm. It must be in the genes". Esmira states as she looks at his physique and the powerful play of his muscles as they ripple under the snug fit of his jeans and chambray shirt " it must be" she thinks to herself. Her mind wanders with thoughts of Jeremy's magnificent body and she thinks to herself "I know it has been seven years since my husband has died, and that long since I've been in a man's arms, but this man appears too good to be true"!

Jeremy has always had an immense respect for the large horses, so his way of saying thank-you was to groom them. While Jeremy was in his own world grooming Blondie he didn't notice Esmira come into the stable? Nor did he notice Esmira reach under the belly of Blondie to accidently brush his waist and then shyly reply "Oh, I'm sorry." Jeremy was surprised at Esmira's playfulness and responded in a low sensual voice "I'm surprised and pleased by the feel of your hands on my body". As Jeremy lifts Esmira on Blondie his rough hands slides down to her luscious breasts and touches them so very lightly before his hands drift down below her skirts and Jeremy says "wait, let's do this right". Jeremy asks Esmira "what do you really want from this partnership?" As her soft and supple feet roam to his waist she says to her astonishment, "Jeremy I want to say I love you, but love is a deep feeling and I feel more for you right now than I did my husband, for fifteen years. So I am going to say it with meaning. I love you! There was a short pause then Jeremy spoke up and said "I am glad that you are able to communicate your feelings. My question is are you sure, because I have deep feelings for you too? As he lifts Esmira off the horse so she is standing right next to him Esmira feels relief and is overjoyed. She knew what she felt for Jeremy was real. Jeremy gives Esmira an approving appraisal and finally rests on her beautiful face and says "not only do I care for you, but I love you too"! Esmira steps closer and presses her body tightly against his waist and reaches out to hug him. Jeremy presses her firmly to his hard body as her heart pounds rhythmically against him. Jeremy reassures her that everything is ok. He lifts her up so they are the same height and kisses her breathlessly. Esmira mouth opens wide to devour his tongue as he strokes her shoulder. The heat just rifles thru her body as an uncontrollable urge. Esmira knows she wants more. Jeremy knows he wants more but would rather have a relationship that lasts. Jeremy carefully lifts Esmira away from his raging body and says "As much as I want you, I want you to be sure of what you're doing and are not rushed into a decision you may regret later. Jeremy's body was screaming for attention, Esmira met his eyes she knew he was a keeper. She had never felt these strong feelings before not even with her husband who she knew she had loved. She wondered if it was wrong to feel this much emotion about a man she had known for such a short time. She didn't think so. If the opportunity presented itself she would make sure that it would be the most sincere advance possible. She would enjoy it. Jeremy came to her and gently turned her around she asked him "do you need some attention" and found no answer coming because he was already kissing her. Esmira knew she was going to let him have her. Jeremy held her tightly as he stated "Do me a favor; let me know how you feel tomorrow. I can promise you I'm not going anywhere. "

It was a new day and Jeremy had been in the barn since five thirty in the morning. He was doing some horse whispering to the appaloosa. Time got away and he noticed it was six fifteen. OOPS he was supposed to meet Esmira in the TAC room at six. He hustled over there and almost caught the TAC door in the face as Esmira came storming out. She backed up a few steps and said "if your think because of what happened yesterday that you have special privileges, you better think again" Jeremy interrupts her to say "I see the barn door from here and if you want me to go, I will start packing right now. I have been here since five thirty talking to the appaloosa and time got away from me. So for the record do I stay or do I go?"

Esmira didn't have a quick answer. She also knew that for a beautiful woman she wasn't dumb. If she said go he would be the kind of person that would never look back. Then she would have to start looking for a foreman all over again. The pickings were very slim. If she said stay they can at least work on some things concerning the ranch. The way Jeremy was with people and animals it would be foolish to let him go. Jeremy was right on how she would feel the next day. It was an indescribable feeling of joy and happiness mixed in. She had never felt that way her whole life. She still felt like her whole body was in heaven... After fifteen years of marriage she never felt an emotion like that. She could still feel pleasure and remember every action and thought of getting there. Jeremy interrupted Esmira thinking and said Ma'am is everything ok"? "Yes" Esmira said "and you are staying. So let's hurry, we've got a lot to do. I will get the Roan if you want to get the appaloosa. Oh, by the way, the answer to your question about yesterday is, I still feel good!"

Esmira and Jeremy went to the stalls to shoe the two horses. Esmira tapped in the two front shoes in no time, and then went to the back. As she lifted up the Roans leg she peered thru two horses and saw Jeremy's' legs as he wass currying the appaloosa. Esmira thought of how one man could provide so much pleasure. Times a wasting, she went over to hurry Jeremy and said "let's hurry with those shoes, so we can ride to the lower forty and check the water." Jeremy lifted her up on the back of the appaloosa and said "well what took you so long as his hands skims over her breast and down to her waist, while he looked into her emerald green eyes for an answer "you have already shooed the appaloosa" Esmira asks. Jeremy pulls his hands down by his thighs and says "Yes" and then adds "if I figured you right we will have a long ride, so I just wanted to get the appaloosa ready"! Esmira smiles from ear to ear. Not because she has been pleased before breakfast but because she does like the way this man takes care of business.

Jeremy takes her down softly from the appaloosa and places her on the ground and asks "are you ready?" Esmira has to gather her wits, because she is feeling very emotional. Jeremy interrupts her again and says "Ma'am is everything ok?" Esmira straightens her blouse and says "why yes, I'm ok. Let's mount! Jeremy turns and straddles his appaloosa and thinks WOW, I love that word mount....maybe again sometime.

Chapter 2

They both ride out of the barn and take an hour ride down to the lower forty to inspect the water. She explains to him that when she lets the stallions out for a good run, this is their watering hole. She goes on about capturing the white mare that has been troubling the herd for the last three years. Jeremy interrupts her and says "if I am thinking right, I'll have her by sundown! Let me try something". He unsaddles and unbridles the appaloosa and gives him a pat on the hind end and says "see ya".

Esmira is horrified. She noticed what Jeremy did and she comes running over to Jeremy yelling, "What are you doing? That is one of my best stallions, well behaved well nurtured and Jim took three years getting the horse right where he wanted." She slaps him right in the chest. Jeremy grabs her hand with his left hand and scoops her up by the right hand and plants a kiss right to her lips' Before Esmira can pull back she sinks toward him with another kiss. Esmira opens her mouth and devours Jeremy's tongue. She hasn't quite figured it out yet what makes Jeremy so attractable. Jeremy carries her right over to the pond and walks up to his waist into the pond and says politely to her. "You need to calm down or I will release you into the water." She flings her arm around his neck and kicks both of her feet to the other arm, so he can carry her. Esmira says "Would you please get me out of here and explain yourself!"

Jeremy says "well, it's really common horse sense! From what you have told me, you have brought all seventeen stallions down here at the same time. This action has scared the young Philly away. She didn't know what to do. The filly's curiosity has not been peaked. By telling your appaloosa to go and swatting him on the behind, I gave the signal to the filly that the stallion was all hers. By me taking care of the appaloosa this morning and currying him down, I have his complete trust, by Sunset he will be back with the Philly over there at that tree" as he points to the west tree. Esmira speaks up "how do you know"? Jeremy reply's "Well that tree is her tree. By watching the Philly she keeps going back to the tree as though she lost something there. The horses will have their romp and she will go back to the tree with her giving herself to him for life." Esmira laughs and says" we'll see!"

Jeremy takes his handkerchief and dabs off his forehead and says "it's getting warm here." He takes off his shirt, tosses it to the ground and walks into the pond. Esmira is only seeing his back, but even that looks good and strong and AHH! Esmira says "what are you doing?" Jeremy says" cooling off, I will be awhile!" Esmira says "you feel pretty confident don't you?" Jeremy strides toward the bank and puts his face right between her breasts and says "I feel very confident" Jeremy lifts his head and says I am hot, I don't know about you but I am going for a swim." The water is crystal clear and just the right temperature, Jeremy disrobes. Esmira is not quite sure how to take all this in. Jeremy must be real comfortable about his sexuality to just take his clothes off. Suddenly, Esmira is feeling the same way. She thinks to herself. I have said I loved him. There is no one else around. What the heck. Esmira also disrobes. This surprises Jeremy but he won't stop her, after all he does love her. Jeremy is fascinated by her lovely body; he has never seen such beauty before. Everything about her is perfect, from her beautifully formed breasts, to her tiny waist and slightly rounded hips. Everything a man would want and more, WOW, was the only way to describe how he felt. They both went for a swim, Jeremy plunged underneath the water and came up behind her back and said "you sure are pretty, the most beautiful thing I've ever seen", Esmira bashfully replies "thank you, you are pretty handsome yourself" as she turns around to face him she takes her right hand and skims across his chest and says "where did you get this muscle". Jeremy says just working on the farm... Esmira thinks of how life was just a week ago, no foreman no direction. Now with Jeremy as foreman she believes she can make the stud farm work. Speaking of studs this guy knows his way around. He swims toward the bank as Esmira follows and as he gets out Esmira looks in amazement at how well his body is chiseled and thinks to herself, "I am glad he decided to stay". Jeremy helps her beautiful body up on the bank and pulls her close to him as he gives her a big kiss and helps her get her belongings back in the right place. Her emerald green eyes look at him with gratitude as he pulls her even closer, he points to the tree. There stands the appaloosa with the white mare. Esmira and Jeremy; both get dressed. Jeremy walks over with bridle and rope in hand and bridles the appaloosa and makes a make shift bridle for the mare. Jeremy thinks to him "It will be an enjoyable walk back to the barn". He asks Esmira" are you ready to mount" and she smiles and says "yes".

As they were heading back Esmira's curiosity had peaked. So she asked Jeremy "how did you know, that she would come back?" Jeremy responded," remember yesterday when I was late meeting with you. I had already talked to the horses and curried the appaloosa down; I had shown immense respect to the horses. That is something they never forget. These horses are known for their loyalty. I gave them a chance to prove it, especially when it came to a one on one basis". Esmira says "in the short time I have known you; you have shown me a total different way of handling my horses. Where did you learn this gift"? "Well, that's a different story for another day" says Jeremy.

"So just for my curiosity" says Jeremy," on a scale of one to ten, how am I doing."" Fifteen" says Esmira, "but don't let that go to your head. Back at the ranch we have a lot more work to do. I am already aware that you know that and from what I have seen so far you fit the bill". "Well I have a surprise for you", says Jeremy. Esmira thinks to herself, from what I have seen so far what else can surprise me? Jeremy says "the mare is already pregnant; it will be interesting to see the colors of the colt!" "Whoa, whoa, whoa. How do you know that" asked Esmira? "I will be happy to go into it on a later date" says Jeremy. "Let's get the horses back to the ranch before it starts to rain."

The rain was just starting to come down. They knew not to rush the horses. So for the next two hundred yards they just walked in.

Everything was soaked, but everyone was safe. Jeremy took both the appaloosa and the mare inside the barn to a single stall. Then he grabbed Esmira's roan and brought him into a different stall. He unsaddled the Roan reached for the curry brush and started to brush the whole animal. Jeremy then took the bridle off and started to talk to the roan as if he was a person. Then he said good-bye and went to the appaloosa and the mare. Jeremy pretended not to see Esmira out of the corner of his eye. He started to curry the mare. He started asking questions about her afternoon with the appaloosa, just as if she went on her first date. From the way the mare was standing he assumed that her afternoon was just as good as his afternoon. The horse shook her head up and down He brushed her mane out and then decided to go the extra mile and braid her hair. It wasn't exactly for her; it was for the appaloosa stud. The mare looked outstanding. Now it was time for the appaloosa to be combed out. He approached the appaloosa in a shy tone because although he was probably the best stud they had, he didn't want to brag about it, especially not in mixed company.

"Boo" Said Esmira. As the horses shied a little bit, Jeremy's' nerves were solid as steel. Esmira knew that when he curried the horses he had a habit of having his shirt unbuttoned half way down. She moved in, toward his chest and kissed his chest and patted his warm muscled body. She moved her hand away from his arousal and back to his chest where she kissed some more. Jeremy held her head gently while she kissed him because it drove him wild. Gosh he wondered what he did to deserve all this. She stopped kissing one side of his chest and slowly moved to the other side. After what seemed like minutes, Esmira stopped and said to Jeremy "if you have some time, can you come up to the house?" Jeremy said "sure, give me about ten and I will be up". Jeremy went over to the end stall where there was a pump and trough. He stripped down to bear naked and thoroughly washed his legs, his chest and his face. He stepped away from the pump and began to shave. He dresses in his coal black pants on, his light blue and black flannel shirt and his eight hundred dollar boots that he won in competition a few years back. He headed up to the house with a bunch of flowers. Jeremy knocked on the door. Esmira opened the door and actually gawked at how nice he was dressed. Jeremy spoke up "ma'am is it ok if I come in?" "Yes by all means, where were my manners." Says

Esmira." "Why you look exceptionally nice, come in, come in." The table was set with an eight pound roast, yams, applesauce and corn bread. There were also two candles and a chilled bottled of wine. Jeremy speaks "My you look nice yourself". This is the first time he has seen her in anything but jeans and boots. To his delight Esmira is wearing a Pink dress with a ruffled neckline! "Thank you" Esmira says "let's sit down for a wonderful dinner." They both sit down almost side by side, Jeremy is ready to eat. Esmira says "I have a lot of questions, the more I ask, the more I will learn. I have had the papers drawn up legally inviting you to be a partner with me to the E&J Stud Farm. This will be 50-50 partnership with no controlling interest on either side. Which in English means you fail I fail or you win I win". To Jeremy's bashful side he would rather sign the papers without anyone else in the room so he asks for a different glass as Esmira goes in to get a different glass, Jeremy signs the paperwork. Jeremy then asks Esmira "Would you like to dance to celebrate our partnership" To his surprise Esmira says "I don't know how!" Jeremy says "don't worry I'll show you how." Esmira agrees. Jeremy shows her where to put her arms and where the hands meet in an old fashioned dance like a waltz. He goes into the box routine left, right, right, left and then into a swirl. Esmira does pretty well for the first time, but he adjusts to a slower dance where they are just holding each other and mildly rotating in a circle. To Jeremy's astonishment he feels his body quickly responding to the closeness of Esmira's softness where it presses against him. He abruptly interrupts the dance and says" let's eat." He walks her over to the table and before he pulls out her chair, he gives her a sweltering kiss to release some of his building desire. Esmira reaches for the arm of her chair and accidently bumps his raging body and says "have you had a rough day?" Jeremy says "No" as he helps Esmira get her chair pushed in while staring right down her neckline to her beautiful breasts. Jeremy thought to himself they were begging to be touched to be fondled; Jeremy had an extremely hard time resisting putting those thoughts into action. Jeremy thought to himself I have to be gentlemen. Her ruffled neckline looked beautiful as he bent down to kiss her. Esmira fought the desire to touch his aroused manhood and said "darling, let's eat." They ate dinner with thoughts of being in each other's arms.

Chapter 3

Jeremy helped clear off the table as dinner was done. He set the last plate into the sink and to his surprise Esmira's gentle hands came around his waist. He turned around and kissed her as she stared at his amazing manly body and wondered what thrilling moments awaited her. The thought that Esmira had of undoing his pants had to be for another time for now she had to be a lady. She moved her hands down to his knees and felt that they were tight. Jeremy put his hands around her bottom and began to massage it. Esmira eyes light up like a Christmas tree, what a wonderful feeling. She said "excuse me I will be right back". Esmira went to get some warm towels and returned. She then rubbed his legs and his backside with the towels. She waited till they cooled a little and then she massaged his whole body. Esmira then allowed Jeremy the same pleasure of massaging her entire body. OMG thought Esmira this is better than sex. They enjoyed one another's bodies until they were worn out. WOW! She thought, do I have to pinch myself or is this a dream? Jeremy picked Esmira up and took her to the bedroom. They both looked at each other tenderly and as if in unionsion both stood up and gently unbuttoned each other shirts. They sat down on the bed and cuddled. To Esmira this was the most sensuous time. The fact that his warm body was so close to hers, the fact that it had been seven years since she had a man with her. Esmira paused but only for a minute as she lay back on the bed. Jeremy lay down beside her as chemistry or magic started to happen. Jeremy says if I hurt you will you let me know. Esmira says "yes, Jeremy knew she was ready. . He touched her womanhood and it felt like it was on fire with all juices flowing, he continued in like manner until he released inside her. Jeremy knew as soon as he released himself inside her that she would be pregnant. Jeremy knew that this was the person that he wanted to share all the joy and consequences of life with. Jeremy was ready to go over to his room which was just off side the tack room, when Esmira said "don't go please stay". Jeremy said "is this the boss talking or my lover?" Esmira laughed, "I would really like to say it is your boss talking, but since you have already signed the papers, this is your lover. Come, oh how I love that word. Come to bed honey!" Jeremy disrobed and went to bed.

It was early dawn and Esmira rolled over and felt that Jeremy wasn't there. She got excited. She thought where is my lover? Jeremy had already talked to the stallions curried the buckskin and was back inside making coffee when his honey showed up. Jeremy said "good morning love, it's a beautiful morning what did you have planned?" Well, she said "you have seen the lower forty, I think it's time you see the upper twenty. It has been awhile since I have been up there. There used to be a fifteen by fifteen cabin shack that would hold around six cowboys. They would either being putting up fence that the buffalo kept knocking over or they got tired of doing the fencing and killed a few buffalo. After that fiasco we had to let the neighbors know that those kind of cowboys were no longer employed at our ranch" "How long ago was that" Jeremy asked. Esmira said "That was over four years ago" "Well it sounds as if we got some work ahead of us" says Jeremy. "I have your roan ready and I am taking out the buckskin today." So Esmira and Jeremy started the two hour ride to the upper twenty.

Upon reaching the upper twenty they saw that the cabin had a few boards from the roof missing and they hoped that the inside looked better. They put their horses around in the make shift stable and headed for the house. Jeremy told Esmira to stay back, something didn't look right. He opened the door and found a two hundred pound cub with his nose in an old coffee can. Jeremy banged on the table three times and told the cub to get out as he chased the cub away. Jeremy knew from past experience that whenever a cub is around that the mama bear is not too far off. He went back outside and got Esmira and asked her if everything was ok? Esmira said "you chase away a bear, you saved my life, and you ask me how I feel! Just peachy but thank-you." Jeremy said" well now that we are inside, I found some nails to fix the roof. I wondered if there was a fresh water supply nearby because I could sure use some coffee". "Well" Esmira said," you get to the roof and I will scrounge around for some wood for the stove and see if I can find some water." About half an hour later Jeremy was done fixing the roof. He went inside the cabin but noticed the horses were stirring. He told Esmira that he would be right back just checking on the horses. He went toward the horses and noticed a man on horseback with a rifle pointed directly at his chest. The man asked "what are you doing on my land, youngster"? Jeremy said "Excuse me! What do you mean your land? Any idiot could tell that my fence is up, why you are going over it" Said the stranger. Jeremy responded "I am moving the fence back to its original location. If you take a look at how this growth on the tree grew over, it will tell you that this fence was moved around three years ago. You see it takes a little bit more than moving the boundaries, to try and make a claim. I'll bet you were reading the part on eminent domain, but old timer you forgot to read the rest of the law which states 'if property is kept up for TEN years then you may file an Eminent domain claim against said owner providing the person filing the claim is also the one that has kept property tidy" Said Jeremy.

"Well before we go any further," Jeremy stated "I already know that you tried to move the fence line three years ago. There is just one small thing you forgot. The land dividers were not the fence line but the only two birch trees on the property." Jeremy turns around and a shot was fired from Esmira's' rifle grazing the temple of the old timer. The old timer gallops off. Jeremy ran inside to see if Esmira was ok. She was just taking off her shirt and was complaining how hot it was. Her hair was long enough to cover her breasts, if she wanted them covered. Esmira said to Jeremy that his coffee was ready, and that she wanted to talk as she flipped her hair away from her breasts so Jeremy could see them. Jeremy wanted to be purposeful about this act of love. He knew the longer he looked at her breasts the bigger his arousal would become. So he had to resist the temptation. Esmira walked over and kissed him and said "how do you feel"? Jeremy said "completely aroused, but confident that our time will come." She walked over and got Jeremy a cup of coffee as Jeremy asked "where did you learn to shoot that way." Esmira said "when Jim had time off we would come up here and practice". Jeremy says "wow, he taught you well. After this cup of coffee I will get out and remove those two fence posts and wrap them around the tree like they were three years ago".

Esmira asked" how did you know it was three years ago?" Jeremy said "that was the easy part. By looking at the lacerations in the tree, I could tell that they grew over. I just counted how many times the tree grew over, similar to counting the rings on a tree. My suggestion to you Esmira is I would come up here more often". Esmira interrupts and says "with you being beside me we will have no problem." Jeremy says "Well, let see. The roof has been patched, the lean to stable is ok and the fence posts have been corrected. Not bad for half days work are you ready to head for home honey"? Esmira said "let's ride". With her shirt still off Jeremy said "I don't mind but some neighbors might." So Esmira reluctantly put her shirt on. She loved not wearing the blouse, especially around Jeremy her lover.

They were out on the trail, just walking the horses when a shot rang out. Jeremy slumped to the left side of his horse and gently laid himself down; at this point Esmira was screaming OMG. Jeremy whispered to Esmira "keep the panic button going". Jeremy thought this would draw the perpetrator closer within rifle shot. The horse was lying down with Jeremy's' rifle over its belly and Jeremy lying parallel to the horse. The person came closer within fifty yards and Jeremy took slow aim cocked the trigger and gently squeezed hitting the person dead smack in the forehead, killing him immediately. "WOW! Great shot" exclaimed Esmira "where did you learn how to shoot!" Jeremy said to Esmira "from Jim, should we go bury him? Esmira replied "No. let the buzzards have a good meal. Hopefully people will catch on and leave this part of the territory alone". Esmira and Jeremy mounted their horses and enjoyed the ride home. How did Jeremy know Jim?

Well, finally back to the barn, a home away from home. Jeremy took the Roan and the buckskin and curried them down, then put them in the corral. This time Esmira was watching and asked Jeremy,"

Why; the corral and not the stall". Jeremy replied, "the horses have had to carry us around for the last two hours and while I am fixing you dinner, I wanted to let the horses feel freedom without the saddle 'till after dinner". Esmira asked "Why"? Jeremy said "these horses know that when I curry them down its stall time. I purposely wanted to thank them by giving them corral time. Not only do they appreciate it but they remember it." Esmira asked "Why would you want them to remember it?" Jeremy said "Dear, remember what happened with the appaloosa and the mare?" "Yes" Esmira said. Jeremy said "Well by me taking immense care of them, and them remembering the care, they still have to make the choice of being well cared for or out on the open range foraging for food and becoming mangy looking. I would be willing to bet on an individual basis I could take any of these horses and do the same thing that we did with the appaloosa and they would react the same way"! Esmira said "you sound pretty confident"! Jeremy said "no not really it was just the way I was taught". Esmira said "if I remember right you said Jim taught you. How did you know him?" Jeremy said. "He was my Uncle and every year he would come home for ten days to two weeks and we would experiment with different teaching methods. That's when we found out that I was good at horse whispering." Esmira asks "When did you know?" "It must have been around ten years ago. I was getting tired of getting thrown by the horses and knew there was a different way to handle them. That's when I knew I had this gift" he replied. Esmira jokes "well you have other gifts' as well". Jeremy smiles and says humbly "thank you". This is starting to make sense Esmira thought to herself. Jeremy has the body of a god, the intelligence of a genius and the skills and ability of horse whispering like Jim. He also had the compassion and patience of a saint. "No wonder I have fallen in love with him" she thought to herself.

Jeremy walked up to the house and opened the door to get to the kitchen. He opened the ice box and saw that Esmira had some deer cooked. He noticed she had kraut in the ice box as well and put it on the table. He looked in the cupboard and found some beans to go with the venison and kraut; he put them in the pot and started to stir them. Esmira, came up from behind him and put her soft hands right around his waist and patted him on the butt just as Jeremy was about to say dinner was done. He turned around and gave her a kiss. Jeremy set the table and passed the food to Esmira. They talked about their day and finished up with dinner. Jeremy picked up the dishes and put them in the sudsy water to clean them. Esmira stood right behind Jeremy and since she had a newfangled corset that opened from the front she decided to test it out. She unbuttoned her purple shirt unlaced her corset and tapped Jeremy on the shoulder. Since she was standing on the chair when Jeremy turned around he couldn't help his face being buried in her voluptuous breasts. Jeremy said "oh, excuse me, I didn't know you were that close". Esmira asked "did that bother you" and Jeremy said "not hardly, I was just caught by surprise and it was a good surprise." Esmira didn't think twice about what some people would call heavy petting; especially to the person you have been thru so much with together. Jeremy finished up the dishes and was walking toward the door to leave. Esmira asked "Where are you going?" Jeremy replied "well I was going to look in on the mare and then go to bed!" Esmira shouted back "would you mind taking care of this one and coming to this bed!" Jeremy stopped dead in his tracks, slowly turned around grabbed the bottle of wine from the table and poured a little in his hands and then unbuttoned his shirt. He put the wine on his lips and before he could motion for Esmira to come over, she was planting another kiss. "Honey" Esmira said. "You are fantastic". Let's talk about the race.

Chapter 4

"Which Stallion should we enter in the race next week?" asked Esmira. Jeremy says "the 'black stallion' he also has enough mass in his legs to take on a three quarter mile. I think he will take it but it will be close". "Oh" says Esmira "what makes you say that?" "Just a gut feeling" replies Jeremy "with 5000 dollars on the line I think the maximum entries will be taken the first day. I will take the black one on a quick ride to warm him up" says Jeremy. Meanwhile Esmira with her red lipstick is busy canning pickles. She remembers how her mom made it look so easy. By boiling the brine with her mixture and pouring them over the cucumbers and praying that the lids seal tight, everything will be done. Esmira was one that had to feel like being in the mood and the lipstick was a factor on doing just that. She would only know how they turned out in a couple of weeks by how they tasted. She looked out the window and saw Jeremy in a slow canter with the black one. She opened the door and yelled out "How did he do"? Jeremy raised his thumb to show that the horse warmed up just fine. Now Jeremy thought, if he can stay this fluid at race time he can win. Jeremy decided to take him into the barn and curry him down. This would show appreciation to the black one and he would remember it at race time. Jeremy knew that the week would fly by and if every preparation had not been made entering the race would be worthless.

The day of the race had finally come and all seventeen entries had been logged in. The race would be simple just once around the three quarter mile track and it would be over. Billie was a youngster, on the appaloosa two horses down, who would not shut up about how he was going to win. The master of ceremonies had raised his handkerchief and said "on your mark, get set, go". Bang went the gun and dust was flying everywhere. The black one was in third place; it wasn't time to let him go. The appaloosa was a nose ahead and Billie was giving the horse everything he had. The switch was flying faster than the horse could breathe. There was a roan that was getting pretty winded that was three feet ahead of the black one. The roan started to fall back. There was thirty feet to go and Jeremy let the black one have his head. He flew like the wind! He caught up to the appaloosa and Billie was switching away. They were nose and nose and ten feet to go. Jeremy reached down and petted the black ones neck. The black one remembered about the curry comb and gave the race a final spurt. It almost looked like a dead heat **finish,** but the judge noticed a red spot on the yellow ribbon. He conferred with the other judges. They had come to a conclusion that between the appaloosa and the black one, whoever had the blood on the nose was the winner. They looked at the appaloosa and saw nothing. They looked at the black one and saw the blood stain on his nose. The black one had won the race and the $5000. Jeremy went over to show sportsmanship and Billie wouldn't have a thing to do with it. Billie shouted "cheater, cheater" Jeremy stood his ground and said "Billie, you know that isn't true. If you had not been switching your switch around and hitting my horse in the nose the judge might have called the race another way. There is always next year.

Now it was time to give back to the community. The 5000 dollars they agreed upon should be re-invested in the community. They were not sure if it should go to the sheriff or to the mayor or to a community. What they were thinking about doing was creation a gymkhana where adolescents 13 to 18 could get involved riding horses or taming them on how to be cutting horses, or doing the broncos or the whispering taught by Jeremy. It was a decision that Esmira and Jeremy had to talk about first. Jeremy knew that he had to get the horse down to the barn for an in depth curry. Jeremy thought that Esmira was up at the house.

Jeremy brought the black one in and started to curry him. Esmira was right behind another horse in another stall eyeing Jeremy doing the curry. Suddenly the black stallion moved and Esmira watched the beautiful animal as Jeremy gently stroked it while calming it down. Right close to the stallion was Jeremy and Esmira wondered how soon she could get some of the same attention. Oh! The thought was too much to bear. Just then she chose to go to Jeremy's tack room where the pump was to get a pail of cold water, she unloosened her beige corset and let her clothes fall to the ground. One could see where the corset imprinted on her skin, she splashed herself with cold water to relieve herself of all the heat. The water that sprayed on her nipples felt so comforting. It was quick, soothing and rather enjoyable. She got dressed and walked toward Jeremy. She had to resist the temptation. Jeremy had won the race and as a woman and lover she wanted to suggest "are you feeling lucky?" She wondered what answer she might hear and if it would be the one she wanted. Jeremy turned around with his shirt unbuttoned 3 notches and Esmira put her soft hand to his nipple and began to play with it. Oh, she wondered, do dreams of this magnitude really come true. Was this going to be enough, and then suddenly the horse whined disturbing the scene and romantic mood bringing them both back to reality. The mood was over it was now time for dinner. Over dinner Jeremy and Esmira began to talk about reinvesting the 5,000 dollars. Jeremy thought it worthy of setting up a gymkhana. This is where riders and their horses would run the barrels, run races and do jumping. On the other note Esmira was thinking of a beginning class for people to learn to ride. Jeremy thought that was a good idea. A part of learning to ride would also be about caring and maintenance of the animal especially after one is done riding. Students would be taught how to curry the horses and how to put the bridle and saddle in its proper place also, sportsmanship the act of getting along with your fellow riders. Jeremy had one more idea of bringing a photographer in to take pictures of horses and riders on a before and after basis. After completion of riding lesson if people wanted to know how to go into the bronco riding and the rodeo stage, they would be allowed to do so. Jeremy would also teach the select few who were interested how to horse whisper. Jeremy and Esmira agreed that this would be the proper way to re-invest the 5,000 dollars in a scholarship for the first fifteen people that would sign up.

It was early morning and as usual Jeremy was up. He had curried the stallions and was making breakfast when sleepy-head Esmira walked into the kitchen. To his astonishment Esmira was naked. Jeremy said" good morning. Esmira noticed that Jeremy's fly had popped open.. She carefully ran her hand over his swollen manhood. Jeremy's sensuality made her mind wander with wild ideas about quenching their desires for one another, she wanted to touch and taste him all over. Jeremy saw the desire in her eyes and lost his self-control. They shared their desires for one another and reveled in the pleasure of making love. Jeremy kissed her forehead and asked' why?" Esmira replied with a" why not? I love you. Let's go eat."

Now, my love, would you like to get dressed" Jeremy asked. She replied" do I have to. I would much rather wear my cranberry lipstick and nothing else all day"" Oh!" Said Jeremy "That wouldn't bother me, but I have some things concerning the ranch that I would like to talk to you today". While in town the other day, a complete stranger asked me if we ever wanted to sell one or more of our stallions. I immediately told him that I would have to consult with my business partner before I could give him an answer. He flipped me his business card and his name is Mr. Sullivan. He wanted to use them for racing. My idea, all though I haven't told him yet, is to see if he has any mares that we could do service with. The cost I came up with is 3,000 dollars for one week in our stables. What do you think, Esmira?" Esmira agreed that $3000 would be a fair price. However, she would have to sit down and interview all applicants for stud fee, first. Then, if selected, monies would be paid in full before any services rendered. Esmira suggested "Let's have some contracts printed up ahead of time so we won't have to keep bothering our attorney". "Honey," as she called out to Jeremy. "Let's run a few ads in the surrounding states letting them know that we are opened for business." "Honey" called back Jeremy "I have to go to town tomorrow to let the paper know how we are to invest that $5000. And I will put the ads in at the same time. Does that work for you"? "Sure" sa id Esmira "As long as I get to come along".

Chapter 5

The next morning they got the buck board ready to go to town. Esmira reminded Jeremy that she was bringing lunch, so along the way; if they found a place to stop they could eat. It was pretty near ten o' clock before they reached town. It was also just when the stagecoach was pulling up. Jeremy was near by the coach and being the gentlemen that he is, put down the step and opened the door for the first person that was to come out. Out came a busty brunette with a crimson dress and crimson hat saying "why thank you, could you please show me the undertaker! You see my husband Mr. Sullivan just died out here while trying to conduct business." As she latched onto Jeremy's arm willing to be escorted to the undertaker's, Esmira quickly unhooked them both and said "welcome, this is my husband, and the undertaker is across the street and take the first left." "Oh!" Linda blurted out "I didn't see that the man was taken he wears no ring". Esmira said "he is allergic to them". "Then I must grant my apology. I hope no harm was done," said Linda. My husband's last letter to me was that he was talking to gentlemen by the name of Jeremy about his horses and the like, do you know where I might catch up with him?" Esmira said "you just did!" "Our business of the stud farm, sometimes reaches out to racing. What are your intentions?" Linda noticed that Esmira was decked out in a light blue plaid flannel shirt and black pants with her expensive boots on. Linda asked "so who takes care of the business side?" Jeremy stated "we both do" As if the glossy stare from Linda was supposed to get a reaction. Esmira buts in and says" I tell you what, you have the undertaker to take care of, and we have our business to attend to, so how about if we were to meet up in an hour and a half?" Linda says "that will suit me just fine" . "I don't like her" says Esmira. "No need to worry my sweet thing. Two can play this game. But I want you to know if she is going to play this game I will guarantee you she will lose. That's my promise to you as a husband and a partner".

Linda entered in to the undertaker's office; he was busy topping off Mr. Don Sullivan's casket. Linda went into the 'woe is me' act. She fanned herself, she tugged on her corset in front, she smoothed her hair, and then she asked "is that him? How much do I owe you"? The undertaker said "that will be $20". She asked him if he could take off the lid for one last look. The undertaker took off the lid and Linda took off his left shoe and found a twenty dollar bill and gave it to the undertaker. Before she left she thanked the undertaker and said "thank God he was always prepared"!

Linda met up with Jeremy and Esmira as planned. Esmira watched Linda's eyes as she talked about business to Jeremy. She noticed that Linda's gaze was fixed on Jeremy's magnificent body. The more she talked about checking out the horses the more she started checking out Jeremy. When the subject of stud fees came up Linda appeared to be more interested in Jeremy's abilities than any of the horses. Esmira had had enough. She suddenly stood right in front of Jeremy stopping Linda's flirtatious behavior and point blank asked her "would you really like to see the horses"? Linda replied, "Sure I would, immediately". Esmira chimed in and said, "The earliest we will be back at our ranch will be 8:00am tomorrow". "Oh, that can't be" said Linda. "I have other things I must put together". Jeremy spoke up." Well you heard my wife. Shall I put you down for 8:00 or 9:00 tomorrow." "Make it 8:00" Linda said! "Thank you for following my lead" said Esmira. "Why did you do it" she asked. "So you can follow mine tomorrow" Jeremy replied. "You will have to give me my head tomorrow and follow my lead if we are to successfully beat her at her own game. Do you think you can do it" Asked Jeremy. "Whatever it takes"! Said Esmira,

The day was a hot one. The temperature must have been in the nineties when Esmira and Jeremy rode up to the lake for a picnic. As they approached the lake Esmira remembered of an isolated place where she and Jeremy could go to have lunch and a cool swim! It was up the road about a mile. They finally got there. As Jeremy was laying out the picnic basket, Esmira stripped out of her clothes and began swimming naked in the little pond. Esmira was enjoying her cool swim when all of a sudden she felt something slithering in the water. She didn't realize until it was too late that there was a snake making its way around her ankles. Esmira suddenly let out a blood curdling scream. Jeremy came running with pistol drawn and shot the bull snake after it had slithered away from Esmira and was coming off the bank. Esmira swam back to shore and hurriedly slipped back into her clothes. Within minutes people came up on horseback to see what had happened. Esmira clothes was soaking wet. Before anyone on horseback could speak up Jeremy volunteered information that it was just a snake, as he showed it to them. Jeremy wasn't going anywhere else without eating he was starved. Esmira laid out all the food and quickly Jeremy reached for the piece of chicken he always reached for, the breast. Esmira said "I noticed that every time we eat chicken that you always grab for the breast! Are you thinking of me?" Jeremy said "no but let me tell you the story behind that. You see me now as a well-built man with abs and everything in perfect position. Is that right?" Esmira bashfully says "yes" "Well growing up" Jeremy continued "it was an entirely different atmosphere. My mother was the one that started the food moving at the supper table. When we had chicken My mother would grab the first piece the breast, she would pass it clock wise to my sister who would take the other breast, then on to my other sister who would take the wings, then on to my other sister who would take the thigh, then onto my dad who would take the other thigh, then on to my other brother that would just pass, then onto my other brother who would take the leg, which left me with the other leg. So when we ate chicken I always had the leg, one scoop of green beans and one scoop of mashed potatoes. When I graduated high school at 4'9" around 93 pounds, I was nothing but skin and bones. I joked with my friends that I was the closest thing of being a cadaver. I just had flesh on me. I knew somewhere I had to bulk up. So I went and visited my grand uncle in Kansas named Ross. He had only one stipulation, you pull your weight, and the sky is the limit. So every day I did the work of three men. I couldn't wait to get a warm meal and start packing the weight on. I was doing enough exercise out on the ranch that I didn't have to say, let me go exercise. The first two months I packed on eighty pounds. My shirt size quickly went into a size 38 in the chest. My waist went to a 30. My legs almost doubled in size. I set my goal for 2 more months. Working like a dog and eating complete meals like a locomotive takes the coal. Two more months I went to a size 50 in chest and 33 in waist. I was satisfied. To answer your question, I choose the breast of the chicken now because I was never allowed to as a child".

Chapter 6

Esmira jaw dropped. She wanted to ask "am I enough for you?" Jeremy motioned for her to come over, and she did. She wanted to be with him completely but she realized now was not the time. They finished up there meal and headed home. Jeremy asked her if she was ok and her response was to lay her head on his shoulder and her hands on his chest. She was happy and content. Jeremy knew they had a lot of work ahead of them, he had to curry and shoe the horses before he could think of more pleasurable activities, all of which would be time consuming. He was feeling a bit gritty, time for a quick wash so he headed for the pump. He used the pump and had no idea that Esmira had come into the tack room. She was sitting on a cube of hay when he came out of the wash room. "Oh! You surprised me" said Jeremy. Esmira asked innocently "does my naked body bother you?" Jeremy replied" hardly". As Esmira looked at how he was built, his chest, and his hair, his everything. **Now** was her moment. Esmira motioned for Jeremy to come over as she unbuttoned his shirt. Jeremy put his hand on her breasts and politely asked "may I kiss them" ? Esmira pulled his neck even closer to her breasts and said "does this give you the answer you have been wanting"? Jeremy told her the plans about how he would trap Linda tomorrow, so there would be no mistake. He told her everything about the plan.

Linda's buggy came up sharp at 8:00a.m. Jeremy and Esmira showed her the barn, the corral and some of the stalls. One could tell she was not afraid of horses by the way she approached them. She stroked the neck, patted the horses in front and almost massaged them before she would go on. Then she would stand directly behind the horse and gently pat the rear and come down on the sides of the horse. She would wait until the horse would adjust itself and if it didn't she would mark in her book. She didn't say she had any mares.

Jeremy told to Esmira to go up to the house and make some coffee. So Linda thought Esmira was going up to the house. Esmira slipped behind a stall as Jeremy and Linda began to talk about her intentions concerning the horses. Jeremy asked Linda" what do you want to do"? As he continued to curry the buckskin. Linda pushed her breasts up against the horse so it appeared that her assets were even bigger. Linda said that she wanted the Roan to mate with her mare and she wanted to take it with her". Jeremy told Linda that he suddenly felt warm down under and mentioned to her that when he is warm like this good things happen for both parties. He told her that he was going to go to the pump right next door to the tack room and that he would meet her near the pump basin in four minutes tops, however she would want to be greeted. Jeremy went to the pump and worked the handle until the water started to flow. Within minutes Linda disrobed and walked within a few feet of the pump expecting to meet Jeremy. Esmira was ten feet behind her and Jeremy came around the corner and said to Linda "may I help you"? Linda turned around and saw Esmira holding her clothes, as she said "don't ever show your face here again!" Linda runs out to the back of the barn totally embarrassed and got dressed. Jeremy and Esmira had never seen a woman move so fast. They both hoped they had seen the last of her!

Chapter 7

"Let's go eat" says Esmira." I have already made tacos with the best guacamole dip one has ever tasted even if I do say so myself." Jeremy says "I will be right up darling, I have to get that strange smell out of the barn that she left behind" referring to Linda's perfume that was still very potent in the air. "OK" says Esmira "but don't be too long. I have a few surprises for you." After Jeremy got that rude feminine perfume out of the barn so his Stallions could breathe easier, he headed up to the house. As soon as Jeremy opened up the door he saw those beautiful legs wrapped in her purple tight jeans with the startling bright yellow sweater that she loved to wear, making those luscious breasts even larger. With the trim 28 inch waist she packed a nice figure. One thing Esmira was blessed with was her beauty. She pulled his chair out for him and as he sat down she dragged her hair across his face. "Well" Esmira said "How is it being chased by two different women in the same day?" Jeremy looked across the table and said "please, I hope you don't think I was the least bit interested!" One woman in any mans' life is more than enough" Said Jeremy."

When Esmira heard this her heart swelled with pride. She stated proudly "nice to know that there is no competition out there that would attract my lover's eyes. Well I got some ideas, with the $5000.00 I believe that we should charge a minimal fee on the first Thursday of every month for a hay ride from 4-7p.m. The children up to age 15 could take part. From 7:30 to 10:30 p.m., ages 16-19 could participate. What do you think?" said Jeremy. Esmira replied "that sounds like a wonderful idea". I have some other ideas about how we can use that money if you got a minute" Jeremy continued. Esmira told Jeremy "I am not going anywhere"! Jeremy continued to tell Esmira about his plans "Well I thought that for the people interested in the 'Whispering" that class would be held at 7a.m. on Monday. For the people interested in bronco riding that would be held at 4:30 pm on Monday. For the gymkhana and the barrel racing and the jumping I thought that we could put that on Wednesday schedule from 1 to 4p.m. The currying can be any morning of the week from 7:00 to 7:30" Esmira said "your business mind must stop now, it is time to come to bed," and the bright purple pants fell to the floor as well as the bright yellow sweater. Esmira leaned over stark naked to Jeremy and said "those are all wonderful ideas that we will implement hem tomorrow when we see our newspaper man." Her delicate hands rubbed his broad back as well as his neck so he could go to sleep.

Jeremy was up at 5:30 and out at the barn currying the stallions. He was going thru the business day in his mind enjoying the peace and quiet of the morning. It is going on 7:00 and Jeremy smelled the coffee brewing and the flapjacks cooking as he went inside. Jeremy said "Honey that smells real good, will I be blessed with blueberries"? "Yes, love" said Esmira. Jeremy sat down and began to enjoy his breakfast.

Esmira was wearing pink lipstick and a full length beige lace dress. Jeremy noticed and said "you look very good today". "Well thank you "said Esmira". I am ready when you are to go to town and finalize all the paperwork to our editor, for all our projects." "If I am not mistaken we have two weeks until everything starts up, that will give us enough time to recheck the upper twenty." Jeremy says "Oh! Will this be a peaceful time for you and me honey?" Esmira says "I sure hope so. Remind me to take the smaller can of coffee up there to accommodate you." "The buckboard is ready" says Jeremy "I will meet you outside". Esmira goes to the kitchen picks up her duffle bag and the picnic basket and is out the door. Esmira puts the basket and duffle bag in the back of chariot and they are on their way. On the way there Esmira rubs and pats Jeremy's leg letting him know everything will be ok. It will be about a forty five minute drive by buggy so there is plenty of time to talk. Esmira has got to say it "Have I ever told you how much you mean to me" Jeremy calmly says "no". Esmira says "After my husband died there was an empty feeling kind of like a void that could not be filled. So I accepted that void not knowing what would come next. Then after Jim died I was just about ready to sell the farm and go to my sisters in Utah. However, something told me that I had to give the farm one more shot. Then you appeared! I have never seen anyone handle the animals, the people and especially me, in such a professional manner. How do you do it"? Jeremy says "Well in all the time that I practiced with Jim he taught me several things in life, but one that stuck with me was the Golden Rule. Treat others as you would have them treat you. So I did, but one day I met this fellow who was the most cantankerous person I have ever met. I treated him nicely but to no avail, he would shout back at me like he was cursing. Then one day when I drove by his farm he was not at the bridge to threaten me. Days later I found out that he passed away. So I asked Jim about it and this is what he said "Sometimes in life you will meet people you just can't agree with, no matter what you do! This is a sad story but true. This usually happens when people do not take time out in their life to love themselves. How can one love another when he can't even love the person that is in his own skin? So practice on knowing yourself and loving thyself, and before you know it you will radiate love wherever you go. So I fell in love with myself at an early age so I could prepare myself for the day that I would fall in love with someone. When I met you I had to see past all the beauty on the outside and see all the good on the inside. Once I knew I passed that test the rest was easy, like seeing fertile ground. So you see when I say I Love you, I really mean it." Esmira thought about Jeremy's words as they quietly rode to their destination. They pulled up to the newspaper building and put the ads in the paper for the ranch. They noticed a family of six children, a mother and a dad and an old gentlemen named Roy. By looking at Roy one could tell that he was very wise but hated to talk. He reminded Jeremy of an old uncle. Jeremy looked over at the children, two male around sixteen and eighteen, three girls around fifteen, fourteen and thirteen and a younger boy around nine. Both the older boys stood six foot plus, the fifteen year old girl had a beautiful build like Esmira, the fourteen year old they called legs, who stood around 5 foot eight with three and a half feet being legs. The thirteen year old could have passed for twenty and built just like the oldest sister around 5 foot and very busty. The nine year old stood around five foot with dusty blond hair as he whittled on his piece of wood.

Chapter 8

Jeremy stepped up and said hello to the mother and father while they introduced themselves as Charlie and Ruth Dunn. Jeremy asked "What brought you into town?" Charlie said "a new law just passed granting squatters rights to any family that could maintain a 3 acre site on land just south of big horn lake that is not already occupied. The law further states that the assessor will come around annually to check on your progress, and after three years if progress of the land has not reached maturity then the squatters have the right either to leave or to have a deed written up and sold to them for so much per acre."! "That sounds great" said Jeremy "I will be your neighbor just west of the big horn lake that we own up there. If you ever need any help, let me know".

Wow! Said Esmira "we might be having neighbors up near the upper twenty. That would be great". "What did you think of them" asked Esmira. Jeremy said "well they look like they come from sturdy stock. I think they will fit right in". Sounds like they are positioning themselves pretty close to the lake for watering reasons. Seems like they are thinking this whole ordeal thru". "Well said Esmira "I think we should be getting back to our neck of the woods honey. Sun tells me that it is just about noon and getting pretty warm, lets head on out." Esmira and Jeremy get in their chariot and go towards home. Since Esmira has the reins she goes up about a half hour to the fork in the road and takes a right. Forty feet on the left hand side right behind the big walnut tree is a crystal clear pond. Esmira pats Jeremy's groin and steps on down from the chariot. Within seconds her beige dress is off and hanging on a nearby branch as she slips into the water. "Honey" she says "are you coming in"? Esmira swims around and bathes herself. She steps toward the tree and is met by Jeremy's wonderful naked body. Jeremy slips into the water and swims around for about ten minutes. Then Esmira says "does that feel better'? Jeremy slyly admits "yes." Jeremy being the gentlemen he is helps her into her beige dress as Esmira kisses his chest. Now they are ready to get back on the main road and head for home. Esmira brought a picnic basket but they both decided to eat while traveling home. Home wasn't far off they could already hear the stallions neighing. In ten minutes they were home. They came pulling up in their chariot with the food all eaten and admiring the horses. Jeremy put the horses up and walked his honey up to the house. It was a hot night, within seconds Esmira had her dress off and hung up. There she sat brushing her long hair that dropped below her waist. Jeremy asked Esmira if he cold brush her hair and Esmira said yes. Jeremy stood in front of Esmira brushing back her thick black hair. He would count to himself how long the brush would take to get thru her hair. Esmira admired Jeremy's muscles It always seemed like he was built for power, it looked like he was always ready to go. Esmira considered herself a very lucky woman.

The dawn had just broken over the ridge and Jeremy was just finishing up currying the stallions. He checked all their shoes and gave them some feed as he headed up to the house. This was their free day not a care in the world a day where they could sip their coffee all morning long. Suddenly there came a rap tap at their kitchen door, it was Margaret Dunn the fifteen year old who was hollering about how her brother was chopping down wood from a tree and how a branch fell on him knocking him out. Jeremy was already to go help and motioned for Esmira to come. Something didn't feel right. Margaret was in a dark black skirt and a purple ruffled blouse. She looked like she was ready for a date. Jeremy grabbed the appaloosa and Esmira the roan and followed Margaret. They came to an old stump that Jeremy knew had been cut down for years. Margaret turned to Jeremy and shouted "why did you have to bring her we could have been alone" Before Jeremy could say anything Esmira interrupted and said "what right do you have even trying for a man at your age? Listen here Margaret you might have the goods on top, and if you have already started sharing at your young age, you will be turned out to pasture before your twenty". Margaret says "What would you know? You own your own land and the horses and got a good looking man to boot" Esmira says "if you only knew the hard work that went behind all that I have. I will bet you money right now that probably the reason why your parents came out this far to start over was due to actions in the last town you were at. Is this true"? Margaret said "yes". Esmira said "well then Alleluia, do you want to have a fresh start, like this never happened"? Margaret says "you could find it in your heart to forgive me and not let my parents know"? Esmira says "have you heard that we are starting up a gymkhana, some horse whispering, bronco riding and an overall class for currying down the horses in our place in two weeks." "No" says Margaret. Esmira says "well you will be my first recruit. I will get with your mom and dad and explain just the necessary stuff, but there is one more thing that I will ask of you before we head out" says Esmira. "Oh! What would that be" asked Margaret. Esmira says "I think that you owe Jeremy and me and apology". Margaret says "you are right. Jeremy and Esmira I was not acting in a way that bests suits me so please take my apology". Jeremy says "you are forgiven; now if you will excuse us, Esmira and I have some unfinished business back at the ranch". They turn their horses south toward the ranch, just waiting to get home and relax. Around twenty minutes later Jeremy has the horses put up and heads for the house. Jeremy asks Esmira if she is hungry for some venison. Esmira says "yes but only the way you fix it". Jeremy goes out back and gets the barbecue pit ready. Esmira stays inside and fixes coffee. There is nothing better on a day off from every worry in the world, than venison and coffee around great company. It seems like they have known each other for a life time rather than five months, but Jeremy and Esmira are inseparable. The fire is just about right now for the cooking. Esmira has her meat on a twig that is long enough to go into the fire without getting burned and Jeremy has found one and is whittling down to a nice sharp point in order to pierce the meat. He gets it on the twig and is cooking his as he speaks; "well honey, what do you think of Margaret?" Esmira says "well, I think she has a lot of good going for her she just hasn't realized it yet.

I think with a little interaction with other people her age she will fit right in. Her only drawback is she looks so much more mature than her age. I believe that she gets around the horses she will forget about her problems." "I believe your right" stated Jeremy "but besides Margaret, who else do we have?" Esmira says" I believe time will take care of the rest of the people that we need to join. We still have two weeks. Tomorrow, would you like to take the roan down to the lower forty. I hear there are a couple of fillies that wouldn't mind making company with our Roan." "Make you a deal" says Jeremy "you take the roan and I will take the sorrel. Let's start out around 6:30 in the morning so we can have enough time". Jeremy asks "you want to put out the fire while I go curry down the horses"? Esmira **says "sure"**

Jeremy goes down to the horses and is caught off guard when they begin to stir. Jeremy thinks quickly to himself either there is a storm coming in or there is a stranger about. The appaloosa is in his stall shaking his head up and down as if pointing to another stall. Jeremy sees a shadow up in the hay loft. He grabs the pitchfork and climbs the ladder. He is just about ready to throw the pitchfork when he sees a boot near the hay. He grabs the boot and pulls. Suddenly there is a scream. Esmira hears it in the backyard and comes running. Audra makes it to her feet at about the same time Esmira makes her way up the ladder. Esmira asks "who prey tell are you, and what are you doing up in my barn?' "I am Margaret's sister, Audra and as you can see my hair hangs to my waist and my mother told me that if I didn't get my chores done on time that she was going to cut my hair" Audra shouted. "Well let's get out of the hay loft and think this all thru" Said Esmira. So Jeremy, Esmira and Audra all climb down from the hay loft as Jeremy prepares the long buckboard for the trip to Audra's home. Jeremy has piled about half a stack of hay onto the buckboard and hitched up four stallions for the journey. Esmira sees what Jeremy has done and trusts him greatly. It was about two o'clock and if they left now Esmira and Jeremy could get back by six o'clock. Now for the explanation, Jeremy tells Audra to listen entirely to what he has to say before saying anything. "The reason for the hay is a peace offering to your mom and dad. I will tell them that you had complete trust in us to bring you all the way back. I will talk to your parents about your concern and tell them about our gymkhana that we are starting up and go from there. "Would you like to be a part of our gymkhana that we will start up in two weeks" asks Jeremy. "Can I, can I, I would love to!" says Audra. So Jeremy says to Esmira and Audra "let's go". Esmira speaks up "I will be right back I have to change". Esmira goes to her room, brushes out her hair and puts on red lipstick and her navy blue dress that fits from the neck line all the way to the ankle. Then goes and gets in the buckboard. Jeremy compliments Esmira on how great she looks. Jeremy helps Esmira into the front of the buckboard as he ties Audra horse to the back end. The drive although long seemed to go rather quickly. Esmira talked about boyfriends and farm chores to cooking and dressing up for particular occasions. These two could not stop talking. It was though they were long lost cousins. They were pulling up as Audra's Mom and Dad were standing on the porch. Ruth told Audra to get inside if she knew what was good for her! Jeremy butted in and said "Whoa! Before Audra does anything I want to congratulate her on not running away from us, when she could of at any time". Charlie speaks up "This is none of your concern. So the quicker you turn that buckboard around the quicker I will be smiling." Jeremy says "well I brought a half of stack of hay to you as a welcome present". Esmira chimes in "and I brought ten pounds of flour along". Just as Charlie was going to say something, Ruth puts her hand over his mouth and tugs on his shirt so he has to turn around, as she says "That ten pounds of flour will last us a year so let's at least hear what they got to say." "Ok" says Charlie. Jeremy says "we have not had time to welcome you. We realize that we all need each other out here if we are going to make it. As of today we would like to invite both Margaret and Audra out to our ranch in a couple of weeks at no charge to you to help us in the day hours with our gymkhana that we are starting up. This will last up to a month. I believe we will both come away with good experiences and wonderful memories". Charlie interrupts and says "You mean you would be willing to take these two head strong young girls and whip them in shape for me, what do I owe you"? Jeremy says "just one thing". Charlie says "oh I knew there was a catch, what is it"? Esmira chimes in "rather than us bringing them back here every day let them stay with us for that month." Before Charlie could get his mouth open, Ruth turned him around and said. "This could be what we were looking for, two less mouths to feed and not that much more work to do". Ruth tells Charlie to Say yes. Charlie says "yes". Jeremy is already backing the horses up to the barn to put the hay in and Esmira is already giving Ruth the ten pounds of flour. Esmira says to Ruth," I hate to be short but we must be getting on down the road". "Boy" Esmira Says "I've had more than I can handle for one day". Jeremy says to Esmira "I haven't had enough time to say I love you honey let's get home and get some rest for a good tomorrow. Jeremy asks Esmira how her your pregnancy coming along. Esmira tells him there is a lot of kicking going on. Jeremy with all passengers aboard turns the buckboard around and heads for home, Tomorrow will come soon enough.

It's 5:30 a.m. and Jeremy is paying special attention to the sorrel and the roan in currying them down. Esmira has forgotten to put her blouse on but she is busy cooking Jeremy's favorite meal, blueberry pancakes. Jeremy comes in and says "everything is ready for the road, WOW you look terrific. Is there a special occasion" ask Jeremy. Esmira says "No, but with all this special attention with these young ladies everywhere I just don't want you to forget me"! "Honey", as he unbuttons his shirt down to his waist and says comes here; I have a present for you, would this action help any"? As he presses his chest against her breasts, Esmira says "you don't have to speak twice." Esmira begins to tickle Jeremy's nipple with her tounge. "Ok, ok, that's good enough" says Jeremy. After getting dressed, they both mount their horses and go on down the road to the lower twenty. Even though the trip is about a half an hour away it goes fast. Before Jeremy has his horse put away Esmira already has the saddle and bridle off and slaps her horse and off he goes. Jeremy is curious about where her horse is and asks where your Roan is? Esmira says "Oh I did the same thing you did last time. So it should work for me too, right." Jeremy says "I have never seen it work before on one that hasn't taken the time to curry him. Let's see! Did you see the mare?" Esmira says "no". Jeremy replied "Well let's give your horse around a half of an hour and see what's happening." Suddenly thirteen horses are following the roan at break neck speed. Jeremy knows what has got to happen. He rushes to his horse undoes his saddle bag and takes out the burlap bag. The fillies will run themselves into the ground unless Jeremy and his sorrel can get in front of them and wave the burlap bag. Jeremy has the right angle in about five minutes he will overtake them and does. He frantically waves the bag and the horses turn east and slow down to a canter as they go uphill toward the same tree that the scared mare round up at. The sorrel and the mares start to walk and Jeremy hardly believes his eyes. Jeremy motions toward Esmira to get the rope and weave it between trees for a make shift corral. Jeremy's heart is pumping crazily he is hot and tired but amazed at what just happened. To cool himself down Jeremy takes off every piece clothing he has but except his boots and walks up neck deep in the cool pond nearby. Esmira is soon behind him; her button down silk dress came right off. Her beige corset lay right beside the dress. Esmira wadded into the water and managed to grab Jeremy's arm where she could feel his strength again. They kissed each other passionately and enjoyed one another's body as they spent time in the cool clean water. When they came out of the water they were cooled down and all the horses remained in the corral. The only decision they came to was to bring the horses with them. It was an hour walk back with the horses and a slow walk at that, because they didn't want the horses scattering. Jeremy got on his sorrel and went up to the leader of the pack carrying Esmira right behind him. Jeremy thought that if the Roan knew that he was around he would be calm. The hour ride back seemed like forever but it came at a steady pace. The stallions were used to staying on the outside if needed. So Jeremy led the roan inside the stable so all the mares would follow. Then he had to put the roan up and made sure that he curried him down. Jeremy could smell that it was going to rain and he knew that it would be a calming one just enough to let the mares know they were safe. Jeremy knew that he had three days' work in front of him tomorrow so he was thinking on just staying out in the bunk house as he heard Esmira say "Oh NO you don't. You know how I am when it rains. Come on up to the house". Jeremy shut all the gates and walked into the house where Esmira had some hot cocoa made. She slipped out of her dress to show Jeremy the new dress that she was saving for the opening day. She put her orange corset on and stepped into the new dress that had tiny buttons from the neck to the waist. The dress was a silky orange that flowed down to her ankles and the sleeves went down to her elbow. The dress fit nicely in the chest area and she liked the way it covered to the neckline. Jeremy bent her over his knee as if he was to give her a spanking and said "I love it" before Esmira could say how do you like it. She was thrilled. It took over a fort night for the dress to get here from out east. She noticed Jeremy was rubbing his eyes and getting sleepy so she unbuttoned his shirt and began to massage his chest which was just enough to get him into bed. Jeremy was extremely tired; when his head hit the pillow he was asleep.

Jeremy was up at the crack of dawn. Yes you guessed it he was already currying the stallions and he had to make room for the mares too. So time was working against him. It must be his senses because he could almost swear that he smelled the coffee and he had five mares to go. He finished up the five mares and went inside and sure enough the coffee was already poured and waiting to be sipped. A good side of bacon was on the stove as well as the flapjacks being made and his cute Esmira was frying the eggs as well. What an accomplished woman, he thought, she knows that the best way to a man's heart is thru his stomach, at least in the morning. In a couple of minutes breakfast was all cooked and Esmira joined her honey at their most important meal of the day. She didn't let her pregnancy get in the way. In the middle of breakfast Jeremy was trying to tell her that it would take most of the day to prepare the wood to construct another corral for the mares. Esmira interrupted and said "that's great; I have been meaning to tell you that at ten o'clock we have two applicants concerning the gymkhana and they should be here by then. Why don't we both interview them"? Jeremy replies "that will be great, how long have you known?" Esmira says "it came in the mail yesterday". Jeremy says "well by ten o'clock that should give me enough time to hall five trees and get back here. Honey, could you make sure there is some warm coffee on the table when I get back"? Esmira winks at Jeremy and says "your wish is my command".

Chapter 9

There was a knock on the door and Esmira answered it. Another new comer, Joe introduced himself and his older brother Ralph and asked if they could come in. Esmira showed them to the side office, where they all sat down. The professional interview consisted of four questions. What do you know? This question gives the people a chance to speak. This is the tricky one. If people just talk and beat around the subject and never come to any point, they are done. How long have you been doing this? This gives a person a chance to give themselves extra credit and a chance to be honest. Why should we pick you over the other candidates? This gives the person a chance to berate the other applicants, build yourself up or be humble about any other individual and just know that you give 110% every day. If we decide to pick you when can you start? This question usually gives a green light on the person's decision if he wants to stay or go.

Joe answers the first question sincerely "I have done a lot of odd jobs but the one I keep coming back to is bronco riding". Ralph answers the same way. He too has done a lot of things but his likes keep him coming back to horse shoeing and metal forging. Jeremy and Esmira like what they hear so far and they jump to the last question. "When can you start" asks Jeremy. Both Joe and Ralph quip "would tomorrow be ok?" "Great" says Jeremy. "We have an outfit ready for you in the bunkhouse. We will meet there every morning at 6:00 unless told otherwise. I will show you the bunkhouse and you are free to get acquainted with the territory". The following morning Jeremy is down grooming the horses at 5:30 and finishes up at 6:00. He meets Joe and Ralph and lets them know that they have to build a corral from the trees on the northeast section. Jeremy asks Joe if he could hitch up the wagon so everybody will be able to go right after breakfast. Ralph helps his brother Joe and within minutes the four horse team is ready. They all head up to the house where breakfast is served. After breakfast Jeremy, Joe and Ralph go up to the section where ten trees need to be cut down, all branches removed by high noon and put in the wagon to come down by lunch time. Jeremy Joe and Ralph hustle thru the project and are ready by 11:30 to head towards the barn.

Kim is busy sewing on her Singer sewing machine back at the Dunn farm. She has realized that she will have to make all her blouses and shirts now and in the future because none of the ready- made shirts at the stores will fit her in the bust. She just assumes it is part of the pains of growing up. She is almost done with her navy blue blouse, just the sleeves she has to put on. She is also planning on making Esmira a peach lace blouse with many tiny buttons from the neckline to the waist with hopes that she gets to join hers sisters in the gymkhana. Kim believes sewing beautiful clothes is the easiest to make anyone happy, so why not just share the joy.

Joe and Ralph reach the barn and all they can think about is a nice cold cup of water that is just inside the bunkhouse. Joe grabs the ladle first and doses his head and neck and then goes for another one to drink from. Ralph does the same before Jeremy calls them into lunch. Lunch is always light like a ham sandwich and some beans washed down with a cold cup of water. It's also a place where they can rest their hats for a half hour before returning to work.

Esmira is showing both Audra and Margaret that cleaning up after the ranch hands is a necessary chore of business. Esmira favorite saying is "cleanliness is next to godliness". She also told the girls "this is an important part of my day, because after I clean up after them, I get to do me. Come here I will show you. She shows them a 6 ft. by 9 ft. room that is only for her. Inside that room she shows them all of her make-up and lipstick and cosmetics. She tells them of her secrets of colors that is her private code but very worth sharing. For example if she is wearing red lipstick this means power. Pink is for passive but alert. Beige is for easy times. Green is for on the look-out. Blue and purple are for being relaxed and orange is for being aware. She also shows them how to put the massacre on and why she brushes her waist length hair differently. She also tells them that she was thinking of putting a sewing machine in their but had never learned how to sew. Audra chimes in "my younger sister knows how, and she has her own Singer machine"! "Really" says Esmira "how old is she, and how long has she was sewing"? Margaret says "she just turned 14" and Audra says" about five years". Esmira says "well, when we go down to your parents place in a week can I meet Kim and see some of her work"? Margaret says "I don't see why not"

Meanwhile back at the ranch the corral is just being finished. It took over three hours but Jeremy is impressed with Ralph's handiwork and asks Ralph "Do you like doing this kind of work" and Ralph answers "well I prefer working with fire and making tools and horseshoes from scratch"." So you would prefer being a blacksmith" says Jeremy and Ralph say "if that is what they call them. I just know I can do it". "Well, can I ask you a huge favor? I have thirteen mares that need to be shod, if I give you a week could you have it done" asked Jeremy. "Well let me see what kind of tools I have to work with" stated Ralph. Do you have a forge, and anvil some tongs?" asks Ralph. Jeremy says "let's go inside and see what we have". They both go inside and Ralph spots in the corner a make shift forge, if used properly it could do the trick. He looks on over to one of the windows and sees some tongs hanging. Now if he could find an anvil and a nice baby sledge hammer, he would almost be in business. Ralph remembers seeing an anvil in the tack room. He goes to the tack room and finds the anvil. Now except for the rods they cut the metal form to make the horse shoes. "When is the next time you going in to town for horse shoe stuff" Asks Ralph. Jeremy says "well it could be in the next few days. I will know better by tomorrow" so all that stuff will work for you Ralph"? Ralph says "yes".

As Jeremy heads for the tack room to get some water he sees Joe grooming one of the horses and asks Joe "'what are you doing"? Joe responds "well, this is one of the horses I would like to bronco ride some day in the future". "So why are you brushing it down?" asks Jeremy. Joe says "well, I can only hope that he would remember me brushing it down and take it easy on me". Jeremy says "I like the way you thought that thru. Have you ever thought of horse whispering"? Joe looks at him with the most peculiar look and says "horse what"? "That's ok Joe, only few people have heard of it and even fewer are successful at it. It's an art that can calm the meanest horse down to where you want him". Now Joe thinks Jeremy is out of his mind and says "I mean no disrespect Jeremy, but what are you talking about"? Jeremy says "You will be riding that buckskin tomorrow. That is when you will find out. Now go call your brother Ralph and bring yourself to dinner".

Esmira, Audra and Margaret had just gotten thru setting the table for dinner. Esmira finished draining the noodles and Margaret finished making the sauce and Audra finished making the meatballs. This is a meal that Esmira puts on about once a month. Joe and Ralph's eyes had never seen such a banquet. All vegetables in one bowl and three other bowls to make the rest. Before Ralph starts to reach for a bowl Esmira states "whoever eats at this table must remember that the meal always starts out with Jeremy and will go clockwise until everyone is served. Does everyone understand?" They all said" yes." Everyone started passing the food around and didn't notice the eyes that Audra was making on Ralph. Jeremy said grace and asked Esmira what her schedule looked like for tomorrow. Esmira said "if everything goes right, I wanted to take the buckboard up and visit Ruth and Charlie and take a look at some of the clothes Kim has made and if everything goes as planned invite her to join our gymkhana". Jeremy says" that sound great, because Ralph and I need to go into town to get some horseshoe rods for the mares". Something was missing, this would be the first time since Jeremy has been on the ranch that Esmira wasn't beside him. Esmira knew that she would have to start out early in order to get up there and back if Kim wanted to come along. It sounded like Jeremy was only taking Ralph and that would leave Margaret and Joe behind. She would have to give orders to Margaret to have his lunch set outside for Joe, when he is done with business. She was confident in Jeremy's decision to go to town but she is worried about seeing more of him before going to sleep. That package that he sports around, below his waist, is starting to look mighty interesting. So Esmira says "it sounds like we have a packed day tomorrow". Dinner was done and Ralph asked to be excused as he winked at Audra.

Jeremy was up and ready at 5: 30 grooming all the horses except for the buckskin. He was half way done with the mares before Joe came out to greet him and asked "can I ride the roan today" and Jeremy said "no, remember the talk that we had yesterday about 'whispering'"? Joe said "yes"." Well you have done your share of bronco riding, let's see what happens on the buckskin" said Jeremy. Joe climbs up on the bronco and lasts about three seconds before he hits the dirt. Joe is determined to get 8 seconds out of this animal before he calls it quits. Joe is ready to climb back on when Jeremy stops him and hands him a burlap bag. Joe, who is thoroughly disgusted at his ride, throws the bag to the ground and said "what is that for?" And Jeremy says "well, if you don't pick it up you can pack your bags now"! Joe shows some embarrassment and picks up the bag immediately. Now Jeremy says "grab his halter and lead the horse into the barn and slowly put the bag over his head, now repeat after me, in a whisper, while petting his neck. You are one of the strongest animals in the universe. I like that. You will be able to carry me wherever I go on my command" Jeremy then says "I want you to keep on saying that to the animal for the next thirty minutes. I will come back and we shall see some results, if you have done exactly as I said." Joe might have a quick fuse but one thing he is not, is stupid. Joe followed the command to the letter and Jeremy came back out in thirty minutes and said "slowly lift the bag from his head while petting his neck and have the bridle nearby. After you take the halter off put on the bridle and then put on his saddle. Then bring him to the end of the corral and sit in the saddle". Joe did as directed. Once at the end of the corral Jeremy asks "Joe are you ready" as he slaps the horse on his behind. The buckskin takes off faster than lighting speed, after about 200 yards Joe comes to his senses and turns the buckskin around. Joe is amazed at just what happened. He comes back to the barn and asks Jeremy "what just happened?" Jeremy says to Joe "you tell me". Joe says" well about forty minutes ago he was the toughest animal I have ever ridden, now he is like the animal that I have spent day and night with for the last two years." Jeremy asks "Would you want to learn more about 'whispering'? Before Jeremy hears an answer he has turned and walked to the barn to see if Ralph is ready to go to town. He finds Ralph ready and is pleased and says "let's grab some breakfast first". All three of the men head up to the house and Jeremy says to both men "can you smell it; it has to be the best coffee this side of the Mississippi". They quickly made it inside where the table was set like a banquet. A big glass pitcher of water, a pitcher of orange juice and coffee already poured for those that drink it, two platters of pancakes, some blueberry, and some plain. Two batches of steaming biscuits with a side order of bacon for anyone that wanted some. But believe it or not all this would be gone within ten minutes with no leftovers just dishes to wash. They were feeding a large crew with Jeremy, Joe, Ralph, Esmira, Audra and Margaret. Now they were ready to work!

Jeremy was going one way and Esmira was going another. They agreed to meet up at the house around four. The ride into town took around forty minutes and they were quick to pick up the supplies, grab some hard candy and check the telegraph office for any mail. There were two more replies by the name of Ross and Byron from Kansas. They were just asking for more information so Jeremy didn't count them as for real. Jeremy thanked the telegraph office and Ralph and Jeremy returned to their wagon for the trip home.

Chapter 10

Esmira was taking the usual way to Ruth's house and in broad daylight she started to point out land markers in case they were on this road alone they wouldn't get lost. The trip took a good hour and Margaret was glad to see her mother. Margaret showed Esmira into the house and into the room shut off by a sheet that Kim used as her sewing room. Kim quickly jumped up and said "good morning" to Margaret and Esmira "is there anything special you want to see?" asked Kim. Esmira said "have you ever put together a dress"? Kim showed her a maroon button down dress that she had made for herself to go to a barn dance. This dress was beautiful. It buttoned down the front with tiny pearl buttons that came right up to the neckline. In Esmira's mind what she saw was enough to seal the deal for her. Any one who could put together a dress with that beautiful had a talent for sewing. She went to Ruth and asked if she could borrow her daughter for three weeks along with her sewing machine so she wouldn't feel lonely. She also asked if all three of her daughters could come with her and return on the same day. Ruth hesitated a bit and Esmira knew if she said anything to persuade her it would backfire. Ruth said "yes but just for three weeks and you make darn sure you take good care of them" as a tear rolled down her cheek. Kim walked slowly with her treadle machine in order to load it properly into the buckboard. With Margaret's help she was able to load it. Then Kim jumped happily into the front seat of the buckboard with Margaret and Esmira and were on their way. It was getting to be around noon and the sun was beating down fiercely. It felt like it was 100 degrees. Esmira knew that to stop and bathe herself and the girls would take too much time. She had enough water in the 3 canteens to get home safely and suddenly there in the road were two boys blocking their passage. The boys told them "get out of the buckboard and take off your clothes". Esmira pulled up closer and said "how much longer do you want to live, because if you look real close I have a gun pointed right at your head and a person in the back with a shot gun that will take your friend out. So either move aside or die". The two boys scampered off like they were having switches taken to them. Margaret and Kim were stunned into silence for a couple minutes and Kim finally spoke "how did you know what to say"? Esmira said "living in this area there seems like there is always someone trying to get something for nothing, and I have worked too hard and too long to let it slip by without protecting myself. I just figured out that I am also going to adapt it in our programs for women only, the ability to take care of yourselves. Now chances are they are not going to tell their daddy that they were out foxed by a woman. If we hurry home we will be there in a half an hour". So Esmira prompted the reins and let the horse start to gallop home. Esmira cooled the horses down to a walk the last five minutes and they were glad to see home. Esmira put the buckboard outside the barn so as anyone in the tack room would not notice and told the girls to stay put. Esmira came into the barn from the left side of the tack room and saw Audra and Ralph kissing. She cleared her throat as they broke their embrace and told Audra to get up to the house and told Ralph that he should go talk to Jeremy immediately. She told the girls to come in the house in five minutes. As soon as Esmira got in the house she asked Audra what she was thinking. Audra said "I don't know" Esmira ripped into her and said "first, you are a very pretty girl. They don't come like you up in these parts. Don't you see that it starts out with a kiss then it moves on to touching certain parts and then it goes to sexual intercourse? Don't ever cheapen yourself like that again. You are better than that. If you like someone and Ralph is a good person to start with take it slow. Learn about him. Share things with him. See if at first you can get along without all the touchy stuff. You have a good head on your shoulders so use it"! Just in the nick of time as the girls enter the door, Esmira says to Kim", let the men get your stuff as we get better acquainted". After Joe and Ralph moved the sewing machine into the house, Jeremy asked if he could have a minute with Ralph. Jeremy said to Ralph that he understood his nature about feeling like a stallion himself and wanted to see how far he could get with Audra. That was normal behavior out here. But on the E&J Stud Farm we look at long term relationships. Then he asked Ralph" is Audra good enough to be your wife"? Ralph said "I didn't quite look at it that way"! "Well" said Jeremy "think of it as a supply store and if you break something in the supply store you have to buy it. You might want to ask yourself a question, would I want to be with her five years from now? Now, let's head up for dinner".

While Esmira had gone up to get Kim, Audra took it upon herself to cook an eight pound roast for supper. This had all the fixings, with sweet potatoes and regular potatoes and carrots with sautéed onions. Water, tea and milk were available to all. This was meeting time as well as getting nourished time. Every night business would be discussed that was to happen the next day. Tomorrow, it was Jeremy, Joe and Ralph going up to the upper twenty to see the rebuilt shack and how the land was holding up as well as the big creek that ran right thru it. If everything held up they were going over to Ruth's and Charlie's to lend them a hand for three days. Esmira mentioned while the men were away she had business concerning the gymkhana and how the ladies were going to fit in and juggle their kitchen chores as well.

Jeremy sometimes thought to himself who needs a rooster to wake up, because he was always down at the stable at 5:30 grooming his horses. Today he had to take a second look on how well the new corral was built because the mares looked happy and content. Jeremy was going to hitch up the buckboard but decided to hitch up the chariot instead. This way he could carry his tools like hammer and nails and drilling Auger if needed. Sometimes that buckboard rode so rough. Jeremy wasn't going anywhere without his morning coffee and a sweet kiss from Esmira, and the men had to have their breakfast. Normally it would be the big breakfast of flap jacks and bacon and biscuits and beverage, but the girls did a twist. This time it was home-made bread, juice and omelets. The men had never heard of this new dish called omelets. The girls had to explain how it was beaten eggs turned into their own little casserole, with ham, green peppers, onions and cheese. One would think that the men had not eaten in days the way they devoured the meal. They took off with hearty thanks and said they would see them in three days. As they took off Esmira had to give Jeremy one more kiss and Jeremy loved it. Jeremy was beginning to wonder if Esmira pregnancy was causing more love. Ralph and Joe got on their horses as Jeremy hitched up the appaloosa, and was off. The ride was about forty five minutes on horseback. The shack looked just like they left it from the front anyway. So Jeremy mentioned to Ralph to get off his horse and walk the rest of the way in as Joe took the right flank to go around the house, and Jeremy would take the left flank. When Jeremy waved his arm, Ralph said" anybody home, just looking for water" This startled the three boys that were inside. As they were making their get- away out the windows in the back Joe and Jeremy were there to stop them. Ralph came in the front and yelled "JACK is that you?" Jack stopped in his tracks and said" Ralph, it's me, With Earl and Bill." You wouldn't believe what happened. A week after you left the abandoned teppes' in Idaho, well Earl , Bill and I took over on a temporary basis the Calvary came in and just burned down everything. Said it had to do something with cholera and the whole acre of tepees was up in flames in a matter of minutes. We have been running ever since. We saw this shack it was a sight for sore eyes. We just got in last night and are very hungry and tired." Joe says" well, I am glad you are all in one piece. Let's look at what we have. I have a rifle with three shots and Ralph has his six shooter. Give us about an hour and we will have something to eat. Jack why don't you make a fire" somebody said. Jeremy assesses what is going on and decides to talk with Earl and Bill. After about ten minutes of talking with Earl who for fourteen stood 6 foot, Jeremy asks why Bill doesn't talk and Earl says that he got a fever when he was young and it took his hearing away. But don't let that fool you, he has like a sixth sense and can figure when things aren't right. Jeremy asks Bill how old he is, and with hand gestures he said he was ten. Jeremy turns to Earl and asks "did you say he was just ten years old" Earl answered "yes, he has always told the truth too." Jeremy says "if I not mistaken he stands about 5'6", and ten years old! If I didn't know any better I could swear I am reliving my youth". Jeremy tells Earl that he has got to do some thinking as he goes outside and talks to Jack. As he is tending to the fire Jack hears two shotgun shells that end with a thud and tells Jeremy "Well, Ralph hit something and we will be eating soon" Jeremy rubs his forehead and says "I will take over cooking duties, I need you three to go down in the creek and take a bath, and scrub hard." Jeremy is worried about the cholera stuff, but he knows that if people are still feeling ok after two weeks then they didn't get hit with it. Ralph brings in a yearling doe with just enough meat to last us six appetites. If everything goes right it will take an hour to cook and ten minutes to eat and we can be on our way. Jeremy puts it on the spit and turns it every five minutes. There is nothing better than a yearling out on the range, to carry a man's appetite. Just about the time the cooking is done the gentlemen come up after taking their bath. Jack, Earl and Bill look a lot healthier. Now let's get some food in them and head on down the road. One could say that they had not eaten in a day or two the way they devoured their meal. Ralph took care of the fire and put it out. Joe looked around back to make sure all the horses were there and Jeremy got everybody together. Jeremy said" It will be about a fifteen minute hard ride from here. But before we go any further we are helping this older couple out and we will be there for three days. We will be working hard and long and maybe not eating like we just did. We have come to serve them, period. If you feel you are not up to it I will understand. But this is where we make the decision, to help or leave. Is everyone with me"? They all say "YES".

 After the hard ride of fifteen minutes and six horses just barreling down at your ranch it's only natural that a Shotgun be raised at you. Jeremy slows everybody and gets off his horse and apologies for the intrusion, but he explains that he would like to help them for three days. So Charlie, a very stubborn farmer is ready to say "what makes you think"… Right about that time the soft hand of Ruth covers Charlie's mouth as she says "Charlie, you scare this help away and I will leave". Charlie says "come forward, glad to have you". Jeremy steps forward and says "I see you have two acres of hay that needs to be cut. I think we can have it done in two days. Would that be ok"? Charlie doesn't understand the strength in numbers, but takes off his hat and says "I think there must be a God, yes, that would be fine." Jeremy looks in the barn and finds that Charlie has two sickles. He looks around and finds some aluminum in the back of the barn and goes to ask Ralph if there was a way he could make two more sickles. If he had a forge, Jeremy thought to himself it just might work... Ralph spouts off "that aluminum has a quicker melting point then steel but that he could do it." Jeremy halls the two foot forges from the back of his chariot and sets him up with coal to start the burning process. Jeremy asks "how long would it take" and Ralph says "give me forty minutes". So Jeremy gets Jack and Earl in the process of using the sickle while Jeremy and Bill are twenty feet behind gathering the hay together in cubes. At this rate, Jeremy thought, we will have a half section done by three. The sun was beating down and was rather hot, thank God Ruth came out with a bucket of water and a ladle to drink from. Each one of them got their turn as the bucket of water was empty when everyone was thru. They thanked Ruth as she walked back to the house. The only thing that kept them out in the hot sun was the thought of a great dinner when they were done at sundown. Jeremy stopped and went into the barn as he saw Ralph riveting the sickles to some old hand rake handles. Jeremy had an idea that would get the work done twice as fast and less back breaking. Jeremy got everyone together for a switch. This meant that Jeremy and Ralph and Joe and Jack would be handling the sickles with Earl and Bill doing the gathering. However, every half hour they would switch doing the gathering to using the sickles until everyone had done both jobs. This worked out great because around eight o'clock, an acre and a half was finished. It was quitting time and time to go eat. Ruth had been making four dozen biscuits along with beans and a new thing called gelatin for dessert, and the entire cold water one can handle. The math wasn't hard to figure out with the eight people they had eating, everyone was allowed at least six biscuits and two bowlfuls of beans. One didn't have to worry about this cherry gelatin either, because it was gone before the water was. Jeremy couldn't wait to share this gelatin idea with Esmira. Dinner was done and everyone took their cue as to go to bunkhouse in the barn to sleep. Everyone was nearby and over in the barn everyone rolled out their blankets to go to sleep, Jeremy was wondering how his majestic Esmira was doing!

Chapter 11

Meanwhile back at the stud farm, Esmira called all the young women together and stated, "During these next two and half weeks I will probably learn more from you then you will from me. I will do my best and I hope you will put your best foot forward and learn to the best of your ability". With that being said Esmira told the ladies to go to the farthest back section of the back yard and she will be right there. Esmira grabbed the rifle with the ammo and a six shooter and headed for the trees. Esmira had some tin cans already set up. She starts with Audra with the six shooter hiding behind the trees. Audra is noticing that every time she shoots the gun, that it has a slight kick to it. Esmira congratulates her on being that aware of the gun. Margaret and Kim take their turns with the gun and notice the same kick. So then it's time to get savvy with a rifle. Esmira instructs Margaret to get in the prone position and take some shots at the can. Margaret hits two out of three. Audra was going to do the same but Esmira suggested that she have one knee down on the ground and the other foot on the ground and shoot. This was painful for Audra but she hit three out of three. The kick from the rifle hurt her shoulder. Now small but busty Kim had to shoot from a standing position one foot slightly in front of the other while slowly squeezing the trigger for maximum effect. Kim managed to hit two out of three and she found out the slower you squeeze the trigger the less kick the rifle has. Esmira said "that will be all for today, I want you to do me a favor, I want you to do whatever you want to do today, if you want to relax then do it, if you want to read or sew then do it, have fun". The three girls decide to walk up the hill. Audra asks Kim "how are you feeling about everything"? Kim says "as long as I am able to sew I will be happy. There are some new patterns that I would like to try and at home I wouldn't of have been given that chance." Kim says to Margaret "I see that you have been giving eyes to Joe lately, do you want to talk about it?" Margaret sounds alarmed when she says "how could you tell"? "Every time he leaves after supper you can't take your eyes off of him" replied Kim. Margaret in denial asks Audra "is it that noticeable"? Audra bashfully says "yes". Kim mentioned to the girls that she didn't know what came after the hill so they should turn back. All the girls turn around to back towards the stud farm where Kim asks to be excused to do her sewing.

As the rooster crows Jeremy rolls over just in time to see the see the sunrise. This is not like Jeremy his biological clock must be off at least a half an hour. He doesn't have the horses to go groom this morning so instead he wakes the whole crew up and gets them started on the day. His stomach is yearning for some coffee, but he is in different territory. Jeremy throws open the barn doors and oh, my, gosh! The smell of coffee has reached his nostrils; he must be in hog heaven. Jeremy is going to have a great day. He knocks on Ruth's door and asks to come in as Ruth answers "yes". There on the table is a huge pot of oatmeal with three pitchers of milk and corn cakes to go around for everyone. Jeremy glances over to the stove and eyes the pot of coffee and asks for some. Either everyone is hungry or excited to go to work because by the time Jeremy is on his second cup of coffee everyone is done. Jeremy politely excuses himself and the crew and reminds his them all that the rotation that worked yesterday would be the same they were using today. Jeremy knows that if he pushes everyone just a little that the acreage will be done around three which will leave time to visit. By one o' clock and Jeremy is feeling hungry. He turns to his crew and says "let's push on and be done around three so we can relax the rest of the afternoon." The crew knows that it starts to heat up around three and there is no better place to be than inside or under some shade. So they all say "yes". Sure enough, just about three all the hay is done and in cubes and everything is cleaned up. There is one thing missing...

food. The crew walks up into the house and two freshly baked apple pies and one peach pie have cooled, just right for eating. Jeremy sees a fresh pot of coffee brewing and looks up to the sky and says "Amen". Charlie doesn't talk much, so Ruth asks all the questions "how are my girls doing? Are they behaving? Are they doing their chores? How is your gymkhana doing"? Jeremy speaks up. "Everything is fine and we will be opening up within a week and will have our hands completely full. Is there anything else we can do for you, Charlie and Ruth" asks Jeremy. Charlie startles everyone by speaking up and says "I like your work ethic young man, its people like you that will make this country strong, no I can't think of anything else that needs to be done". Jeremy asks "would it be ok if we just visit with you and take leave tomorrow morning"? Both Charlie and Ruth say "yes".

Esmira has the girls picking watermelon from their garden. This will be a nice treat she thought because of the way she will decorate the melon. Audra brings it in and Esmira appoints Kim to do the carving because of her sewing ability. Esmira puts an outline on where she wants Kim to cut. She tells them this is a dish that takes several hours to prepare because of the cutting and the other fruits that will be added. After Kim has the zig-zig pattern cut atop the melon, it will take Margaret to pull up on the middle and Audra to pull up on the other end. The top of the melon came off without breaking. They turned it over and scraped with a spoon the excess melon. Now, for the tedious part, the inside of the melon had to be carefully sliced because grapes and cantaloupe and honey dew would be added to the inside. When completely done the dish looks like something the newspaper printed because of so many colors. Two and a half hours later the dish was done. Esmira was amazed at how well the girls did and invited them outside to the barn. Esmira wanted to show the girls about beauty, so she went over to the pregnant mare and brushed her mane out. Then she told the girls to watch how she braided the horse's mane. After everyone looked on and took their turn the white mare was done. Esmira invited the girls back up to the house and into her parlor to begin showing them what colors of blush and rouge to use on the face. Then she took Audra, whose hair was waist length like hers and showed her how to brush her hair backwards. The girls were becoming so absorbed into brushing their hair that they forgot about everything else. Next she showed both Kim and Margaret why she loved to wear the Garibaldi blouse. Which was a loose fitting blouse that was gathered at the waist band and worn over the skirt? It also had what the stylists called bishop sleeves which looked like puffy sleeves. In fact the shirt hugged the body and it gave a silhouette form allowing a woman to be covered but still allowing them to be feminine. Esmira pointed out how important it was to always make a good first impression. "The gentlemen are coming home tomorrow and let's look good for them" says Esmira. Esmira looked at the bolts of fabric that she had and draped certain colors over the girls to see what they looked good in. Kim looked good in a peach color. Margaret looked good in navy blue and Audra looked good in pink. Esmira took Kim aside and asked "is there any way that you can sew this fabric up as a Garibaldi blouse before tomorrow"? Kim said "Oh, that will be a snap, but it will take a little time". "Great, take all the time you need and thank-you", said Esmira. Kim goes over to her treadle Singer sewing machine and gets to work as Audra and Margaret follow Esmira into the kitchen to start preparing the ham for tomorrow. It was getting to be around 4:00 o'clock and Esmira knew that it would take three hours of cooking before everything is done. With Kim upstairs Esmira knew that she would be one short for fixing the meal, but she would make do. Esmira gave instructions to Audra and Margaret before she went out to feed the horses. Audra took it upon herself to set the table with all the silver ware and plates and glasses. Kim hollers from the parlor to have Audra come in and try the almost completed blouse. Audra tries on the bountiful sleeved blouse and teases Kim by saying "look I have huge arms" as she lets out a gentle laugh. Kim replies "very funny" as she grabs Audra's arm and measures from shoulder to wrist and then says "you are done". As Audra exits the parlor Margaret is busy checking the ham stirring the green beans and checking on the sweet potatoes. Everything seems ok for now. Margaret finishes off the tea as Audra and Margaret both sit down at the table enjoying the refreshment. Margaret sees Esmira coming up to the house and dashes into the kitchen to get Esmira's favorite drink. By the time Esmira reaches the door to come in, Margaret places the tea on the table. Esmira speaks up and asks"I wonder how the men are doing"? Audra states "I hope they are doing ok" and Margaret says with hope in her voice "how could they be doing anything else but perfect"? Esmira gets up to go to the parlor as Kim calls Audra to come into the parlor to try the finished product on. Audra takes off her blouse and tries the new pink garment on for size. Audra looks stunning in it, so much that she is held speechless as Esmira looks on and says to Audra "Well what do you say?" As Audra blurts out" Oh! Oh thank-you, Kim, how do I look". Esmira interjects "like a lady that knows what is happening". Kim who is in the background is now working on Margaret's navy blue Garibaldi blouse... Esmira is overwhelmed with delight. She has found a young lady with 100% heart and seems very dependable for a fourteen year old. It is nearing six o'clock and the ham won't be done for another hour. So Esmira believes this is the best time to show the ladies how to dance. She goes over step by step on how the waltz is done. She makes it known it is very important to follow the man's lead. After Margaret and Audra both practice trading off who was the lead and who was the follower, they believed they could dance if asked. Kim was finishing up on Margaret's blouse and since Kim and Margaret were the same size she just measured her shoulder to wrist and put together the sleeve. Margaret had her black pants on and when she tried her navy blue blouse on, she had the same effect that Audra had. Another, stunning sewing performance by Kim. Esmira announced that dinner was done. Over dinner Esmira complimented Kim again on her sewing and this one time excused her from the dishes afterward, so she could get her own Garibaldi blouse done. Just about time the dishes were done Kim had only to add the sleeves. She added them on, and tried it on and entered the living room where everyone was at to show them. Peach was definitely Kim's color. Everybody sat around drinking tea and just relaxing. Time went by before they knew it and it was 9:30. Esmira told them that she was headed for bed and they might do the same because 5:30 came early and they all had to be out grooming the horses.

 Five-thirty came before they knew it. As they were leaving the house Esmira pulled Margaret aside and asks if she would fix the breakfast that would make this house famous, the blueberry pancakes, the sunny side up eggs and bacon and or sausage for your choosing. If Esmira's timing was right by the time she, Kim and Audra groomed the seventeen stallions and brushed down the mares, everyone would be ready for breakfast. The sun was just coming up over the trees and it looked like a single ray was aimed at the barn, the mares were filling the warmth. Margaret rang the bell and Esmira was right, they were finishing up the horses. Esmira ate light; something told her that Jeremy would be pulling in around ten-thirty. Kim and Audra ate like they had never seen food before and Margaret ate moderately. Margaret was one of those taste testers as she cooked. Esmira told the girls that after cleaning the morning dishes she wanted them all to get dressed in their brand new Garibaldi blouses and skirts to just relax.

Jeremy got the whole crew together. He could only imagine how Esmira would feel when he pulled in with three more people and the possibility of two more! He would have a fun time sharing the news of how the team helped Charlie and Ruth. Jeremy and the whole crew said good-bye to Charlie and Ruth as they headed on down the road. The Sun was getting a little warm and the canteens were full. Jeremy was in no hurry so he was just walking the horses. It got to be a lot friendlier on the long drive because of all the information that was shared. They almost felt like a big family. One more hill to go and they were home. Jeremy went over the hill and saw Esmira in her beautiful blouse with the tiny pearl buttons from her neck to her waist that she only wore on special occasions. Esmira went back inside and told the girls to wait inside until the men come in. Jeremy pulled the Chariot into the barn and waited 'til everyone had put there horse in the barn and all six of them lined up single file and headed up to the house. Esmira and the girls were on the other side of the living room, so they would be the first to be seen when the men opened the door. All the guys, Bill, Earl, Jack, Ralph Joe and Jeremy went inside in that order. Bill's eleven year old eyes opened to twice the size. Earl, Jack, Ralph and Joe all took their hats off, and Jeremy wore a big grin on his face. The sight of Kim in peach and Margaret in navy blue and Audra in pink was a refreshing picture. Audra broke the ice and said "well come in, put your hats up and stay awhile, what you would like to drink, lemonade or tea?" Kim went on over and shook Bills hand and said "what is your name"? Earl interjected, "his name is Bill, I am his older brother Earl and this is my older brother Jack. You see Bill had a fever when he was two and it took his hearing, so he never learned to talk. But I never saw anyone that could read faster than Bill. So if you see a lot of notes around you know Bill has been close by". Esmira looks at everyone and then gives Jeremy the eye. The kind that means you will explain all this. Bill and Kim stay together most of the afternoon. Audra greets Ralph with a hug, while Joe, Margaret and Jim are getting to know each other.

Esmira grabs Jeremy gives him a big kiss and takes him to their room and says" please explain"? Jeremy tells Esmira the complete story of how he met the gentlemen their circumstances and then how they all worked at Charlie and Ruth's and what kind of heart they really had. Esmira, Jeremy says "I love you, and these gentlemen are keepers." That's all it took, Esmira felt like melting into Jeremy's arms, but lunch was ready.

Kim motioned to Bill to come to the parlor in order to get more chairs for the new people that will be joining the table. There is nothing better after a long ride than a ham sandwich on warm bread. Jeremy wanted to know what all happened while they were gone. He already noticed the wonderful blouses that the girls were wearing. He noticed the meal, which was outstanding. He wanted to know the details if time permitted. Half of his mind was on what happened while the other half was on the business of running a stud farm. The business won out. Jeremy could find out the details tonight behind closed doors. Jeremy directed everyone outside to the bunk house. He mentioned to Joe to show the bunk house to Jack, Earl and Bill. Jeremy took Ralph to the back side of the barn and asked Ralph "would this be a good place to put up the forge on a permanent basis"? Ralph looked around at the enclosure to make sure there was no drafts coming inside the barn and answered "yes". Ralph followed Jeremy over to the bunkhouse where he met Joe and the others and motioned everyone to come to the tack room. Jeremy pointed to Bill and then pointed to the curry comb as he spoke out loud, "Everyone will be required to be up at 6:00 o'clock and to be ready with curry comb in hand" as he raises curry comb for Bill to see "and curry comb five horses before 7:00 o'clock, everyday, unless directed otherwise. Since there are five of you here, each one of you will be responsible for having a clean tack room. I will tell the individual that morning who will clean it out. Let's all go over there now and clean it up so the person tomorrow won't be taken advantage of". The tack room took ten minutes to clean. The bridles all were in order the saddles were in place and all curry combs were in their home. Jeremy talked to Ralph and said "I think Bill will be a behind the scenes person likes yourself. Would you mind taking him under your wing and teaching him what you know." Ralph says "no". Jeremy needed to show everyone the importance of respect to the horses, so he gathered everyone together at the mares corral and said "pick out one of the horses that you curried combed and I'll meet you back here in ten minutes to be ready to ride." Jeremy needed to get inside for a cup of coffee and a gentle kiss from Esmira. He headed to the house walked in and caught Esmira teaching the girls about beauty tips, and lost his train of thought. Jeremy saw Kim with mascara on, Margaret with bright red lipstick and Audra with light blue eye shadow, and stood there with mouth opened until Esmira said "Honey can I help you with something?" Jeremy shook his head, closed his mouth and was too embarrassed to get a kiss and said "just coming in to get a cup of coffee". Jeremy sipped his coffee until it was gone and then went outside to his horse as everyone was waiting on him. Jeremy mounted up and took his horse about a half a mile up the road and turned around. He pointed to a section just east of the mare's corral where he wanted the gymkhana. He talked it over with Ralph on where he wanted the barrels placed, once placed there, the barrels would stay there. There was already a chute there for timed races and the broncos coming out. Jeremy went over to Jack and asked "where do you think we should put the jumps?" Jack said "with the barrels already out there, it would look confusing to put them anywhere else. I believe that you should have the barrels removed at the end of the activity and put your jumps in then." Jeremy thought about what Jack said and it made sense to him. He also thought to himself that it was a pleasure having other people around him with good horse sense. So he visualized the bronco riding going first, the barrel racing going next and the jumping last. Then he sent Ralph and Bill over to the stallions corral to make sure all the horses were shod. Then he sent Joe, Jack, and Earl to bring the stallions out for them to do some bronco riding. They bring three horses out and Joe was the most eager to show his skills. So Jeremy told him to get on the palomino. Joe secured his grip; and he was ready. Jeremy motioned to Earl, to let the door open and the bronco riding began. The horse went left came down and did a circle went up again and turned right, and off Joe went around four seconds.

Joe picked himself off the ground dusted himself off and was frustrated with himself. He has done better than that in the past. Jeremy sees this and will get back with him on this. Jeremy knows that Joe would be a prime candidate for whispering. Next up was Jack he got in the chute fixed his hands and almost the same thing happened but Jack lasted six seconds. Earl was up, this was his first time, and he fixed his hands, than motioned to the chute opener that he was ready. The chute door swung open and another second Earl was down on the ground. He too, dusted himself off and wondered where he went wrong. Jeremy called them all over and told them that was enough for one day. He asked them all one question. "Did anyone of you groom these horses this morning"? No one answered. "That's what I thought, if you don't respect the horses first, how can you expect any respect in return"!

It's coffee time Jeremy thought as he walked up to the house. He believed it's time to introduce Joe to horse whispering. Jeremy opened the door cautiously; he remembered what happened last time. However, this time Esmira met him with a kiss. She also introduced two new individuals that wanted to join the gymkhana. They were Ross and Byron. The interview started and Ross passed with flying colors. Byron got three of the four questions right. It was the honesty question that was disturbing Jeremy. Jeremy dismissed Byron and headed into his bedroom. Jeremy was busy rubbing his forehead. He walked over to the side of the bed as he bumped into something that startled him. He took his hand down from his forehead and looked to see what he had bumped into. Esmira says "hello, honey" as she reaches for his waist "you have always taught me if something is troubling you, do something different. What were you thinking about?" as she winks at him and then gives him a kiss. Jeremy says "thank-you, the decision that I had to make becomes clearer now." Jeremy decided to have Byron join the team. It was midday and he ran into Margaret as he left the house and grabbed his coffee.

Esmira calls all the girls together and tells them how beautiful they look. All of them are wearing dresses in their favorite colors; Kim is in peach, Audra in pink and Margaret in navy blue. Esmira kept on teaching the girls how to keep the men pleased. Esmira told them to get the lemonade and the tea ready to drink with enough glasses for everyone. Esmira went out and rung the triangle with her bar so people over in the next acre could hear. All the men looked at Jeremy as he motioned to them to come up to the porch for a break. Byron motioned to Ross to go get his Banjo as Byron dug his mouth harp out of one pocket and the harmonica out of the other. As everyone got to the porch Ross and Byron had already started playing their music. Esmira and Jeremy look at each other and are already thinking of a way to incorporate this music into the gymkhana. Joe is having eyes for Margaret and Ralph is having eyes for Audra and both Jim and Bill are getting better acquainted with Kim. Jack, Ross and Byron are more concerned on keeping their life's in one piece. A full hour must have passed with the nice music being played. Jeremy calls out "I hate to rap this up but the mares corral needs mending". As everyone broke apart Jeremy went over to Ross and Byron and asked "where did you learn and how long have you been playing?" Answer came back, "while mom and pa were out in the fields we were left behind with Pa's sister and she sang all day long. We picked up the music so we could have our own thing going on and before you know it we were playing at barn raising's and the like. Pa's sister got married and moved out east and our music went away for a while. It was nice playing again so we know we still have it inside us".

 About an hour later Esmira calls over to Jeremy to see if his crew is done. Jeremy says "that he will be done in a half an hour". Esmira says "great! We are having the oldest fashioned dinner anyone can ever have". Jeremy says "let me guess, beans and rice". Esmira says "how did you know"! A half hour passed and Esmira and the girls had set the table where all twelve of them could feast. Jack, the curious one asked Jeremy at the dinner table what was on for tomorrow. Jeremy said "I am glad you asked, Kim has sewn together a banner to put on the fence to welcome everyone. Near this banner will be a little booth selling pies and accepting donations on the gymkhana. We are hoping that the two weeks of the gymkhana will bring over two thousand people both new and familiar to this territory." "We will make sure that this booth is well put together by the hands of Ralph and Bill. Then we will take practice runs on setting up the barrels and the jumps, so we will be ready when the real thing comes". Dinner was almost over so Ross and Byron asked if they could play some music. Jeremy and Esmira said "yes". Ross started playing The Battle Hymn of the Republic on his fiddle and Byron followed with the melody on his harmonica, next was an old fashioned Yankee Doodle song. They played for another hour before they wrapped it up.

Another day started with Jeremy grooming the stallions. He finished up and saw everybody flood out of the bunkhouse. This startled Jeremy; this was the first time in two weeks that they were right on time. Jeremy directed them to the mares for grooming. A half an hour passed and Jeremy came and looked at the mares. This was outstanding. Not only were the mares groomed but all of the manes were neatly braided, all thirteen of the mares. Jeremy said "congratulations, now let's go eat the kind of breakfast the frontier is known for, pancakes, eggs, bacon, toast and orange juice or milk". The neat and beautiful girls met them at the door with smiles. Ralph winked at Audra, Joe smiled at Margaret and Earl and Bill shook Kim's hand. Jeremy reminded them to eat hearty because there was a lot of work to be done. Thirty minutes later all the males were out by the mares corral setting up Kim's banner. Ralph and Bill went to a corner of the barn and started to make the booth. It would be a three sided booth because the back of the booth was already in place. Two hours later the booth had been made and put into place.

Jeremy took Joe aside and told him that he had been watching him ride the broncos and mentioned again, if he was interested in whispering he would be available. Joe told Jeremy "let me think about it". Jeremy reminded Joe that it was only three days until the start of the gymkhana and if he was going to at least start it that he would need to know by tomorrow morning. Joe said "I will have an answer by tomorrow." Although Joe was completely capable of making a decision himself he felt that he had to include his brother Ralph on this decision. That night before they went to sleep Joe called out to Ralph "you know Ralph, all the other bronco riding I have done has been like one snapping a finger, get on the horse, eight seconds later the bell rings and I get off the horse. But out here something has gone awry. It's like I am a rookie, can't last more than four seconds, and this grooming thing I have never even heard of before. You know, one is just supposed to get on the horse and show him who is boss, end of story. I am perplexed"! As he takes off his hat and rubs his brow. Jack over hears the conversation and says "excuse me, I overheard the grooming part and what I think is going on is just a mere respect factor to the horse, I mean." Joe says "it's not my way; I never had any respect for nothing my whole life. Why the heck should I start now?" Earl leans in and says "sometimes when you start something new it's downright irritating, because you are expected to catch on and get with it". Joe interrupts "are you calling me stupid"? Earl says "no, that's not it at all. There is just another way of doing things and to get better results. I mean try it his way, you have done everything else and I think you will be surprised". Ross chimes in "hey Joe, do you like my music?" Joe says "what the heck does that have to do with bronco riding?" Ross says "just about everything, if you knew that some of those pieces we play took about a month to learn. Now think about it, we play over thirty different pieces and if every-one of them took a month to catch on, that would take thirty months to put together. Think of it this way, what do you have to lose?" Joe says "well first off, I have never been in this kind of situation before. I have never been around people that care what I do. I am a grown man and this caring and respect stuff makes my stomach go flip flop. I got my answer. I will tell Jeremy yes in the morning. Thanks guys".

Joe was the first one up. He slipped into his boots and met Jeremy grooming the horses at five thirty. Joe said to Jeremy "my answer is yes." Jeremy says "oh what changed your mind?" Joe replies "I just had to think it over and got a different perspective when I mentioned it to the guys". Jeremy says "Well I think you have made a good choice, let's see how many horses we can groom before the others get up!" Joe groomed six and Jeremy groomed eight by the time the rest of the crew came to the barn. Jeremy told the crew to get the rest of the horses done by seven. He pulled Joe aside and told him to get the appaloosa. Jeremy had to test Joe's decision making by allowing him to have the most spirited horse on the land. Jeremy showed Joe how to stroke the horse's neck while putting the burlap bag over his head. Jeremy also showed him why the burlap bag was used. Jeremy then told him to talk to the horse like he was your long lost friend to pay close attention to his breathing. If for some reason the horse starts to breathe faster, talk to him about how much you missed him, calm the horse down and relax him by the way you whisper to him. Remember to tell the horse that he likes to listen to your voice, and only your voice. Jeremy watched Joe whisper to the horse for thirty minutes. Then Jeremy told Joe to tell the horse that he will be back tomorrow at the same time, but now he has to go. Jeremy showed Joe how to take the bag off; nice and slow while still stroking his neck. Joe did exactly that as the horse remained calm. Jeremy told Joe "you did a good job for just starting. Now let's go eat".

Kim, the young fourteen year old had been extremely busy at the sewing machine, with bolts of fabric that Esmira had gotten from the store in town. She was able to make a lime green dress for Esmira, a peach one for herself, a navy blue one for Margaret and a pink one for Audra. It was extremely tough for her to work on the bust line because they were all so busty except for Audra. She whipped thru hers with a breeze because of her average bust and long legs. It was the buttons that made the dress so tough since it had forty buttons from neckline to the waist. Kim thanked Esmira for allowing her to display her talents. Esmira was just finishing making up all the girls right before the gentlemen walked into the house for breakfast. It was a moment to be seized, as the men all dropped their jaws in disbelief at the beauty that stood before them. Esmira announced "you can all put your tongues back into your mouths. This is just the effect that we want to have on all the public that visits here for the Gymkhana. I am completely surprised at the way Kim undertook this project and great thanks to her. Audra and Margaret have put together wonderful cooking talents to help this gymkhana get under way. We are two days out and I know the girls are ready. So if you will please sit down to the pancakes and omelets and bacon that Audra and Margaret have fixed, and have a great day". Jeremy goes over to Esmira and says "my you look stunning". Esmira says "how my great man doing"? She pats him on the back and grabs his hand to lead him into the bedroom, she calmly squeezes his hand and whispers into his ear "don't the girls just look beautiful?" Jeremy takes Esmira in his arms and says "not as pretty as the one I have in my arms" as he gives her a squeeze. Everybody sits down to enjoy breakfast. Over breakfast Jeremy states "this is the walk thru of what will happen in two days. If everything goes well on this walk thru then so will the real thing". Everyone excuses themselves from breakfast as Jeremy goes over to get another cup of coffee. Esmira wraps her tiny hands around his face and kisses him twice, once for today and once for tonight. Jeremy kisses her back and turns and walks outside with his coffee and his crew to Ralph and Bill's station where they will be making horse shoes. He continues to walk through the stations as it will be that first day when they will be showing their skills off to the public. Everybody will see the mares first then the stallions which will lead to the bronco station where they will show both Joe and Jack ready to mount their horses. Next will be Kim, Audra and Margaret showing off their foods with Ross and Byron nearby playing fiddle, banjo, harmonica and mouth harp. Then as the people look to the west they will see the land that we have available to keep this stud farm going. Jeremy took this information to Esmira and they discussed the plans and other things behind closed doors. It was forty five minutes until lunch and Jeremy congratulated everybody and gave them the rest of the day off. Jeremy went in the house and to the bedroom where Esmira had just unbuttoned her dress to the waist. Esmira knew it was a hot day and just wanted a hug. Jeremy came over gave her a hug and stroked her long and lovely hair. Now Jeremy was ready to talk business. Jeremy mentioned that the only place that might need improvement was a Kim's station showing, off her sewing talents. Esmira answered"do you want to move that machine out there or do you want to show off the products that Kim has made"? Jeremy answered "I think it would be better just to show the garments that she made, with that change everything looks great"! Jeremy said "I gave the gentlemen the rest of the day off" as Esmira interrupts "I gave the girls the rest of the day off, we think alike. Now that you have me burning with desire, may I give you some attention"? As her dress drops to the floor exposing her perfect breasts and developing baby bump how can her man say no? She knew that this action would come more often because of what she felt. She didn't mean to seem selfish but it felt so good. She kissed him every time she could. Jeremy and Esmira finally had some time to release all the pent up desire they had been holding on to. Esmira felt quite happy now that she had fulfilled her desire and even happier that she had quenched Jeremy's. Now it was back to the stud farm, Jeremy got up, got dressed and made sure Esmira was ready before they went to the door.

    Kim, Bill and Earl were busy playing hide and go seek. Ralph, Joe and Jack were busy grooming the mares and talking about which one they liked the best. Joe took the pregnant mare and Ralph took the palomino and Jack took the appaloosa probably because of its spots. Audra and Margaret were walking near the canal, which was very tempting to take a swim, when they heard the lunch bell ring. Audra said to Margaret maybe some other time we could go for a dip. Margaret spoke up "I would like that very much"

Everybody filed up to the outdoor patio where sandwiches are served with tea and lemonade. Jeremy congratulated everyone for being so prepared the day before the gymkhana. Since it was a cooler day in August, where everyone could enjoy themselves it was a good day for taking some time for relaxing. Esmira tried to warn everyone about the crowd that could be showing up in the days to come. Esmira explained "every time we went to town to get fabric we checked the telegraph office, we will be expecting over eight thousand people over the next few weeks. If everything goes right our dream of makeing this gymkhana a rodeo within a few years will become a reality. Some people will only be looking at our studs, some will be of the competitive spirit and some will just come for the barn dancing. Everyone was astounded by the news and cheered with loud Whoops of excitment! Jeremy gives Esmira a sharp glance because he forgot to mention the dancing. So he interrupts and says" right after lunch for about an hour we need to clear the area to give Ross and Byron enough room to play their music."

At five-thirty in the morning Jeremy is up and down at the stallions doing the grooming. Ten minutes later Joe shows up and starts to do the regular grooming. Jeremy speaks to Joe "why the change" Joe says "sometimes I don't do the brightest things, but I realized that I wanted that eight seconds more than anything and if horse whispering will help me get there then so be it". Jeremy says to Joe "hum, those where my exact words about eight years ago" Joe looks at him with alarm and says "you mean you used to ride?" Jeremy says come here Joe as he takes Joe into the parlor and unlocks a footlocker that no one has seen in years and shows him the saddle, the belt buckle and the key to the city as well a newspaper clipping that he saved. Joe asks "do you still do bronco riding?" Jeremy says "not now. I decided to turn my love for horses into this gymkhana so others could enjoy the gift that I gave up. I turned that gift into horse whispering and knowing that there are only a few of us in the states, I will always have my passion".

Joe looked stunned. He had never met someone at a young age such as Jeremy that was so involved with helping people and liking it. Jeremy had already achieved what Joe wanted to do. Joe was so focused on the goal of being a state rodeo champion, and now he saw what the next step after the rodeo might look like, WOW was all his mind could comprehend! It was nearing six-o'clock and everyone was starting to line up in the grooming area. Joe returned to groom the mares. He felt like he knew where his future was going now. As he groomed the mares he hummed his own private tune. Everyone finished up the grooming early and went to the house. Thanks to Audra, Kim and Margaret another breakfast banquet was ready, pancakes, sausage, omelets, biscuits, bacon and orange juice and milk. Esmira stands up and wishes everyone good luck on the first day of the gymkhana and to meet at the side booth around noon for lunch and any other directions.

Around eight fifteen in the morning Joe is on horseback, ready to do his bronco riding. He has already said his short prayer and done everything he could think of to prepare for these eight seconds. He grips his rope a little tighter and the chute opens. With his left arm raised in the air for balance the horse heaves up into the air. Joe digs in his spurs as the horse lands on the ground for another heave up in the air. This horse is mean and he turns when he moves on the land again. Joe was ready for it, he turns with him. The horse heaves into the air again. Joe spurs the horse again and is ready for a turn when the horse lands as Joe loses his hat and the eight second buzzer goes off. Jack is there with another horse along the side of the bronco to pick him up. Joe is grinning from ear to ear. Next in the chute is a walk-on named Chip. He raises his arm as if he is ready and the chute opens. Chip is grabbing for more rope like he was not ready. He is thrown off the horse at five seconds. Chip lands on the ground, picks himself up and gets out of the bronco's way. Next in the chute is Jack. Jack gives the sign that he is ready and the chute flies open. The horse flings his head to the left as he lurches up in the air. The horse lands and lurches again but this time to the right. This got Jack off guard but he adjusts himself as he digs his spurs in the horse. The horse gets near to the fence as Jack pulls his head the other way to avoid danger as the eight second buzzer goes off. Joe rides along the side of the bronco and picks Jack off the horse as he tells Jack "good job". Then he suggests they go over to the booth to see the girls, Jack agrees. Jack sees Kim and walks right up as if this has been the girl that has been waiting for him. Jack compliments the dresses as he notices the handicraft and love that has gone into each piece. Jack touches the navy blue dress that Kim has made Margaret and says "this looks beautiful, did it take long to make?" Kim replies in a professional manner "I am not sure I just love to sew" as she places her small smooth hand on his rough hand and looks up to him with a smile. Jack realizes she is the one for him. Joe is off talking to Margaret, asking how her day has gone thus far. Margaret winks at him and says "well it just got a whole lot better since you came by". Joe asks if she wanted to slip away and get something cool to drink. Margaret replies "I would love to but Esmira doesn't want us to leave our station until five this evening, when the gymkhana is done for the day". Joe asks "well, then would it be ok if I bring you something cool back"? Margaret says "that would be nice but not necessary". Before Jack and Joe manage to pull away, an older couple steps up to the booth and greets Audra, Kim and Margaret and says "Are they treating you right here?" Kim calls out to Jack and Joe and says "I would like for you to meet my mother and father"! Joe says "Oh, we have met. I have never tasted a better apple pie in my life." Kim, Audra and Margaret did not understand. Charlie opens up and says "I have never met a better bunch of men in my life, the way they took care of the hay that one sweltering day. My hat is off to them. Jack and Joe have you met my three daughters, Kim, Audra and Margaret?" Jack and Joe innocently say "we have now, as they excuse themselves. As they start to walk away Charlie says "young men, what do you have in your future?" Jack speaks up "well we both like bronco riding when we get a chance!" Charlie says "After your bones are rattled, have you thought of settling down." Joe says "no, haven't gave it much thought". Charlie says "if you are interested you might want to take a look at my daughters." Jack says "ok, I hate to be rude but we must be getting along". Charlie says "Have a nice day." As they walk away, Joe says "man; that was close, and akward. Instead of being chased away like hoodlums we are welcomed with open arms. That is something I have to get used to!" Jack says "you can say that again. I know those girls are cute but are you ready to settle down Joe?" Joe says "let's save that question for another day."

Chapter 12

Ruth is being busy asking all sorts of questions about how the girls are doing and how do they like the stud farm. Kim answers with "I am able to develop a talent that I wasn't aware that I had." Audra and Margaret reply "Mother I have been taught some cooking tips that would land any man, now it's up to me on who I choose." Audra says "me to, I never realized that one person could have so much knowledge about different things. Esmira has taught us so much". Ruth says "Now don't get to picky. You might just pass by the one that's right for you". All three of them chime in "Yes mother". Ruth yells at Charlie "we should be going".

Kim says "what do you think about, I mean when this gymkhana is over, are you ready to go back to the farm?" Audra and Margaret look at each other with eyes wide open, as if a rattle snake was close by. Kim says "any answers?" Audra and Margaret say "well we are working on a plan" Kim is over joyed with excitement and says "please let me know". They huddle momentarily and Margaret says "nothing would please me better when this gymkhana is over to be married to Joe". "Really" says Audra "I have been thinking the same way about Ralph". "That's great" says Kim, "I want the same for me and Jack." "What" says Audra "you are going on fifteen. What do you have to offer"? Kim flaunts her best assets by drawing attention to her lovely breasts with both hands and says "I have a start". Margaret who remembers how sternly Esmira ripped into her about kissing Joe interrupts and says "if that is her dream let her stick with it. I think she would be good at whatever she decides to do. Now all we have to do is hook our men!" Audra says "by the time this gymkhana is over I plan to be married"!

Bill and Ralph are busy keeping the fire hot for making the horseshoes fit just right. This will be an all-day affair and anyway they have seventeen stallions to do and thirteen mares to take care of. Jeremy couldn't think of a better way to show off their talent and get the horses shod at the same time.

Next up was the barrels and Earl was on the appaloosa, as the chute opens he was off, he rounded the right barrel without touching it went for the left barrel curved around it then shot for the top barrel and went for the finish line all under seventeen seconds. This sport went fast; no sooner was Earl across the line the chute opened for Bill. He was on the Roan, he took the right one headed for the left went around it and headed for the top barrel and passed the finish line at sixteen seconds. Bill was smiling from ear to ear. Next up was Byron he did everything just like the ones before him and tied at the finish line at sixteen seconds. Ross was up and sped thru the barrels just under sixteen seconds on the palomino. Everybody could hear the applause. Ross was happy. It was also time for lunch. Esmira had thought ahead, if her people would want to eat outside there was a white ribbon that they had to show for free eats. Somehow Jack, Ralph, and Joe ended up at the booth where Kim, Audra and Margaret were serving the hundreds of people their Fried chicken, potato salad and beans. Ralph saw the opportunity to be next to Audra passing out the chicken so he stepped in and helped. Joe saw the same opportunity with the potato salad by helping Margaret and Jack followed by helping Kim with the beans. It made the line go much faster. Within an hour and running out of food Kim had set three plates of food aside for Joe, Jack and Ralph. Jack felt proud that his girl would think of being considerate and setting things aside. Margaret gave permission to the fellows to go ahead and eat because she knew that the jumping exercises were coming right up. Audra made sure their glasses were full of water.

The jumps had been erected. Jeremy, Ralph, Jack, Earl, Bill, Ross and Byron were all ready. Each one is well trained in each jump but this time they broke it down singular so as not to take too much time. Jeremy took the steeplechase jump. Ralph took the bush jump. Jack took the water jump. Jim took the brick jump. Bill took the pint sized steeplechase jump combined with a water jump. Ross and Byron took the valley jump. This is where you go downhill and uphill and right at the top of the hill is a jump. If this was lengthened to its rightful time, it would take around twenty minutes per individual. Joe was waiting for things to come to a conclusion, because he was up next with the horse whispering.

Joe was up. Joe slowly put his burlap bag over the horse's head, while stroking the horse's neck for around ten minutes Joe would whisper to the horse. For five more minutes with the sack still on the horse head he would walk him around the barn. Then he would put the blanket on followed by the saddle. Then he would take the burlap sack off while putting the bridle bit into his mouth and get on the horse. Then everyone started to clap.

The people's attention was then directed to Kim's booth where she had just sold the emerald green dress and the navy blue dress for one hundred and fifty dollars each. Kim knew that it would be left up to her to sew more dresses as well as the bridal dresses for herself, Audra and Margaret. She didn't have a lot of time. How could she sneak enough time in to make all those dresses and then the bridal dresses? Kim got together with Audra and Margaret, told them the plan, to see what they thought. Margaret who was a little older, but built exactly like Kim, could appreciate her dream. Imagine, just for a minute, that over one hundred men have noticed you, thru the gymkhana, and all this fourteen year old could think about is how she can give to her older sisters. Her dream included herself and Jack and the others involved, and the time line was less than two weeks away. So for now all anyone had to know is that she was making more dresses for the gymkhana. She had the patterns for her build and Audra's build and that was enough for her. The gymkhana was wrapping up for the day and she still had to hint around to Jack about what was happening without spilling the beans. So she said "Jack although I really want to be with you, I have to make two dresses tonight because of the ones I sold today." So Kim excused herself and went inside to her sewing parlor. She put together both wedding tops for Kim and Margaret and managed to put an emerald green dress together in Audra's build. It was definitely time to go to bed; five thirty would come soon enough.

No sooner then she closed her eyes did it feel she was waking up again. She went down to make breakfast and saw Esmira. Kim told Esmira of her plans and asked to be excused from making breakfast. Esmira said "although I normally wouldn't do it. This is extending circumstances, so go". Kim made it to the parlor and stared at a plum dress with buttons down the back that looked like it was made for Margaret. Kim put the buttons together first, that was the hardest part and the button holes matched up perfectly. Kim barely got it done, had time for breakfast and was out the door. She thanked her sisters for carrying her role in the breakfast making knowing that tomorrow she wouldn't have that luxury. Esmira stayed back in the kitchen making another eight pounds of potato salad as Jeremy was putting together all the chicken that need to be cooked by noon. Now it was time for the grooming of the horses. Bill took one of the mares and Earl took one of the stallions and for the next hour showed why it was important for the grooming. They even checked the hoofs to make sure that no mud got up inside the shoe. This gave Joe enough time to groom his stallion and get ready for the horse whispering. The timing was perfect. Bill and Jim had just got finished as the audience was directed to Joe and the appaloosa. The reason why the appaloosa had been picked was because of his high strung temperament. If Joe could show that a temperamental horse could be calmed down, then more people would be interested. Joe captured the audience by stroking the neck of the animal for ten minutes then covering the head with the burlap sack. Joe gently stroked the horses back for five minutes before putting the blanket on. All this time he kept on whispering to the horse. He put the saddle on and people noticed a little skip to the horse. Joe spoke to the audience and reassured them that this was normal for the additional weight that has been distributed to his body. Joe lifted the sack from the horse's head at the same time that he put the bridal into the horse's mouth. Joe then led the horse around for ten minutes and before mounting him and starting to ride him. The audience was impressed. Some of them went to find Jeremy to see if they could be trained in this horse whispering. Now it was to the barn for blacksmithing.

 Everyone went to the barn to see Ralph and Bill demonstrating bending the horse shoes into the right fitting for the horse as the hammer clanged against the anvil. Now it's time for Earl to show his mastering of the bronco riding. He completes his eight seconds which doesn't make Joe feel too happy. Then it's on to the jumping which is mastered by two strangers that no one knows, and off to the barrels that are completed by three unknowns. Their times were held at eighteen seconds, still an impressive show. During this time three dresses out of four Audra had made were bought for one hundred and fifty dollars apiece. The navy blue, the peach and the plum all went to the same customer. She had one dress left and it was ten minutes to noon. Kim went to Esmira and asked what to do! Esmira asked Kim if she wouldn't mind staying in the house and doing her sewing while her sisters took care of the booth. Kim replied "that would be ok". What an opportunity! Hopefully she could put together the bottoms of the wedding dresses and then go on to put three dresses together that would match Audra's build. She had fabrics in nice carnation pink, peach and a sky blue she could use to put together the dresses. The bottoms of the wedding dresses took about a half an hour a piece. She looked outside to see if anyone was coming, no one in sight. She went with the sky blue and as soon as she was done she took it outside. She told Audra if she could relay a message to Jack. The message she wanted told was "Let him know how much I care for him and then let him know that I will meet him at the dance tonight". Audra said "ok". Kim went in and sewed the peach and the carnation dresses within the hour. She returned to the booth with both dresses and set them down. She noticed Joe and Ralph were getting extremely close to Audra and Margaret. She didn't mind, she had to go back in and get her wedding dress made. Since Margaret and Kim were the same build, she wanted to put more flowering along the bust line so they could tell the two dresses apart. Kim had just finished her wedding dress and put it up when everyone was walking in the door. Another day at the gymkhana had passed and Margaret told Kim the sky blue dress had sold for one hundred and seventy five dollars. Kim had one more dress to sew and forty five minutes to do it. So she put together a sky blue dress in her build for bustier customers. Now it was time to pull out the pork roast that she put in the stove around three hours ago. There was some left over potato salad and Audra was just finishing up the green beans. This was going to be dinner fit for a king. As soon as the dishes were washed she would be getting ready for the dance. Kim pulled

Audra and Margaret aside and showed them the wedding gowns. Both Audra's and Margaret's mouth gapped open in astonishment. "Oh, you shouldn't have" came from the sister's mouth. Kim said "It's ok. Now just hook your man". All three put on their Sunday best and walked across to the barn, where Ross and Byron were getting their instruments warmed up. Songs were played like Onward Christian Soldiers, There is a Green Hill Far Away, The Little Old Log Cabin in the Lane, Beware, Looking Back, Good-bye Liza Jane, Mollie Darling, plus many more just to name a few. The playing lasted until at least 10:00 p.m. when Jeremy stepped in and said that two more songs could be played before calling it a night.

Five-thirty came early and Audra, Margaret and Kim were ready with the food to beat all, flap-jacks eggs, bacon, and sausage, feeding twelve people. Kim now also loved to cook and she kept on learning from her gifted sister Margaret. All she could concentrate on now was eating, washing the dishes, and getting to her sewing. If she could sew five dresses by the end of the day, she would be caught up. She would really like to know who the lady was that kept buying her dresses. Kim had an idea. Today she was going to put together a pant and suit jacket for women, three dresses all of different builds and a bonnet. She had a cherry color, a teal color, a beige color, a white color and some plaid for the suit jacket. Kim knew that Jack was bronco riding again today. So she would have to break away in an hour to see Jack ride. She woild take some lemonade up to her sisters with the hope of catching Jack ride. The grooming would just be finishing up. Right now the barrels were being run and it looked like Bill had the best score just under sixteen seconds. Kim was just starts up the steps with the lemonade when she heard the chute open. She hurried and tried to get there on time. She missed the ride but found out that it was Joe that had just finished with his ride. Jack was up next. Kim looks on as Jack secures his grip, motions to the chute opener that he is ready, and out the bronco leaps. It is like someone put the cinch on to tight. Jack is expecting the horse to roll. He digs in deeper with his spurs, as the horse rises back trying to confuse the rider. Jack is aware of what the horse is doing as the buzzer sounds and Joe is riding alongside the horse to pick Jack up. Joe tells him good job, as Kim clenches her fist and says proudly to herself "that's my man". As Kim is walking back to the house Esmira notices and asks where she has been. Kim just says that she brought lemonade to her sisters. Kim gets back inside and starts on the plaid suit jacket. Instead of putting a zipper inside the pants she puts a set of four buttons with a flap that conceals them. She cuts the pattern out, sews the back on, then the arms, puts a collar on the back and is done with the suit. Next she follows the pattern for the bonnet and within ten minutes she is done. Now she decides to give the first dress a small bust line with a longer length for more leg room. She takes the cherry color and is awed at the beautiful color. She puts the buttons on one side and matches the other side with the button holes. She measures the small waist size and then finishes up the dress. It is getting close to noon and Kim is hungry. She cuts off some ham that has been cooking in the oven and makes a quick sandwich. She washes the sandwich down with the lemonade and is back putting the beige dress together. This time it is a big bust line and a tall length that takes her about an hour and a half to put together. Now she puts the Teal dress with a big bust line and a smaller leg room very similar to what Esmira would wear. It is getting close to four thirty and the jumps are just about finished. Kim decides to stay put with her older sisters and is just about to fold up shop when a lady comes around and buys the plaid pant suit for two hundred dollars. The buyer is just about ready to take off but spots the bonnet and pays thirty dollars for it. Kim is just about ready to offer her the other dresses but that means she has to sew the rest of the night, if she sells them. Kim is getting tired and she knows that she still has to go help with the dinner tonight. Maybe this is what Pa meant when he said the spirit can be strong but the flesh is weak. "Excuse me young lady, may I see that teal dress?" "Why, yes" said Kim, as she hands the dress over to the lady. "This is beautiful; it is so hard to find a big bust line with smaller leg room. Who made this"? Margaret and Audra sing out "she did"! The lady looks at Kim and says "then you have some talent that needs to be exposed. What's your price?" Kim bashfully says "two hundred" as the lady puts her hand into her purse and gives Kim four fifty dollar bills. This lady knows that back east she can easily ask double the price and get it. However, this dress is put together so well she just might keep it for herself. It's about ten minutes to quitting time and Kim suggests closing early because she knows she still has to help in getting dinner.

She is just about ready to fold the beige dress up and a tall woman about six feet is at the booth. The lady asks "may I see that dress"? Kim gives the dress to the lady. She holds it to her body presses in at the waist and says "this is perfect, how much"? Kim speaks up "that usually goes for three hundred but if you want it today it's yours for two hundred and thirty." Before Kim gets the last word out, the lady stuffs her hand full of money and is off. It's five o'clock. "Excuse me can I see that cherry dress" says a gentlemen standing six foot five. "That looks like that would fit Betty, my girl. How much"? Kim boldly says $250.00 as the man shuffles thru his wallet and pulls the money out, Kim says "thank-you". Audra, Margaret and Kim head for the house. As soon as they enter the house and give the money to Esmira, they are shown to the dining room table, where mutton and hog roast await them. Lamb on one side, ham on the other, where sweet potatoes and potatoes adorn the spread and bread butter and beans round out the rest of the meal. Esmira speaks "I can't thank you enough for the tireless work that you have put in to make this gymkhana. I am already looking forward to next year, with the hopes that we as a team can recruit even more people just like you to duplicate the effort. If you do decide to take the offer it will be a dollar a day plus free room and board. So please eat till your heart's content". Everyone was sitting down and Kim, Audra, and Margaret were sitting right across from each other. With their shoes off the girls play underneath the table with their men's boots so as not to attract any unwanted attention. Supper lasts a good hour and Kim is concerned with the fact that she has no dresses to put out for tomorrow. So she asks Esmira what to do? Esmira says "take an hour later in the evening and sew what you can. Right now you need some friendship time with everyone here so, go relax. Then in the morning when everyone else is out there under the sun put some time in here doing what you do best". WOW! She thought. Someone that understands that hard work needs to be nourished by pleasure time. Kim finds Jack and before she can say anything Jack blurts out "will you be my girl Kim" and Kim answered back "what took you so long, of course I will!" What a good feeling to finally have, a total euphoria came over both of them. Ralph had finally caught up to Audra and he too ask the question "will you be my girl" and Audra with a little tease in her voice said "well what can you offer this country girl" and Ralph said "I got the best craft going, and there will always be horses to shoe, so I will always have enough to take care of you". Audra then says "well the answer is yes, than." Ralph is extremely excited he can't wait to tell his brother Joe. Margaret and Joe are busy talking, but the conversation is centered on Joe and what he wants to do with his life, not even considering a place for Margaret. Ross and Byron find an opportunity to bring out the fiddle and the harmonica to play' Yankee Doodle', The Battle Hymn of the Republic and some more favorite tunes. Esmira and Jeremy find their own private time to engulf each other with love. The hour is 7:00pm two and a half hours until the sun began to set. Everyone went their own ways to get ready for tomorrow. Ralph couldn't wait to share his excitement. Once inside Ralph tells Joe and Joe replies "are you nuts. She is a young girl, and you haven't turned eighteen yet. How will you take care of her"? Ralph interrupts Joe and says "wait a minute, I shared with you the best time of my life with my girl and you are going to question me! Who do you think you are? Oh the big brother that has yet to put anything solid in his life. I have a craft that will last until the cows come home. So if you can't share in my happiness then don't say anything at all!" Ralph sets a stare at Joe that would stop time, but looks away. On the other hand when Jack tells Bill, Jim, Ross and Byron they are elated. All of them pat Jack on the back and give encouragement and say if there is anything they can do just name it. Jack looks at Ross and Byron and says "do you know any wedding songs?" Ross and Byron both say "yes".

 Kim shares the news with Audra and Margaret and Audra beams "me too" but they suddenly see the sadness on Margaret face when she doesn't come forward with any information. So they asked Margaret what was going on. Margaret just replies "he talks about 'his future, but I am not aware if I am in those plans". They offer her encouragement by saying "if you're not, it is his loss". Kim excuses herself as she goes to the parlor to sew another pant suit together. She knows five thirty in the morning comes awful early.

 It is breakfast time and everyone rushes through breakfast because they realize that the specialty in the gymkhana today is the grooming phrase. Jeremy starts out by explaining why it is a good idea to groom the horse a practice based on respect to your animal. If the horse feels that the respect from his companion is true, the experience of riding the horse that day will be much better. Always let the horse, smell you first, let him or her know that you will be advancing toward them, but take it slow. Jeremy starts out at the top of the mane, Joe starts at the bottom of the mane and Jack starts on the body with long sweeps gently talking to the horse. After the body is done unless one wants to do the tail, one is finished.

Joe meets up with Jeremy and says "do you have a minute"? Jeremy says "sure, what's up?" Joe says "I have noticed that Jack and Ralph are head over heels in love with their girls. Personally, I think their crazy". Jeremy says, "Joe believe it or not they do not need your permission and they probably don't care what you think. If they had shared this good news with you they were probably under the mistake that you would wish them well!" Joe ponders for a minute and says "what do they got going for them"? Jeremy says "That is a judgment question and I will not answer that and you should not either. They probably already have a plan and that's between them. What plan do you have for your life Joe"? "Joe says "we have already gone into that". Jeremy says "yes we have, but what happens if you never reach that goal? Are you going to be a broken down cowboy the rest of your life? I have already started to show you about whispering and there is more to show. However, only you can answer that question, and if you truly decide to commit to horse whispering then you have a bright future!" Joe stubbornly says "why does it always have to be someone else's path." Jeremy cuts him off and says "Joe, let me tell you a story about a young sapling. This young tree would always look to the big oak near the house that it stood. To the sapling it was a huge tree, looked about five feet wide and about forty feet tall. The sapling told itself that someday it would be just like the big oak. The next day it stormed hard and the sapling went this way and that way barely able to control its stand. Then that night the storm calmed down and the sapling felt better. It didn't even notice three more shoots that he sprouted for branches. Years went by and the young sapling grew. People would stop by and be amazed how the tree still pushed toward the sky even though its trunk was a little curved because of the storm. Some branches were also bowed but were still thick and growing. If the big oak could talk would he say to him 'thanks for not giving up". Jeremy says to Joe "are you going to be like that tree?" and before Joe has a chance to answer, Jeremy says "I have got to get back the jumping is starting"

Kim and Audra were busy talking about their plans. The idea would have to be spectacular and the plan that had to put in place had already begun. No one knew that the vivacious young Kim had already sewn all the wedding gowns. It was up to her to keep it a secret until the wedding day. So Audra kept on talking about how she wanted a long train on her dress and Kim quickly talked her out of it. Then Margaret appeared in tears with the explanation that she didn't want to go back to the farm with Mom and Dad when the gymkhana was over. However, that seemed like what was going to happen if she didn't somehow lasso Joe into marriage. Kim walked up to Margaret and calmly soothed her fears by saying "didn't you always tell me it gets dark before the storm ends and the light that appears was worth the wait?" Margaret says "yes, do you know something that I don't"? "Well" Kim says "I see Joe talking to Jeremy all the time and maybe he is asking for advice on how to ask you". "What" Margaret says "he does everything else pretty reckless, he knows how to talk, what are you saying?" Kim reminds Margaret of the cow they had on the farm, and every time we went to milk her we had to prod her first. So next time Joe talks to you just listen. I mean listen.

Joe knocks on the house door and asks to see Margaret. Margaret comes to the door and says "hello". Joe and Margaret walk outside and Joe walks with her to the big oak near the house. Joe wrings his hands and says" I don't know how to say this but I have feelings for you unlike I have had for any girl in the past. Margaret are you listening"? Margaret nods her head yes. Joe says "I am just a cowboy that has a lot of dreams and some of those dreams just haven't come" true yet. I am beginning to believe that I am supposed to include you in my dreams, but don't know how". Margaret nods her head. Joe keeps wringing his hands as Margaret turns around and heads for the house. Joe sees her leaving and chases her down and kneels before her and says "will you be my girl forever and ever"? Margaret nods her head, Joe is perplexed and says "speak to me" as Margaret says "yes, but I got to go". Margaret runs to the house, races thru the door and goes to the parlor where Kim is sewing another bonnet and says "YES", Joe asked me to marry him". Kim stops what she is doing, leaps up and hugs Margaret and says

"I knew that it would happen, somehow I just knew". Margaret asks "where is Audra? She has to know also. Kim says "she's with Ralph". Margaret says, "Oh, we have so much to do, the dress has to be made. Kim would you mind making me a dress" Kim says "I don't know I have so much on my plate, I mean sure if they give me enough time to do it. We only have three days until the gymkhana is over, and so much to do". Kim stands up and stretches showing off her perfect model form. She says "I will be back in a bit I have to go for a walk". She goes down to the big oak and happens to see Jack finishing up on the jumps. Jack walks over to the tree to give Kim a kiss as Jack says "it's a warm day". Kim replies "yes it is, how are you holding up"? Jack replies "well as long as I can get a cool drink of water from the tack room I will make it to see another day" he grins, as he heads over to the tack room. Kim realizes he is busy as she turns around and heads for the house. Audra, Margaret and Kim all meet inside the house in the parlor sharing their excitement about the wedding day. But the only one who knows when the magical day is Kim. Audra and Margaret believe that it will be soon but do not know what day. Kim excuses herself, takes some elastic from her sewing bench and sews it into Esmira's dress. She finishes up the alteration in Esmira's dress and neatly lines it up with the other three dresses in her footlocker chest. Kim excuses herself and meets up with Jeremy down at the mares corral. Esmira sees this and gets jealous. By the time Esmira gets down to the corral, Kim has made her way back up to the house. Esmira asks Jeremy "what is going on"? Jeremy explains that Kim was just looking for Jack, and Jeremy said that he hasn't seen him. Esmira begins to say "well what does that"…… as she is interrupted with a kiss from Jeremy. "We have been pretty busy but I have a gift for you" he says. Esmira looks down at his rough worn jeans below encasing his powerful body and says "why yes you do" as her soft hands rubs his muscular chest he gives her another kiss and says we will continue this later". However, right now I have some unfinished business to take care of in town. So I should be back in two hours". Jeremy mounts the appaloosa and is gone like the wind. Esmira has never seen such urgency on his face before. She wonders why he couldn't tell her. Jeremy reaches the Sheriff's office right before the shift change and asks the day sheriff if he wouldn't mind being the justice of the peace for a couple of weddings that will happen in a couple of days. Tom, the sheriff says that he would be glad to. Jeremy gives the time at high noon on Friday at the house. Jeremy thanks him and says he has to go. Jeremy mounts back up on his appaloosa and heads for home. He gets home after an hour and a half and meets Esmira in their bedroom for business and pleasure. After the pleasure Jeremy has to make sure all the arrangements are being taken care of. Jeremy meets with Kim and finds that all the dresses are ready. He meets with Audra and Margaret and asks how the lunch is being prepared for the big party for this Friday and they say that everything will be ready. He gets in touch with Byron and Ross about the music around eleven thirty. Jeremy gets back in touch with Esmira an hour later explaining what he has going on Friday. The only ones that knew what would happen that day are Jeremy and Kim.

Chapter 13

It is Thursday, another beautiful day at the stud farm. All the activities are going off as planned. The girls are in their booth with dresses that Kim has sewn and food that Audra and Margaret have cooked. The day has been busy and everybody had a chance to see some new talent on the activities. In a half hour, the gymkhana day will be done. An hour after that Charlie and Ruth will be pulling up in time to visit with their daughters and hoping that the Gymkhana has made great ladies out of them. Jeremy sees Charlie's and Ruth's buckboard coming up the way and intercepts them. He maneuvers the buckboard behind the mare's corral where Ralph explains to Charlie and Ruth about his blacksmithing and asks for Audra's hand in marriage. Ruth says if it is ok with her you have my permission. Joe was putting up the appaloosa for Jeremy and overheard the conversation and walked right in and said "while we are at it, my name is Joe and I wish to have Margaret's hand in marriage". Charlie spoke up and said "that's fine". Jack was just coming out of the tack room from getting some water and humbly approached both Ruth and Charlie. He explained who he was that he has a job at the gymkhana, getting a buck per day and wished to have Kim's hand in marriage. Charlie agrees only if they stop by once a year until she is fifteen. Jeremy overheard this and says well isn't that in a few months"? Charlie says "yes" and Jeremy interjected "if there is anything I can say to help change your mind"? I know this man and he will provide for your daughter". Ruth speaks up and says "what he is meaning to say is yes. He is inviting Jack and Kim back to the house for her birthday that is all." Oh Thanks" says Jack to Charlie and Ruth as he leaps to his feet and tells Jeremy he will be grooming a mare. Jeremy goes out to Ralph, Jack and Joe and tells them to be quiet on everything. He has some more plans that he has to talk over with Bill and Earl. He goes to Earl and tells him to have four horse and buggies set up for tomorrow with a 'just Married' sign on the back. The wedding will be at noon so twelve thirty the buggies have to be ready.

Jeremy greets all the gymkhana people at breakfast and tells them that he didn't want the booth out there today instead he wants the girls on horseback opening the last day at the gymkhana. The girls will ride around till eleven and then get off their horses and go around and greet people in the audience. Jeremy walks by Kim and tells her that time is your time to get everything ready with the girls. Jeremy says he will be at the house by eleven. All the activities began at nine o clock and the girls looked so proud in their plaid shirts and blue jeans. They rode around until eleven and then Kim said she wanted to talk to them back at the house. So Audra and Margaret met Kim back at the house. Kim walked Audra and Margaret over to the footlocker and opened it up. Jeremy was nearby and helped hold the dresses up until the girls got over their shock about putting on their wedding dresses for today! Audra and Margaret in unison both speak up and say "it fits perfectly, you shouldn't have"! But Kim had one more trick up her sleeve as she asked Jeremy "could you bring Esmira here?" Esmira came into the room and Kim pulled her aside and said" would you put this gown on"? She said "how can I? I am pregnant". Kim said "I know. There is some magic that I did with elastic and you will look beautiful. The gown will conceal most everything." Esmira begins to cry and says "no one has ever been this nice to me, unless they wanted something". "Hurry" says Kim "I still have mine to put on". Within thirty minutes every girl is lined up ready for their wedding.

Earl sees the Sheriff coming over the bluff and tells Jeremy. Jeremy rides out about half way and shows them where to go when they arrive. The wedding will be outside and when the music starts the gentlemen will be coming from the tack room and the ladies from the parlor. Ross and Byron begin to play the Wedding March, and the wedding begins.

It is standing room only but Jeremy and Esmira have a lot of space. Since all three girls that walk down the aisle have the same dad, he walks each one down starting with Kim then Audra then Margaret. Then Esmira walks down half way and is met by Jeremy who escorts her rest of the way down the aisle. The sheriff greets everybody and before he even begins he raises the question "does anybody have any reason why these people who stand here today should not be married? Speak now or forever hold your peace"! No one speaks. The Justice of the Peace made it quick by simply asking "do each of you take the other in sickness and health for richer or poor so long as you two may live". All parties said "yes". So the music played on. As the crowd began to clear the Brides changed their clothes to get ready for their honeymoon. Esmira had changed and put her foot up to the carriage and her foot slipped. Jeremy asked what was wrong. Esmira said "my water just broke" Jeremy stood up in the carriage and yelled as loud as he could "IS THERE A DOCTOR IN THE HOUSE" A doctor heard the call for help and came quickly to help Esmira and Jeremy and asked "is she strong enough to make it to a bed?" Esmira said "yes". The doctor quickly asked for some hot towels. As he was getting the first set of towels the baby boy came. The doctor sent him down for more hot towels and by the time he came back up a baby girl was born. The doctor told Jeremy and Esmira this was the first time that he delivered twins. The doctor told Jeremy that Esmira will need rest for the next couple days and that it will be very normal that the babies start breast feeding immediately.

 The girls wanted to stay around and Esmira answered "that is entirely your choice, but don't keep your man waiting on my account." Kim the youngest of the girls had an idea. Her suggestion was to stay around for a week and then since she came up with the idea that she and her husband should go first to the shack on the upper twenty for a week and then come back so another could use the shack. The girls finally agree that would be a great idea. They elect Kim to go ask permission from Esmira and Jeremy. Kim does and Jeremy and Esmira both agree. Kim tells Jack the good news and Jack goes inside the barn to get the horses ready. Jack grooms the horses down quickly and both the Roan and Palomino are ready. Kim kisses her sister good-bye and begins the hour and half journey to the upper twenty. Esmira has told Kim what to look for when she pulls into the shack area.

Jack and Kim are happily married and happily going toward the upper twenty. Kim tells Jack about the dreams she has about opening up a boutique for all her dresses that she has been making. Jack agrees with her and compliments her on her gift. Kim asked about where they might settle down after the honeymoon and Jack says "I have been meaning to talk to you about that. I have two offers, one from your dad and one from Jeremy. Now your dad's offer is room and board in exchange for farming with a forty per cent of any profits that the farm would bring. Now Jeremy's offer is a buck a week with free room and board and ten per-cents of the profits of next year's gymkhana. Kim thinks it over and says "well if we go back to my parents' house, I am going to feel that I am still under their rule and I think it would be more trouble than it's worth. But on the other hand being at the J.&E. Stud farm I will have more time to develop my sewing craft, and if we play are cards right, I will ask for forty per-cent of the profits off all the stuff that I sew. I saw eighteen hundred dollars go thru my hands on the clothes I made. If you take 40 per-cent of eighteen hundred dollars I would have received seven hundred and twenty dollars. After one year that would be enough to buy a five acre stretch with a house and have my own sewing room." Jack says "Sounds like you have thought this thru pretty good my darling, that's one of the reasons why I love you. I see that the shack is just over the next hill. Let's approach the property cautiously; I think I saw some movement". They climb the last hill and Kim sites movement also. She says "Esmira told me that there might be some strangers around the place, wanting to move the boundary lines for water rights." Kim says to Jack "I will stay here. I will let you go ask him why he is on our land". Jack slowly walks his horse up on the property and flanks the Stanger so he will be coming around his back side. Jack has him in his sights as he is pointing the gun right as his chest and says "may I help you?" The intruder who has just wrapped the wire on another tree to make the water rights his, turns around and pulls his gun as a shot rang out. He is struck in the heart as he falls to the ground. Jack looks up to see Kim topple from her horse because of the kick of the thirty .06. Jack looks down seeing that the intruder is dead and gallops off toward his bride. Jack gets to the horse that was standing still and jumps off his horse to ask are you ok? Kim says "yes". Jack is startled and asks "where did you learn to shoot like that?" She states "Esmira taught us". Jack says "I will have to go change the wire back to its original tree, but Kim interrupts and says "I will have the coffee brewing". Jack goes and mends the fence, tying it around the other tree. He can smell the coffee brewing. He hurries back to the shack but first stops to bring the hard tack in from the saddle bag. The hard tack was similar to hard biscuits. This and coffee would be it for dinner tonight. Jack was still amazed of how his young life had been spared by his wife's marksmanship. Jack stepped inside the shack and asked his young wife again "who did you say taught you how to shoot again"? Kim says "Esmira did." Jack says "I can't thank you enough". "Oh" Says Kim "don't worry about it", I was aiming for his knees the kick of that rifle must of raised the shot enough to kill him. "My shoulder is still feeling the kick." "Let me see" says Jack as he unbuttons her vest and then begins to unbutton her tightly fit shirt. He gets the shirt fully open and there her breasts sit as a picturesque as a statue, so beautiful. He looks at her shoulder and says "yes, it's already starting to bruise up. A couple of days being sore and you will heal". Jack finally notices that he is extremely aroused. Kim says to Jack "come to the shack and let's finalize this deal". Kim was ready for action, she believed that her heavy breasts needed to be kissed and fondled. She dreamed of rubbing her breasts against his chest and kissing his beautiful body. Kim and Jack's clothing drop to the floor and the marriage was sweetly consummated. Kim explored all of Jack's body and was well pleased with what she found. The love making began and continued for some time. When it was over Kim said "don't leave just lay awhile. Jack remained for some time and when he got up he told Kim that he loved her but was awful hungry. Kim got up, got dressed, and heated the food over the fireplace.

 They both nodded off and woke up to a scratching of the door. They opened the door to find a 6 month buffalo calf at their door in which they shot immediately for food. Kim says to Jack "I hope her mother didn't hear that shot. However, we do have our food for the week." Jack says "I believe there are some hooks out in the lean-to where we can drain all the animals' fluids so I can properly butcher this buffalo". Kim slowly puts her shirt on and meets Jack as he is finishing up. After ten minutes Jack asks why we don't we see what we have around here?" After 3 hours of looking over the land, Jacks spots the watering hole. He feels dirty. Within seconds Jack has discarded all of clothes except his boots and is in the water. The watering hole is shielded by the forest on one side so no one can peep in. Kim wades in clothes and all and then Kim asked "are you cool, now?" Jack says, very!" Jack got dressed and both Kim and him mounted the horses and rode back to the shack. Jack checked the buffalo and decided he could take it down before animals started coming in and to help themselves. Kim goes inside to brew more coffee. After the coffee is done she takes off all of her clothes and sits at the table naked. Jack comes in and Kim says "I will never get a chance of doing this again, so I want to take full advantage." Jack looked across the room at his beautiful wife. Everything was perfect! Jack decided to put the buffalo on the spit in the fire place knowing that it would be three hours or more before being done. WOW! He thinks to himself, I am married to the most beautiful woman in the world. I am a lucky man. With the income coming in from helping the stud farm, we can stay there a year until the plan of Kim and her sewing dream comes true. It won't be as hard because I have known horses all my life. Kim has good people skills and wonderful sewing skills so we will have a wonderful future.

There comes a knock on the door. Kim grabs her clothes and puts them on. Jack reaches for the rifle as Kim opens the door and hides behind the door. Jack sits down in the chair aiming the rifle at the person's chest and says "How, can I help you?" The bearded man who looks like he is sixty asks "have you seen my boy"? Jack immediately thinks of the trespasser that Kim killed earlier and asks "What did he look like? "OH he stands around 5 feet 8 inches blue jeans and red bandana and answers to Larry". "No, can't say that I have, but if I do meet him is there something you want me to say to him"? "Well, just tell him that his boy took a mighty turn for the worse and get home." Jack replies "I will do that, hope everything turns out ok". No sooner than Jack closes the door and puts the rifle away than Kim has removed all of her clothes again and says "this feels so comfortable". Jack says "right now we have dinner to get to". Kim knew that Jack was right, but damn, a girl can't let a good looking man go unfulfilled. Jack carved up the buffalo and Kim scooped up the beans. Kim wanted to hurry up with dinner because of the way she was feeling, but she would follow her mans' lead anywhere. Jack was always a fast eater and Kim was one that chewed every bite. Jack finished his meal and got up from the table and put his dish on the counter. He came over and started running his hands thru her hair Jack helped her out of the bed while he looked for a sheet or blanket for the bed. Jack said "well, tomorrow will be a new day." As he threw some more logs on the fire and said "let's go up to Elk Horn River to see what's up there." Kim replied "sounds good to me, my hero, you coming to bed?" as she pats the bed.

Kim woke up to some scratching at the door, and saw thru the window that it was just a raccoon trying to explore. Well as long as she was up she decided to make coffee for her and her wonderful man. The smell of the coffee woke Jack up. He decided to be bear naked until after the coffee was drank. Kim thought to herself that she was the luckiest woman around, as she went thru all of Jack's attributes and said "yes" as Jack said "did you say something"? Kim said "Oh just thinking out loud." Jack says "well as soon as I get dressed, let's head out". Jack gets dressed and grabs his rifle and Kim follows right behind. Jack looks to the sky and sees vultures circling. He notices the horses are stirring also. Jack goes to the horses and calms them down. Jack asks Kim if she could curry the horses while he goes up to the hill and see why the vultures are stirring. Sure enough, this is the intruder that Kim killed while he was pulling a gun on Jack. Jack threw some dirt on the birds as they flew away. Jack knew he would have to bury him. He went down to the lean to and got a shovel and began to bury him. Around an hour later Jack was done with the shallow grave and the rock as a marker. He went down to Kim and said before we start out do you have any coffee"? She said "I thought you might ask there is some over the fire." They sat and drank their coffee and then mounted the horses and off to the river they went. As they approached the river they noticed a cattle drive coming toward them. The cattle were around thirty minutes away. "At the top of the hill is probably where they will rest the cattle for water. Jack said to Kim "well this is not going to be an option for a couple of days so let's go back to the shack and look over the land to see if any of this land up here is tillable.

Meanwhile back at the stud farm, Audra and Margaret are helping Esmira with her new borne. The hustle has been great here. It seems like one baby would finish nursing and the other would get their turn. Margaret and Audra were doing everything they could and then some just to keep up. Audra and Margaret knew that when there was a minute of peace that was their cue to start lunch or dinner for the men that were out doing chores.

So back at the honeymoon, at the shack, Jack sizes up the land and says that about five acres would be tillable. So that meant it could support some cattle. He wondered if it would be worth the time.

It was days like this that Jeremy's sixth sense came in awful handy. Jim, his uncle taught him to see this way. Jim always said that if things were extremely calm a storm was right around the corner. Jeremy took a good look at his twins and kissed Esmira good bye. Jeremy said that he felt something was wrong at the shack. Jeremy knew if he rode hard he could make it in an hour. Jeremy grabbed the black mare the one that had been warming up all day. Jeremy saddled her and took both of his rifles and his two six shooters, just in case. Jeremy felt that there was trouble up by the shack. Jeremy pushed the horse hard. All the way up there Jeremy knew he had to keep his mind blank. It seemed the ride was just a blur. Jeremy knocked on the shack door and Jack and Kim opened the door and stated "thank God you are here". Kim said", we noticed the cattle drive wanting to cross the shacks portion of the river in order to save themselves the route of seventy five miles. They will be up on the water in fifteen minutes. What do you want to do?" Jeremy said to Kim "Get on your horse but stay one hundred yards away sporting a rifle. Jack you get on your horse and follow me down, to the river." So Jack and Jeremy went down to the river where the fence was wrapped around the correct trees. So far everything was ok. Jeremy saw two men coming toward him on horseback and said "state your business" The guy with a patch over his left eye introduced himself as Chris and the gentlemen that he was with introduced himself as Ronnie. Chris said the he wanted to cross here and get the cattle watered and be on his way. Jeremy yelled out "I understand you would be saving your whole herd of a thousand if I allow you to cross. Is that right? Chris said "yes" Jeremy yelled back "if you don't want to turn back, so you don't lose your cattle at a dollar a head. I will let you rest and be watered for fifteen cents a head. Chris says "I won't get paid until I deliver the herd." Jeremy says" I have already thought of what we need to do. Fifteen cents a head equals out you leaving one hundred and fifty head behind. We will watch the cattle take care of them for two weeks, which will allow you to get back and get your cattle for fifteen cents a head. This will help pay for the cattle and for us taking care of them. Chris says "well what if I don' want to do that?" Jeremy motions his arm to the individual on the hill sporting the rifle. Chris says 'WELL, it seems like you have this well thought out. You win. As Chris reaches for his gun Kim lets out a shot, showing that Jeremy meant business. Jeremy says "put your guns down or someone is going to get hurt." Chris and Ronnie both put their guns down. Jeremy asks again "do we have a deal?" Chris says "yes" Jeremy replies let's start separating the 150 head now so you can be on your way. Just one more thing if two weeks from tomorrow have gone by and you haven't come back to get them you will forfeit all rights to the cattle. Do you understand? "Yes" said Ronnie and Chris. The 150 head were separated and Chris and Ronnie were on their way with the remaining cattle. Jeremy spoke and said you have an hour to get off the property.

As Chris and Ronnie were gathering up the cattle to move on, Jeremy turned to Kim and said "I have a funny feeling about this. I don't think we will ever see them again." "Oh" said Kim "what makes you say that" Jeremy says "just a gut feeling". Kim replies "I sure am hungry". Jeremy says to Kim "Would you get a hold of your husband and send him over to me?" Kim says "I'll send him right over". Kim goes over to the other side of the cattle and tells Jack the message, Jack comes over to the side where Jeremy is as Jeremy tells Jack to get the biggest cow out of the herd and fix it for supper. Jack had no reason to question his boss. Jack went and got the biggest cow out of the herd and took care of it.

Ronnie and Chris had taken the cattle down about an hour south and rested the cattle. Ronnie couldn't wait to get to Denver and dump off his half of the cattle. This is a life that Ronnie couldn't stand. The only reason he did it was because it was a dream of his dad's to be a success. If his dad had not died in his arms, he would have told him not on your life. But he promised his mother that he would take all of

Dad's cattle to Denver to pay off his dad's mortgage. Half way down coming from Seattle he met Chris with five hundred head going to the same Denver drop off. They decided to join forces for the next nine days. They never expected to be confronted like this. They had six more days from there resting place. This meant sixteen hours in the saddle in order to reach Denver on time. Chris was proud of the things going on and he knew it could be a lot worse. It was time to catch some shuteye. Chris said good night to Ronnie.

Ronnie was already asleep. Tomorrow would hopefully be a better day with a new and fresh start. Morning came soon enough. It wasn't a bitter cold just a kind of cold that would make one want to have a fresh cup of hot coffee. Chris was getting the horses ready for the ride. He had a nice saddle that was handed down from his grandpa. No one had ever seen a saddle quite this black with trimmings all around. This was a constant reminder to Chris of how to get thru the rough days. You see Grandpa Joseph had won it via the rodeo. Chris would think about it often especially on the long grueling ride to Denver. Chris shouted out to Ronnie "hey, sleepy head the daylight is burning we got to get going." Ronnie returns with a reply "I am glad I have the privilege of waking up before the darn rooster crows" Chris says "I will check on all the cattle making sure we gather up the wanderers and meet you back here in an hour. That should give you enough time to have a cup of coffee ready when I get back." Ronnie yells back "if you're lucky".

While Chris was out getting some calves separated from the bushes they got themselves into, Ronnie was making the coffee. Chris mentioned to Ronnie that if they can get an eighteen hour ride into today it would make the rest of the ride more bearable. Ronnie said "why not, it's not like I have a girl waiting for me".

While back at the E&J stud farm, Margaret was waiting for the end of the week to come because she and Joe were up next for the shack. Margaret and Audra have been so busy helping out Esmira with the twins, they were lucky to get their own chores done. Joe and Earl had been taking over the duties of grooming all the horses on a daily event. Bill and Ralph were busy at their blacksmith duties. Esmira was missing Jeremy. She knew that something was up but she had pure confidence in Jeremy's leadership. Well, the twins are starting to rouse and it's feeding time. Since Esmira was breast feeding Audra had to be close by because when she got done with one baby, she would hand off to Audra while Margaret would give Esmira the other baby.

Back at the shack Kim was helping Jeremy look over the cattle as Jeremy came up behind and said "boo". Kim jumped a little bit and that's when Jeremy said "Look here young lady. I know your sewing machine is not up here and I appreciate you helping me with the herd but this is your honeymoon and for the next couple of hours I am relieving you of your post. Go take care of that husband of yours." Kim looks back at Jeremy with a grin and says "Why thank-you" and was off lickety split. Kim ran into the shack threw her arms around Jack and kissed him a bunch of times. Jack said "what do I owe this pleasure" as Kim said "just sit back, relax and let me make you feel like a man" Jack relaxed and enjoyed all the extra attention that one receives on a honeymoon.

Ronnie wasn't much for hard work and cattle stuff. He couldn't wait to get paid at the end of the drive get drunk and gamble a bit. Ronnie was thinking that he could double his half of the money, which was four hundred and twenty five dollars. He could then get back to Seattle, pay off his dad's mortgage and go down to Sacramento, California where he thinks it's sunny all day. Chris was more concerned about getting back to his girl Mandy, to make a future with her. Another day was done and if they were lucky it would be only four and a half day until they rolled into Denver.

It's not like Esmira didn't have her hands full with the twins, but she was missing Jeremy something fierce. It wouldn't be right for the twins to endure a ride up to the shack. So Esmira felt like she was home bound. Esmira had just got her walking legs back and was beginning to stir around the farm. She was tempted to go down in the tack room. That was where Jeremy did his best work. He loved grooming the animals and doing his whispering. Esmira motioned for Audra to come over and said she was getting dressed to go to the tack room and would she mind looking after the twins for fifteen minutes. Audra said "she wouldn't mind". Esmira went down to the tack room and she knew she was feeling a whole lot better because she was feeling excited. It was like a new life swept within her. Some would call it getting a second wind. She grabbed a grooming brush and started grooming one of the studs while thinking of Jeremy. She knew she couldn't be long here because of the babies back at the house. But, just coming out here was refreshing.

Well, three more days have passed and Margaret is extremely excited when she sees Jack and Kim come over the bluff, Margaret yells to Joe. "Joe, quickly come here. It's Jack and Kim they will be here in ten minutes. Do you have the horses ready?" Joe said "no, but he will go get them ready right now." As Jack and Kim approach the barn, Joe is coming out of the barn with the horses. Jack fills Joe in on what has happened up at the shack and not to be surprised about watching over some cattle. Joe replies "well, we will have to see. Margaret is going to have to come first". As the sisters get a chance to share all their news, Margaret warns Kim that sometimes she might be up in the middle of the night helping Esmira with the twins. Kim remarks "Oh that is ok as long as Jack is taken care of, as she winks at Margaret and they both smile. Jack and Kim put their horses up as Kim goes inside the house to see everyone and Jack stays in the barn removing the saddles so he can brush them down. Kim catches up on all the news since she has been away from Audra.

"Oh! My aching butt and back" says Ronnie. "The first thing I will do after we get paid is to take one of those luxury baths to loosen my bones". "Oh quit complaining, you act like you never been on a horse" says Chris. Ronnie quips back "not for these many miles". "So let's go over to the cattle barn and get paid" says Chris. Ronnie and Chris get paid as Chris takes his half and walks over to the bank to deposit four hundred. Eight dollars is enough for supplies to get back up and get the rest of the cattle. It's getting pretty dark so Chris decides to get a bed at the hotel and head back up tomorrow. Well, daylight has broken and Chris went down to the livery and paid two bits to get his horse out, as he leads his horse over to the saloon to get some fresh black coffee and a rib-eye steak before he starts his trip back. Chris puts his order in to the bar keeper and out of the corner of his eye he sees Ronnie at a table gambling. Chris walks over and sees a bunch of money all spread out on the table and questions Ronnie. Chris says "what about your dad's mortgage?" Ronnie says," I am winning". Chris says "yes. This hand, from what I can tell you has twenty five out of your four hundred and twenty five left." Ronnie says "shut up Chris it's none of your damn business". A local who is winning at this hand says "I have a gun turned right on you and if you know what's good for you, you'll go away. Chris steps backward until he is back at his bar stool, where his steak has just arrived. He doesn't realize that he is sitting next to the town's sheriff. Chris finishes up his breakfast and is standing up as Ronnie approaches Chris asking for more money to gamble with. Chris tells Ronnie "you have gambled away your dad's fortune, which means your mother will be on the street begging for handouts. You have been playing with professional card sharks. You are a born loser. Chris turns his back takes three steps and Ronnie pulls his gun and fires, hitting him in the back and killing him. The Sherriff stands up and shows him his badge and says "you are going to jail". Then tells Ronnie "as a witness, I saw it all, and the second circuit district judge arrives tomorrow you will be hanged before next Friday". Ronnie puts his head into his hands and weeps.

Meanwhile back at the shack Margaret and Joe are just arriving. Jeremy greets them and tells them what is going on. Jeremy says "I might need help from time to time but I will not expect too much because of your honeymoon. Now go and enjoy yourself." Jeremy gets back on his steed and corals the cattle as well as gives them water. Margaret and Joe go inside the shack where they immediately disrobe. Just in case Margaret has her night clothes nearby. Joe tells Margaret "you are the most fascinating person, I have ever met. I want to go thru this whole world with you and I hope that God blesses us with more than a handful of children. Margaret replies "I don't have a problem with that as long as you keep on working and let me raise the children. So why are you keeping me waiting?!" Joe is astonished. It takes him a few minutes to realize that he has everything he wants right at his fingertips. Then Joe starts to kiss Margaret and Margaret rubs his chest before kissing it tenderly. This arouses Joe as he kisses her breast. He allows Margaret to take the lead and consummates the marriage. From this love action Margaret knows that she is pregnant and in due time can't wait to tell her sisters. As Margaret got dressed Joe went outside to ask Jeremy in for dinner. Joe tells Jeremy how elated he is and brags about this marriage by saying it is the best thing that ever happend to him. This makes Jeremy think about how much he misses Esmira.

So back at the stud farm, Kim begins to tell Esmira about the intruders. Esmira wanted to know the whole story but Kim only gave her an editorial version. Kim kept it simple by Jeremy allowing the intruders to water their stock for fifteen cents a head. So that meant one hundred and fifty cattle had to stay behind until they came back and gave them one hundred and fifty dollars or keep the stock. Esmira was ok with that, but she had a question that she needed to get answered herself. The question she needed an answer to was 'whomever came up with the quote', "absence makes the heart grow fonder" but by how much? Esmira was really missing Jeremy.

Time came and went at the shack for Margaret and Joe. Joe helped Jeremy numerous times with the cattle and was thanked for it. Now it was time for Ralph and Audra. Although Ralph was a very mechanical man and love putting things together he knew that Audra was more experienced in the love role. One must remember that Audra was very proud of her long legs. On the other hand Ralph was extremely proud of his chest muscles. Audra was proud of what Ralph's chest had to offer, so she began to kiss his shoulder and chest to see if this would get him aroused. She was right. Audra squeezed his waist bringing him closer to her. Audra slipped off her skirt showing off her legs. She held Ralphs hand onto her leg and allowed him to stroke her body. That was enough. Audra was aroused. Audra decided to take the lead and help Ralph. What seemed like a long time to Ralph was probably ten minutes, but the marriage was consummated. As soon as Ralph was ready he came out and helped Jeremy. While Ralph was sitting on his horse he would count all the cattle to make sure they were there. Jeremy rode up and said to Ralph "I have a huge favor to ask of you. If this ram-rod doesn't come back to claim his livestock, I will be forced to move them on down to the stud farm. Would you help?" Ralph says "I would be delighted to . . . When will you know?" Jeremy says "at the end of the week, when everybody will be leaving here anyway". "Ok" says Ralph. "Let's go eat". Audra knew they had just enough provisions to last them thru the end of the week. Dinner was getting a little old when it was beef and hard tack biscuits but it was better than going hungry. As Jeremy excused himself and went back outside to watch the cattle, Audra asked Ralph what was the matter. Ralph said "I can't hold it inside any longer, I hope you are not upset with me by being a novice at this love making" Audra interrupted and said "don't you worry your sweet head about it Ralph. I am blessed with having the ability to teach you and that is what is going to make our future the greatest. You have the blessing of being a blacksmith and I have the blessing of being a mother and a terrific wife. I will take care of you in ways that you haven't thought of yet. You just keep blessing me with children. Do you have any other concerns?" Ralph shook his head no, with a big grin on his face.

Before Ralph and Audra knew it time flew by and it was time to head on back to the E&Jstud farm. Jeremy thanked Ralph again for helping out especially with moving the cattle. It was only eight in the morning and Jeremy was getting everyone ready for the drive back to the farm, my how he missed Esmira. Ralph knew that Jeremy missed Esmira a whole lot also. Ralph was ready for the rough ride and it was nothing to Audra because she was used to moving. Sometimes the cattle would wander but it was nothing to get them back in line. It seemed like the ride took longer than it did. Just as Esmira saw Jeremy comes over the hill. She was on her horse and met Jeremy half way and got as close as possible to give him a kiss. Jeremy told Esmira that after they got to the barn, they needed to talk. They reached the barn and Jeremy asked Ralph to take care of the horses. Ralph said "sure"

Esmira couldn't wait for her man to come inside because she missed him so badly. As she hugged and kissed him Jeremy said" we have to talk" "Sure, said Esmira is there something wrong?" Well, not really. As you can see we came into one hundred and fifty head of cattle. We can turn our gymkhana into a rodeo next year with roping calves events. However, I have decided to give Joe, Jack and Ralph a split with thirty eight head a piece. We will receive thirty six. Ours will not be cut from the herd until we want them so it will appear that Jack, Joe and Ralph will have fifty head apiece" Said Jeremy. Esmira says "I trust you, so what is the difficulty" as she kisses Jeremy. Jeremy said "There is no problem. I love you enough to let you know what I was doing". Esmira says "let's go eat lunch"!

As the women were setting the table, Esmira rang a bell and shouted that it was nice to have everybody back. Since the twins are sleeping Jeremy has some good news for everyone. Jeremy says "I am proud to know all of you. I have decided to split the herd four ways but it will look like three. I will take twelve out of each of your herd leaving you with thirty eight head apiece. So by giving you the herd I already know that your determination will match your responsibility." Kim stands up with tears of joy running down her cheeks as she says "a month ago I was just a lost child on a broken farm with no future in sight. Now that I have experienced the gymkhana and the opportunity of sewing and selling my wares as well as getting married I feel like I have matured greatly. I couldn't of done this without your opportunity so thank-you." Joe stands up and bashfully admits that a month ago he was bound and determined to do bronco riding his way until he met Jeremy and found that there were different ways of arriving at the destination. He continues to say "thank-you". Then Joe's brother, Ralph, stands up and says "I think I can speak for just about everyone here, we probably looked like a lost bunch, but with this gymkhana opportunity, we have all changed considerably. So thank you.

In the upcoming years the E. &J. Stud Farm gymkhana expanded their events so they could be called a rodeo. Bill and Ralph remained behind the scene as coordinators. Audra and Margaret developed their cooking skills to a world class level and Kim was noticed especially by the eastern sea coast for her dresses and bonnets. Ross and Byron kept up their musical talents and traveled extensively to other rodeo's as they promoted their start at E&J stud farm. Joe and Jack became junior partners in the E&J stud farm while developing the cattle side.

Chapter 14

Kim, the young sixteen year old had been extremely busy at the sewing machine, with bolts of fabric that Esmira had gotten from the store in town. She was able to make a lime green dress for Esmira, a peach one for herself, a navy blue one for Margaret and a pink one for Audra. It was extremely tough for her to work on the bust line because they were all so busty except for Audra. She whipped thru hers with a breeze because of her average bust and long legs. It was the buttons that made the dress so tough since it had forty buttons from neckline to the waist. Kim thanked Esmira for allowing her to display her talents. Audra and Margaret had wonderful cooking talents to add to the success of the gymkhana so the whole crew sampled pancakes, omelets and bacon as they prepared for the days to come.

While reminiscing with her sisters Kim asks "what do you think about, I mean when this gymkhana is over, are you ready to go back to the farm?" Audra and Margaret look at each other with eyes wide open, as if a rattle snake was close by. Kim says "any answers?" Audra and Margaret say "well we are working on a plan." Kim is over joyed with excitement and says "please let me know". They huddle momentarily and Margaret says "nothing would please me better when this gymkhana is over to be married to Joe". "Really" says Audra "I have been thinking the same way about Ralph". "That's great" says Kim, "I want the same for me and Jack." "What" says Audra "you are going on fifteen. What do you have to offer"? Kim flaunts her best assets by drawing attention to her lovely breasts with both hands and says "I have a start". Margaret who remembers how sternly Esmira ripped into her about kissing Joe, interrupts and says "if that is her dream let her stick with it. I think she would be good at whatever she decides to do. Now all we have to do is hook our men!" Audra says "by the time this gymkhana is over I plan to be married"!

Kim had just finished her wedding dress and put it up when everyone was walking in the door. Another day at the gymkhana had passed and Margaret told Kim the sky blue dress had sold for one hundred and seventy five dollars. Kim had one more dress to sew and forty five minutes to do it. So she put together a sky blue dress in her build for bustier customers. Now it was time to pull out the pork roast that she put in the stove around three hours ago. There was some left over potato salad and Audra was just finishing up the green beans. This was going to be dinner fit for a king. As soon as the dishes were washed she would be getting ready for the dance. Kim pulled Audra and Margaret aside and showed them the wedding gowns. Both Audra's and Margaret's mouth gapped open in astonishment. "Oh, you shouldn't have" came from the sister's mouth. Kim said "It's ok. Now just hook your man". All three put on their Sunday best and walked across to the barn, where Ross and Byron were getting their musical instruments warmed up.

It is Thursday, another beautiful day at the stud farm. All the activities are going off as planned. The girls are in their booth with dresses that Kim has sewn and food that Audra and Margaret have cooked. The day has been busy and everybody had a chance to see some new talent on the activities. In a half hour, the gymkhana day will be done. An hour after that Charlie and Ruth will be pulling up in time to visit with their daughters and hoping that the Gymkhana has made great ladies out of them. Jeremy sees Charlie's and Ruth's buckboard coming up the way and intercepts them. He maneuvers the buckboard behind the mare's corral where Ralph explains to Charlie and Ruth about his blacksmithing and asks for Audra's hand in marriage. Ruth says if it is ok with her you have my permission. Joe was putting up the appaloosa for Jeremy and overheard the conversation and walked right in and said "while we are at it, my name is Joe and I wish to have

Margaret's hand in marriage". Charlie spoke up and said "that's fine". Jack was just coming out of the tack room from getting some water and humbly approached both Ruth and Charlie. He explained who he was that he has a job at the gymkhana, getting a buck per day and wished to have Kim's hand in marriage. Charlie agrees only if they stop by once a year until she is fifteen.

 Jack and Kim are happily married and happily going toward the upper twenty. Kim tells Jack about the dreams she has about opening up a boutique for all her dresses that she has been making. Jack agrees with her and compliments her on her gift. Kim asked about where they might settle down after the honeymoon and Jack says "I have been meaning to talk to you about that. I have two offers, one from your dad and one from Jeremy. Now your dad's offer is room and board in exchange for farming with a forty per cent of any profits that the farm would bring. Now Jeremy's offer is a buck a week with free room and board and ten per-cents of the profits of next year's Gymkhana." Kim thinks it over and says "well if we go back to my parents' house, I am going to feel that I am still under their rule and I think it would be more trouble than it's worth. But on the other hand being at the J.&E. Stud farm I will have more time to develop my sewing craft, and if we play our cards right, I will ask for forty per-cent of the profits off all the stuff that I sew. I saw eighteen hundred dollars go thru my hands on the clothes I made. If you take 40 per-cent of eighteen hundred dollars I would have received seven hundred and twenty dollars. After one year that would be enough to buy a five acre stretch with a house and have my own sewing room." Jack says "Sounds like you have thought this thru pretty good my darling, that's one of the reasons why I love you." With tears of joy running down her cheeks Kim is overjoyed as she states "a month ago I was just a lost child on a broken farm with no future in sight. Now that I have experienced the gymkhana and the opportunity of sewing and selling my wares as well as getting married I feel like I have matured greatly." Audra and Margaret developed their cooking skills to a world class level and Kim was noticed especially by the eastern sea coast for her dresses and bonnets. Ross and Byron kept up their musical talents and traveled extensively to other rodeo's as they promoted their start at E&J stud farm. Joe and Jack became junior partners in the E&J stud farm while developing the cattle side.

Kim had new ideas for the future of her family, she setting herself up against the odds. This was something that she was already familiar with. By selling those dresses at the Gymkhana and getting the prices she wanted. Kim had to set her sights on a new vision. There were two secrets that she was keeping involving her dresses and the attorney that she met in town. Her first step was to get a team player that could hold down the business in the states, while she traveled abroad. Once she got abroad Kim would study the fashion and implement her secrets.

Chapter 15

And the year was 1870 and Victoria had just opened a letter from her cousin in Boston Massachusetts. If as she was overwhelmed with excitement on the young lady her cousin had met in a Gymkhana near Big Horn, Wyoming. Usually the letters she would receive from her cousin would be about a page in length, more or less just to tell Victoria the updates on the family. However, this time was different. The length of the letter was at least four pages and couldn't stop talking about Kim the young lady that sold her a beautiful dress at a price that she could double her money back east. These dresses were not some material that one could just throw together in a matter of minutes but extremely detailed. She went on to tell her that she revisited this Gymkhana four more times to admire and buy the dresses that she was making. One particular dress that she was fond about was the maroon dress with a bigger bust line than most but the forty two buttons that lined the front made the dress look exquisite. This dress looked like one would wear it to the ballroom or dance floor. Victoria after reading this was so intrigued that she would have to meet this person face to face. Victoria sat down and replied to her cousin that she would be there in May just to meet this young lady. This meant traveling across the Pacific Ocean on a twelve day cruise, just to meet this young lady that turns cloth into magic.

Over in Big Horn, Wyoming Joe and Margaret agree that three days up at the shack away from the stud farm would do them some good. It wasn't that they were bored, but the stud farm and the twins kept everyone busy all the time. Audra agreed to watch her sister's twins for those days. As long as when she returns that she would do the same for her and her husband Ralph when she got back. Margaret agrees. Jeremy asked "Joe to check up on some things when he was up there. To check the boundary lines to see if they have been moved and the roof of the shack." Joe agrees. Joe saddles the Palomino for him and the sorrel for Margaret. It was about 9:30 in the morning so the hour trip up to the shack would not be in the mid- day heat. As soon as they get on the road away from anyone to hear, Margaret tells Joe how much she loves him. Joe says "thanks, are you in need of some extra attention?" Margaret replies" oh, it's not that, it has been extremely busy taking care of the twins and just getting everything done." Joe agrees and says "yes, taking on those cattle has been quite time consuming. Right when you think you are getting on top of things and you take a deep breath, there is a mother cow calving. This little get away will be enjoyed right after I look at the things that Jeremy wanted me to check on."

Joe and Margaret finally reach the shack and Joe checks the boundary lines and the roof and everything is in order. The door on the shack is ajar so Joe tells Margaret to stay put until after he checks it out. Joe carefully opens the door and sees a cub wandering around. Joe yells "Get, get you little monster". As he motions with his hands and opens the door so he scampers away. Joe motions to Margaret that it is okay to come in. Margaret comes inside and says to Joe "let's just sit awhile. All I want to do is relax".

Back at the stud farm Audra is taking care of her twins as well as her sister Margaret's. While Ralph is busy shoeing some of the horses. Audra thinks to herself and how lucky she is. She has a husband to call her own a set of twins and a promising career as a professional cook all at the young age of seventeen. She knows that if she was back at home with her mother and father she would just be doing the farm chores with no future in sight. It seemed like it was just yesterday though, if this gymkhana had not come around she would still be there. Her attention is immediately turned to Ralph as he enters and asks "is there anything I can do to help"? Audra kids with Ralph and says "it's too bad you can't nurse, I would gladly give you the other twin. I know that as soon as I get done here Margaret's twins will be hungry. Please just sit with me and tell me about how our time in here will be shared." Ralph who is not one for talking begins to dream out loud. "Well, first I would take you in my arms like we were dancing and whisper sweet things in your ear. Then I would wait for you to respond. Who knows one thing might lead to another. But most important of all is that you are happy. "Audra interrupts his dream and says "get a towel and help burp the baby, as I get the other twin feeding" Ralph loves his wife deeply and would follow her to the ends of the earth. As he says "Sure honey."

Well, the horses are stirring and neighing as Jeremy leaves the barn. He looks around to make sure no company is coming down the road and then remembers that this is the horses' way of saying thank-you. As he approaches the house he begins to smell the best aroma anyone could smell, and that would be the smell of fresh brewed coffee. Dog gone Jeremy thinks to himself I'll bet that is also the smell of blueberry pancakes. Then he talks out loud to God thanking him that he has enough chickens to feed this whole crew.

Back at the shack, after relaxing a spell, Margaret fixes Joe and her some lunch. To some people this might look like a rundown shack from the outside. But on the inside, with a little imagination, this could be a castle. The kitchen was spacious that could lead into a family room, which led to the bedroom. With a little of dusting and a table cloth and a nice blanket for the bed, this place would look inviting. But for right now, eating and just relaxing was the only thing she was thinking about. It seemed like Joe just inhaled his plate of ham and beans. Margaret would take the slow and comforting way. After lunch she already had a plan to sit in the rocker and gaze across the field and dream. Joe would go out and curry the horses down and check the boundary lines. To Joe when he would curry the horses down, it was more than that. He learned the lesson well from Jeremy, it was about respect. So a twenty minute brush down was perfectly okay by him. Imagine your major mode of transportation and not respecting it. Unheard of. As Joe was wrapping it all up he could see Margaret waving for him to come to her. Joe approached Margaret as she said "can you see a café on top of the hill, where the pony express riders would exchange their horses, or stop for a great meal that Audra and I have fixed? "Joe responds "I understand that you are indeed relaxing, and I can see that. No one could make better food than you two. What would you serve?" Margaret says," steak and vegetables with hot bread straight out of the oven. Then if they didn't mind I would sit a spell and talk with them, just to see where they have been and where they want to go. I get so many new ideas about food when I talk with them." Margaret blinks her eyes and the dream vanishes. My, how time does fly, as the clouds were coming in and it was nearing dinner time. Margaret jumped into Joe's strong arms and says "buffalo steak is coming up served with corn on the cob." Joe didn't have any concerns when it came to having food cooked. As far as he was concerned Margaret was the best. It seemed like dinner and the rest of the night went faster than the blink of an eye. As they both drifted off to a wonderful sleep. Then says Margaret to Joe "if that rooster hadn't sounded off I would still be sleeping. Now let me get my where abouts as you go outside and hustle up some eggs, so I can get them cooking. "After about ten minutes wrestling with the hens, Joe brings in a half of dozen eggs. Joe loves scrambled eggs. So Margaret puts all the eggs in the pan and starts to scramble them. After breakfast is served and cleaned up, Margaret is just going to relax. That is exactly what happened for the next two days.

    Meanwhile back at the ranch, Jeremy talks to Esmira over the breakfast table about the gymkhana that will start in a week. Jeremy understood that he has two more recruits that want to join the ranks, but he is worried if he can use them. Joe and Margaret have just come down from the shack to help prepare for the annual event. Margaret's sister, Kim already knows that her talent of sewing will be used with the proceeds of the dresses sold to go to the gymkhana fund. Kim struck a deal with Esmira that an addition to the house will be made into Kim's boutique in trade for her sewing ability. What Kim is not expecting is the visitor that she will meet at the gymkhana that will change her life forever. As Margaret and Joe pull up to the house Jeremy comes out and says "good timing, we have a place at the table set for you". Joe "hollers back thanks". Joe gets out of the carriage and helps his stunning wife Margaret to get out of the carriage. They follow Jeremy up to the house. "It's so good to see you, come let's eat breakfast and you can tell me everything." They all sit down at the table and the picturesque Esmira opens with a statement. "It's all so great to see you under one roof again. I won't make this long, but we all know the work that has to be prepared for the gymkhana and I want to thank-you in advance for the work that you will accomplish."

Jeremy says "let's bow our heads to say grace and be thankful for our loved ones as well as our bounty that the good Lord gives us. Amen." Jeremy is content with people just enjoying the food no need to bring business talk up just yet. Esmira asks all the girls how the twins are doing and each one of them say "good". Esmira knows that Audra and Margaret love to cook so she asks them if they have anything new? Audra says "I have been reading about bread pudding and I will try it tonight at dinner." Margaret looked at her recipe and saw that it took 2 cups of milk 1/4 cup butter with 2 eggs slightly beaten ½ cup sugar with one teaspoon ground cinnamon or nutmeg 1/4tsp. Salt 6 cups of bread cubes ½ cup raisins if desired and heavy whipping cream. Heat oven to 350 degrees until butter is melted and milk is hot. In large bowl, mix eggs sugar, cinnamon and salt. Stir in bread cubes and raisins. Stir in milk, pour into round pan bake for 45 minutes. Since Margaret was the most shy of the sisters she wasn't aware of how to accept praise. That night when her and Audra had completed the bread pudding recipe and set it in front of the whole crew, Audra liked to take the credit even though in this particular case Margaret did most of the work. One would think that the whole crew was starving as they inhaled the bread pudding. Margaret and Audra didn't need any thanks; the proof was in the eating.

Chapter 16

Victoria had just boarded the ship in London, England with her assistant Elizabeth. Elizabeth is to meet her cousin from Boston Massachusetts at the gymkhana near Big Horn, Wyoming. The trip on the ship would take twelve days and eleven nights. This was okay with Victoria because she needed a long rest from the royal duties she had to perform. Absolutely no one knew she was of royal rank and that is the way she preferred it. She dressed like she was a commoner, that of almost middle class. She loved to dabble in painting, faces are the ones that she preferred. She had six or seven with her that she took everywhere. To her these were pictures that represented the different paths that went thru her nobility. These were her keepsakes. Now was Victoria's time to practice being a commoner amongst the people. She didn't have to walk far on the ship when she bumped into a young lady that was busy crying. She interrupted the sobbing and said "dear, whatever is the matter" The young lady says "My fiancé said that I wasn't worth the dirt I was made of. "Victoria interjects, "Say, young lady just for being ornery let's play a small trick on him. Are you up for it?" The young lady dried her eyes and said "what do you mean? "Victoria hands her a pouch full of unbelted flour some Indian meal and oatmeal. "Shake this up and put it in his drink. Trust me on this." A few hours later they both were drinking and she slipped this powder into his drink. Around an hour later Tom, her fiancé got severe stomach cramps and nausea resulting in diarrhea. Naturally, Tom was beside himself, so Pam left for a half hour. When she came back, Tom pleaded with her for help. Pam answered back, "two hours ago I wasn't worth the dirt I was made of, and now you want me to help you. The true colors are coming out in you, why would I, who am lower than dirt, help you?" Tom begged and said "I am so sorry, I was out of line". Pam stepped it up a little bit and said," we are going to part are ways as soon as the ship docks. Here is your ring back. I don't need a man in my life to validate me. You see Tom if we were to be married I would need to know that we would be a team. You haven't shown me that you can carry your own weight. If all you need in your life is some kind of sleazy tramp, they are at the next watering hole. Do you understand me so far?" Tom who could barely stand up says "I haven't ever seen this side of you. I was definitely the one who made the error in judgement. If you could find it in your heart to help me that would be comforting." Pam leaves for ten minutes and comes back with two apples and two oranges and tells Tom to eat these as quick as possible. Within ten minutes you will feel normal. Tom does and is very glad. The next day Pam meets Victoria on the deck and shares with her that Tom definitely needs to work on his people skills and for right now its better that Tom goes his own separate way. However, I believe that Tom would like to do otherwise. So it's completely up to him. Pam was curious on how she knew this remedy would work and Victoria just replied that she learned it thru her travels. Pam said "thank you" and excused herself. Victoria looked across the ocean and said to herself, "could this young lady that she will soon meet, meet her expectations. "If so the patent rights would make her extremely wealthy. This would even be better than collecting taxes from the people. Victoria looked over the ocean and thought to herself that only time would tell. The following day Pam meets Victoria and introduces her fiancé Tom to her as Victoria asks," how do you feel about Pam as Tom says "it's the best decision I ever made". Well great says Victoria "I hope you will always feel that way!" Tom says "I will." Elizabeth who is Victoria's assistant and right hand person, interjects and says "Victoria it is time for tea. "Victoria excuses herself and says until we meet again. Victoria talks openly with Elizabeth over tea and asks, "Why do you think this young lady Kim is so special". Before Victoria says another word Elizabeth says "look "as she points to the cream colored dress she was wearing. Elizabeth points to the sleeves that were made in three quarter length. She points to the length of the dress and the full blown bodice of the dress with a wonderful neck line. Victoria does take a second look at how well the dress fits and is amazed. "I see "says Victoria. The ride on the ship was about to end, and tomorrow she would board the train that would take her to Sheridan Wyoming where she would meet Elizabeth' cousin. From there they would take horse back up to the gymkhana where it would be the day before it opens to the public.

As Victoria and Elizabeth depart from the ship, they wave good bye to Tom and Pam. They get their belongings loaded on the stage and are off for a two hour drive to the train. Once on the train it will be another two hours before they reach their destination. It seemed to Victoria that a lot of time was consumed with loading and unloading. Oh well, this must be the price of success. Once on the train Victoria asks Elizabeth for a summary of the trip. Elizabeth was always concise with her answers. "Well the voyage on the ship was rather relaxing. The stagecoach ride reminded me of muscles that I had forgotten about and the train was just enough to regroup my thoughts". Victoria responds with "you took the words right out of my mouth. I can't wait to meet Kim. "All they saw as they looked out the windows were mountains in the background and curvy plains everywhere else. Everybody on the train were minding their manners and that was quite okay with Elizabeth. The train whistle blew as the train was coming into the depot. The porter yelled out thru the train that the depot was coming up, so anyone departing could get ready. As they were getting off Elizabeth spotted her cousin with two other mounts and her buck board. Now they only had a two hour trip before they reach the stud farm. Victoria could tell that Elizabeth was in a chatty mood. So that meant Victoria had to be in the listening mode. Just like clockwork as soon as everyone got loaded and comfortable, Elizabeth started in. Elizabeth bragged about all the comforts of the ship and how good it was too relax. As her cousin drove the buck board she couldn't get any questions in anyhow. After an hour of listening, her cousin said "my ears need a rest how about you, Elizabeth?" Elizabeth apologized for carrying on. They finally arrive at the E&J stud farm. Normally Esmira would have sent them back into town, but she wanted the company and had a spare room. Elizabeth introduces herself and brags about her experience with the gymkhana last year and how she enjoyed buying the dresses from Kim. Esmira has to interrupt her to ask the name of the lady she is with. Elizabeth apologizes and says "oh please I forgot my manners with your different activities including the dresses and the food. I guess I carried on so much she had to see it for herself. This is Victoria." Esmira adds "well please come in. Jeremy will take care of your horses."

Audra and Ralph return from the shack as Audra tells Jeremy that everything is okay at the shack as Ralph takes care of the horses. Ralph helps Jeremy with the currying of these new horses, as Audra goes in the house.

Jeremy looks over the horses as he is brushing them down. He notices that both of the horses were pure white and they were mares. He looked over his mares and noticed that he only had the one white mare. This would be the first thing that he mentions to Elizabeth after he finishes brushing them down, but before he finishes this task Bill interrupts Jeremy with news of the other mare having trouble fouling. Jeremy races to the tack room and gets his full length shoulder glove and races over to the mare corral. The foul is turned around an instead of coming out legs first the foul is coming out head first and is kicking to get out causing the mare great discomfort. Jeremy asks both Ralph and Bill to comfort the mares head and keep her busy so as not to squeeze her stomach. As Bill and Ralph are holding her head and petting the head, Jeremy reaches up the birthing canal and pulls with all his might as the colt comes out. Immediately, Jeremy tells Ralph and Bill to let go of the head to see if the mare will care for her colt. The mare goes for the colt cleaning her up. Jeremy tells Ralph and Bill to thank their lucky stars that they were done. The rest is up to Mother Nature. He takes time to thank them for what they did and invites them up to the house for lunch. As he heads up to the house he talks to Ralph and Bill and says "can you smell that wonderful aroma of coffee"? Ralph says "yes". As Jeremy walks inside he looks at the table and is graced with an eight pound ham and three freshly baked loaves of bread. He thanks Margaret and Audra for their wonderful act of cooking and asks Jack if he would say grace. Jack begins with the thanking of the company and for blessing all the wives with twins and prays for a successful future of the gymkhana and for a beautiful day. Jeremy breaks the news about the colt and says "let's eat." Over the table Esmira acknowledges that all the twins are growing like weeds and very healthy. Audra and Margaret express their hope of opening a restaurant in town, which is about forty five minutes from the farm. Jeremy asks Elizabeth on where she picked up the horses. Elisabeth says "there was a gentleman at the livery stable near the train station that was closing up his shop for the day and I asked about the two white horses and he sold them to me." Esmira catches Jeremy's look and completely understands what his next move will be. Jeremy asks Victoria and Elisabeth "how long are you going to be around?" Victoria answers with "probably until the gymkhana ends or until you get tired of us". Esmira speaks "Well this year we have extended the gymkhana to two weeks and have added some different activities, but we will be happy to have you for that time." Victoria and Elizabeth both echo "thanks". Jeremy says "Thanks." again to Margaret and Audra and excuses himself from the table and mentions to Esmira that he will be in the bedroom. Esmira enjoys the chit chat at the table and excuses herself from the table and goes to the bedroom. Esmira closes the door behind her and immediately embraces Jeremy and kisses him. Jeremy brings her closer to him and presses her picturesque body tightly to his. After a minute embrace Jeremy releases and says "are you thinking what I am thinking"? Esmira brings Jeremy closer to her and gives him another kiss before she answers. "My stud, what are you thinking"? Jeremy answers "I believe I will put the two mares in a private corral with the palomino for a week and then the sorrel for a week just too see what happens". As Esmira pulls him tightly toward her picturesque body and gives him a long kiss and says "I like the way you think". Jeremy reaches for the door as he expresses "I love you, my tempting one!" Jeremy catches Ralph before he can go outside and says "can I talk to you?" Ralph walks over as Jeremy whispers to him "put the palomino stud in with the white mares only." Ralph nods his head up and down as he departs.

Chapter 17

Jeremy goes to the back of the barn and begins to talk to the musicians Ross and Byron. Jeremy asks Ross "if he is ready for the next two weeks and he says "yes". Byron mentions that they have written some new songs that are ready for the occasion. Jeremy says "I just want to thank-you in advance because I know you will do your best."

Joe and Margaret introduce themselves to Victoria and Elizabeth. Joe asks the ladies if he can show them around. Elisabeth quickly answers "yes". Joe points to the field to show them where the jumps and barrels will be, and explains the horse whispering and "bronco riding." Victoria quickly interrupts and says "what did you say?" Joe says bronco riding. Victoria says "no before that." Joe says "oh the horse whispering." Victoria says "oh are you going to tell the horse a secret or what"? Joe says "it's better explained when you see it yourself!" Joe quickly inserts to the ladies, "well, what brings you ladies here?" Victoria says "Kim," Joe says" I'm not sure I understand". Connie says. "I know you remember me from the last gymkhana because I was here every day buying up dresses and bonnets. I was so thrilled with Margaret's younger sister, Kim, I mentioned it to my cousin, Victoria, and she just had to come out here to see for herself." Joe says "I see, that's enough for one day let's go have a sneak preview of what's going to be for music. "They all stand right outside the west side of the barn as they hear Ross and Byron warm up with different tunes.

They purposely didn't want to be seen, they didn't want to disturb the musicians.

It seemed like they had just had lunch but the hours fly by so quickly when you keep yourself busy. Audra was in the kitchen waiting for Margaret to start her part of the roast dinner. It was Margaret's time to peel the carrots, potatoes and onions. Margaret didn't mind she always loved the way the peelings came off her vegetables and transformed into a delight. Audra had to go get the wood and fill the stove and get the fire going, as well as getting the water from the stream. Since everything was going as planned it would be about two and a half hours before everything was complete.

Kim was busy completing her fifth dress for the gymkhana. Her dresses that hung in the closet were of different styles and shapes. Her pink one was for a small busted lady of average height of five foot two and a full dress all the way to the floor. Her teal green one was for a large busted lady with a full length gown for a lady that was between five ten and six foot. Her maroon one was for a lady of Kim or Esmira height between five foot and five two but very large in the bust area. Her fourth one was a deep purple one smaller in the bust, but a full gown for someone like her sister Audra who stood five eight. This fifth one was a peach color with a big bust line and a full gown for someone that was five foot four. She was just putting the buttons on when Victoria interrupted and said "if I remember correctly you are the young age of fifteen and married with twins. I congratulate you, not only on your twins and your marriage but on your uncanny ability of sewing as well. As you know Connie was the one who bought the maroon, the silver and the sky blue from you all for around six hundred dollars. Connie was the one that told me about you. I had to come see you with my own eyes. Kim you are like an artist with your sewing machine. I understand that it takes time and effort on each of your dresses. This must be a passion for you. For I see that others would labor fiercely to accomplish what takes you a couple of hours. I apologize that the oceans separate us. For if they didn't I would commission you as head seamstress to the Royal Crown. This would unfold many favors for you as well as setting new designs for a fashion industry. I will give you my private resident address in case you will ever change your mind."

Chapter 18

Victoria is also amazed at Audra and Margaret's cooking talent. If only Victoria could have a crystal ball and see in the future, where a picture of these meals could be sent around the world in split seconds. Right now she would have to communicate via telegraph, put out the recipe and hope for good.

Wait! What's that sound, the horses are stirring? Victoria and Kim look outside to see the doctor coming down the hill in his buggy. Victoria, Kim, Audra and Margaret meet him outside and ask him if there is anything wrong. The doctor replies "Well, I am hungry. I heard the great cooks were in town and I wondered if I could trade my services for those wonderful blueberry pancakes and such. I will look over all the twins as a check-up in return for those pancakes. "'Audra and Margaret were so pleased they both echo "sure" as they ran up to the house and into the kitchen to put the wood in the stove and get it lit so by the time their batter was made the pan would be heated just right. The doctor took his time looking at the three sets of twins and all the checkups went okay. Margaret and Audra were busy spilling in the blueberries and Margaret said to Audra "I have an idea, I have some raspberries in the ice box and let's see how they taste" Audra says "that sounds like a novel idea, let's ask Victoria and Doc to taste them first so their taste buds wouldn't be confused if they tried them after the blueberries." "Good thought "says Margaret. The front door opens and in walks Jeremy and says "The mares and stallions are groomed and dog gone I came out of the barn and smelled the coffee and if I didn't know any better I believe blueberry pancakes were in the making." Margaret comes around the corner and sees the whole crew of Jeremy's following Jeremy and says to Audra "let's get another dozen of eggs going the crew just came up". Audra says "my pleasure" as she starts to cook an additional pancakes with blueberries inside and a blueberry syrup that she made days ago to compliment the table. Audra motions for Doc and Victoria to come inside the kitchen where two barstools were set up amidst the built in nook to taste the new cuisine. Margaret says "Audra and I need for your honest opinion while tasting this" Victoria has one pancake and one sunny side up egg, and Doc has one pancake with scrambled eggs. Victoria comments on Doc's scrambled eggs and ask for a bite. He says "sure". They both try the cake without syrup and comment that it is a little on the dry side. Once syrup was involved it was a sweet tasting breakfast. Immediately Margaret introduces a new cake and asks for an answer. Doc and Victoria immediately ask for another because it is so sweet and delectable. Audra gives them both another and Margaret asks "Doc what did you experience?" and Doc says "it was very moist. Making my pallet want more!" Doc is intrigued and asks "what was the difference", and usually Margaret would say "that's a secret" but today she said, "I warmed the berries on the stove first so that when I put them in the cake in the pan the juice would begin to ooze out". Doc comments "that's pure genius, but your secret will stay with me." Victoria thinks to herself, I must remember that. As Audra brings out the pancakes, Margaret follows up with the eggs. It seems like it is just minutes for the crew to inhale the food that Margaret and Audra spent time cooking. That's okay, because it gives Audra and Margaret hope in their dreams of opening a café in town.

The crew and Jeremy excuse themselves from the table and are ready to do the farm chores. Victoria, Audra, Kim, and Margaret do the dishes and as soon as they are done, Esmira comes around the corner and startles everyone by saying "let's go outside for practice". Kim, Audra and Margaret know exactly what she is talking about. Victoria ask "anything special". Kim says "target practice". Victoria eyes brighten up. Esmira invites Victoria to go first as she hands her one of her favorites a Remington Rolling block rifle. Esmira told

Victoria that the rifle was ready for shooting. So Victoria stood up behind a tree and shot at the cans hitting all five of them dead center. Esmira is astonished and comments have you done this before and Victoria quickly says "no" because she wasn't going to give the truth that back home she is considered a marksman. Esmira looks deeply into Victoria's eyes for a couple of seconds and then goes to get her 1847 colt 45-walker revolver for more practice. Victoria knows that she can do the same with the revolver but doesn't want any more attention and hits one out of four. Esmira suspicion is taken away. Kim, Audra and Margaret all do their practice and Esmira is very pleased with their practice. After all the rifles and revolvers have been put away, Kim gets Victoria alone and asks her "where did you learn to shoot like that?' Victoria says "we do fox hunts at home and ever since I was eleven my mother told me to always be prepared, whether it be with guns or knowledge." Victoria concluded "please do not let anyone know about this!" Kim replies "I won't, but I have to check on the twins and start my sewing today". Jeremy enters the house to get a cup of coffee and asks for Victoria. Esmira over hears this but before she could get to the parlor they have left. Esmira is furious with jealousy. She knows that she has to get these emotions under control, but Victoria is a very tempting woman. She is a moderate built woman with a smaller bust line than Esmira but with thicker hips. However, Victoria has a smile that could that could charm a polar bear out of his fur. Esmira knew something was not right but for right now she couldn't name it.

Chapter 19

Jeremy took the appaloosa and saddled the palomino for Victoria. Up about ten minutes on the road but still on the property was the pond that Jeremy wanted to show her. They finally reached the pond. Jeremy wanted to know why this particular pond that looked like it measured thirty by forty was outlined in limestone. He was amazed that at any time of the year this pond was extremely warm. He had never seen anything like it "do you have any ideas "said Jeremy. Victoria spoke up with her thick accent and said "she knew that the limestone was like a filter and that was why the pond stayed crystal clear but she would have to do research on why it stayed warm. Are there any geysers or underground streams around?" Jeremy asks "water that flows underground, how does that happen?" Victoria says "if it is just peaking your curiosity that is fine, but I would leave this kind of information up to the geologists!" Jeremy asks "what's a geologist?" Victoria says "it's the study of the earth's structure" Jeremy says "okay' we should be getting back to the stud farm". Victoria says "that sounds like a plan."

Jeremy and Victoria ride in and see Esmira standing on the porch with arms folded and fuming. Jeremy takes both horses into the barn as Esmira walks pass Victoria and is tempted to say something, but doesn't. She sees Jeremy putting the saddles away in the tack room, as he gets ready to start brushing down the horses". Esmira comes up to the backside of the palomino and says "what were you doing?" Before

Jeremy answers he lifts Esmira up as she locks her legs around his waist and Jeremy gives her a sweltering kiss. He is about to set her down but her legs remained lock so Jeremy gives her another kiss and then sets her down. Jeremy asks "what were you saying?" Esmira says, as she was trying to catch her breath "I must have lost my train of thought". Jeremy tells Esmira that he took Victoria down to the pond to ask her why the pond stayed warm year round and remains so comfortable. Esmira cuts him off and says "what makes you think she would know anything about it?" Jeremy says "I have listened to her accent, were you aware that she is not from around these parts. That she comes from overseas and I wanted to get her view about it". Just for good measure Esmira wraps her small hands around his waist and presses her body into his as she kisses him. Then says "I just want you to remember there is more where that came from". Jeremy winks at her and says "thank-you". Esmira gets to the front of the barn and turns around so Jeremy can get a side view of her as she waves her hand. Jeremy looks at Esmira and thinks by gosh she is a picture worth looking at.

Ralph comes up to Jeremy and says "the forge is ready, and how do you want that brand on the cattle?" Jeremy says as he takes a stick and writes in the dirt. The letter E will be above the J so the whole brand can't be copied. Ralph tells Jeremy that he and Bill will get right on it.

Jeremy heads up to the house as he smells the coffee brewing as he hears Margaret's twins crying to be fed. This was a usual sound, it seemed if it wasn't Kim's twins or Margaret twins or even Audra's twins it would be Esmira twins. This noise was pure joy to Jeremy. This was history in the making. Before they knew it the twins would be running around asserting their independence.

Jack who is married to Kim and Joe who is married to Margaret are busy at feeding the cattle. It's a mild day and Jack and Joe know that when they are done here they have to go look in on the stallions. They hear that in three days they will be having a visit from Mrs. Morgan. She will want to look at the appaloosa, the palomino and the thick black one, although the thick black horse is just a tad shorter than the other horses. Mrs. Morgan will probably be intrigued by this horse. The three days have passed and Mrs. Morgan is here. She asks Jeremy "if she could take the black horse for a ride?" Jeremy would normally say no but this time he felt differently. So he said "yes. "As Jeremy took the black horse to the stall he mentioned to Mrs. Morgan that he was going to take ten minutes to brush him down. She resisted and commented "why"? Jeremy insisted "that if he had to explain WHY… then his offer to ride the horse would be taken back. "Mrs. Morgan did fume a little but remained calm. When Jeremy was done grooming the horse he put on his saddle, the one he won eight years earlier in Colorado. Jeremy took the horse to Mrs. Morgan. Mrs. Morgan looked at the horse, then looked at the saddle with eyes wide open as she asked "where did you get this saddle?" Jeremy boasted "eight years ago in Colorado by winning the rodeo". "Hmm I see, yes I know my nephew happened to be there with two points behind you and claimed second." Jeremy said "oh, I didn't know, is he still riding?" "No, he was killed a year later when getting ready to go to his next rodeo. He was favored to win that rodeo, but that time is long gone". Jeremy says" I am so sorry to hear of your loss". Mrs. Morgan said as she climbed on the black stallion, "maybe that's why I have such a strong liking to this black stallion. You see the last horse he rode looked exactly like this one except for the star in the forehead". Jack is on the palomino showing Mrs. Morgan where to ride. The ride was a quick mile as Mrs. Morgan took the horse out for all he had. The horse handled beautifully as she told Jeremy she would take him. Jeremy told Mrs. Morgan that he would have to talk to his partner before completing the sale.

 Jeremy talks it over with Esmira and they both agree to the price of $10,000.00 for the stallion. They also agree that if for some reason the sale could not go thru a plan B would be offered. Plan B would be a stud fee of two thousand dollars to be bred with a black mare. Jeremy and Esmira talk it over with Mrs. Morgan and she agrees with plan B. Payment will be one thousand now and one thousand when the colt is born. The deal was sealed.

 Kim had just gotten thru measuring Victoria when jealous Esmira walked into her boutique. Esmira asked Kim if she could have a moment. Esmira meant well she just wanted another dress for herself but this time in yellow. Since Kim and Esmira had the exact same build there was no need to measure her. So Kim's next few days would be a purple dress for Victoria and a yellow one for Esmira. Kim's twins were crying and Kim politely asked Esmira if she could peek in on the twins. Kim had another dress already made for the opening of the gymkhana tomorrow. But, she had five other dresses prepped to attach the fronts to. It was so much easier building the dresses in parts. This made it similar to an assembly line. So the next step was to attach all forty two buttons to the front as they prep the bodice. Then attach the bodice to the skirt part making the garment beautiful.

It was five in the morning Jeremy was starting to groom the stallions. This was his heaven, time to give to the horses. A time for respect and peace. This was his time to gather his wits and prepare for the day. All the mares needed to be groomed and everybody's day will start within a half hour. The first day of the gymkhana is always the busiest. Dog gone it, the half hour has passed because Jeremy could smell the coffee brewing. The rest of the crew will groom the mares while Jeremy heads back up to the house for his coffee. As he is sipping on his coffee Margaret and Audra are making an award winning breakfast for the crew. Flapjacks, eggs and bacon all you can eat. Esmira comes up to the backside of the palomino and says "what were you doing?" Before Jeremy answers he lifts Esmira up as she locks her legs around his waist and Jeremy gives her a sweltering kiss. He is about to set her down but her legs remained lock so Jeremy gives her another kiss and then sets her down.

It was five thirty in the morning and Jeremy was just walking in to the barn carrying his usual cup of coffee. He checked in on the Palomino and the white mare as he saw the palomino shaking his head up and down as though trying to communicate that everything was going as planned. Jeremy has a smirk on his face and the Palomino knew everything was okay. Jeremy had to get to the tack room to get his brushes for the grooming of the day, especially today because for the opening of the Gymkhana the horses had to look their best. Jeremy was at the top of his schedule; he would have eight horses done in the half hour before his crew would come in and take care of the rest of the horses. Jeremy gave directions to the crew as he walked up to the house and could smell the waffles and something else. He couldn't make out the smell. This must be something new that Margaret and Audra were trying out. As Jeremy walks in the front door his picturesque wife greets him with another hot cup of coffee and a sweltering kiss. Margaret is right behind her, full of joy and excitement asking Jeremy if he will try her new dish called Polenta. Jeremy quickly takes a bite and states "this really good. What is it?" Margaret adds "This is fried cornmeal. I have been writing a friend of mine down in Louisiana and she swears by it." Jeremy adds "well, I would have to agree with her." Margaret says "thank-you". Margaret turns around and races to the kitchen to tell Audra the good news. The breakfast would be set in fifteen minutes with sausage, cornmeal cakes, blueberry waffles, bacon and eggs with plenty of milk and coffee to go around. Esmira says grace and goes over the plans for the Gymkhana and thanks everyone in advance for all the work that will be done.

Jack, Earl, Bill and Ralph head toward the barn to saddle the horses in their exquisite gear for the day. They lead them up just south of the mare corral and tie them up. The field is starting to fill up and within minutes the count of the people will be beyond three thousand. Esmira is dressed in her fine dark blue dress riding side saddle and is accompanied with Margaret, Audra and Kim as they walk their horses thru the arena with their banner. This took fifteen minutes just long enough for the men to get the brahma bulls set up for the bull riding. This event that usually took an hour before it was completed was the perfect event to start out with. The men would gather around with their cigars and pipes almost drooling over the talent that is coming out of the chute. Here is one now. The bull comes out of the chute with a mean shake to the left. The experienced rider digs his spurs into the animal as he shakes to the right. The animal tries to heave the rider off as he keeps bucking and turning. The buzzer sounds and the rider has made his eight seconds.

Kim was walking around the arena when out of the corner of her eye she sees one of the riders leaning up on the fence and kissing this young girl. Kim was about eight feet away when she saw him reaching for her busty breast and started to feel them. Kim got closer and stopped his hand from going any further and said "stop"! The man took his hand away from her hand and was ready to back hand her, when a booming voice from the background says "Do you want to try someone your own size?" said Jeremy. Fear gripped a hold of him as he said "Why don't you mind your own business?" "This is my business and you are on my land do you need any more explanation?"' says Jeremy. The young man says "never mind "and is ready to leave as Jeremy grabs his arm and says" I like your spunk, I want you to see something come with me" As they walk off Kim turns toward this girl and asks "what is your name, and how old are you." The girl says "Gala and I am fourteen and a half" Kim speaks out loud and says "I should of known" Gala says" What do you mean"? Kim says "we will talk about that later. What were you thinking?" Gala rips into Kim with the statement. "My Dad ran away when I was three, my mom has done whatever it took to get me to ten years old and I have had to do the rest" Kim interrupts and says "I am sorry you have been dealt that hand in life, but if I could show you a better way, would it be worth it to you"? There is a little pause from Gala and then she says "why sure." "Well, the answer to your question that you asked a little bit ago when you said what do you mean? I was in the same boat a little over a 1year ago, I thought I had the world by the tail. As she shows Gala her fine busty physique. I thought this was all the men in my life would want. However, I began to notice that I was setting up a pattern. We would heavy pet and then they would leave and another would take his place and the cycle began over again. Does this sound familiar?" Gala blushes and says "that's exactly what happens, as she puts her hands under her breasts and says "I know full grown women that don't have what I have on top and yet they seem happy. What am I doing wrong?' as she begins to weep. Kim holds onto her hand and says "Come with me".

Chapter 20

Jeremy starts to walk to the barn as he says to this fellow, "what is your name"? "I go by the name of Marc." Replies Marc. Jeremy says "what brings you around these parts?" Marc says "well my three brothers have done bronco riding their whole life and so I thought if it was good enough for them, then I might as well try it." Jeremy opens up the stall and shows Marc the beautiful Appaloosa and says "do you want to ride?" Marc enthusiastically agrees. Jeremy saddles the Appaloosa and then invites Marc to get on. Marc gets on and Jeremy slaps the animal's backside and the horse immediately goes into the 'bucking bronco' mode. Marc manages to stay on for two seconds before he hits the ground. Marc gets up and is thoroughly disgusted with himself. He dusts himself off and says "that must be a high strung horse that has never happened before." Jeremy says "now what if it did? What if only twenty per cent of your rides were successful? That would mean for every five times you got on the horse, one ride would be successful." Marc snarls back "YEAH, I KNOW! But that would really suck." Jeremy interrupts and says "follow me", as he goes into the inner tack room and gets his burlap bag. Jeremy instructs him to put the burlap bag over the horses head very slowly and start stroking his neck while saying "you are the most powerful animal in the whole world, thank-you for letting me ride you"! Now say that for ten minutes I will be right back. Marc continues to say this statement over and over in a soft voice until Jeremy comes back. Jeremy instructs

Marc to leave the bag on but walk the horse around the corral while continue to talk to him. Marc does this for five minutes and then stops the horse. Jeremy then tells Marc to slowly take the bag off and mount the horse. Jeremy opens the corral gate as he points down the road and tells Marc to run the beast hard. "Ye Haw" Marc yells out as the horse goes into full stride for two miles and Marc turns him around and does the same back to the corral. He can't believe his eyes. Marc asks "what did you do? This was like a changed animal!" Jeremy says to Marc "you have the power, follow me".

Jeremy leads Marc over to the arena where three thousand people are watching. Jeremy announces to the public about horse whispering and tells the audience that Marc will demonstrate from the beginning of how horse whispering works. He shows the whole audience from the burlap bag, to the removal of it and the racing. The crowd is stunned. If they had not seen it for themselves they would not have believed it. Jeremy thanks Marc and is ready to leave as Marc speaks up "I want more of what you got" Jeremy turns around and asks "what do you mean?" "You are loaded with success. A wife, land and horses what more does one need?" says Marc "I'll make you a deal" says Jeremy "if you can apologize to Gala for what you were doing, I will show you success as you know it". Marc says "I was just having fun" Jeremy turns around and heads for the gymkhana gate as he hears Marc says "wait, wait you win" Jeremy tells Marc "I thought you might come to your senses."

Kim and Gala reach the house as Kim introduces Margaret and Audra to Gala. They were on their lunch break as Audra offered her a sandwich and told Gala they had to get back to the gymkhana, but it was nice to meet you. Kim had a few minutes and showed Gala her boutique. She showed her the dresses and the sewing machine that she used extensively to make the dresses. Kim asked Gala if she ever thought of wearing something nice like one of these dresses'." Gala says "they are way too expensive!" Kim speaks up "I will make you a deal, if you can apologize to that gentlemen for making yourself look easy, I will show you how you can make yourself a dress just like what you see here." Gala gasps and says "you will do that for me?" Kim says "yes, but we should get back to the gymkhana."

As they were going back over to the gymkhana Kim and Jeremy and Marc and Gala meet half way to the gymkhana and Marc speaks up first and says "My cruel and insensitive side got the better of me and all I could think about was me and I am so sorry". Gala says "you are forgiven, but I too must say that I am sorry for making myself so freely available and giving off all the wrong messages" Marc is astonished about what he hears and forgives Gala.

Ralph, Bill and Earl are busy watching the barrel races and are wondering if the best time of seventeen seconds will hold up. Wait, there is one more contestant, looks like she can barely fit in the saddle, probably five foot. The gun goes off and she is just circling the left barrel as she turns her bay horse toward the right barrel. The horse has an unusual large gait and is just turning the right barrel as she gives the horse a kick as she races for the top barrel. The audience is concerned about the time she is making. Will it be enough? The horse and the rider stretch across the finish line as the judges' call out the time of sixteen and nine tenths of a second. She is the winner. Just as she crosses the line Earl's stomach begins to growl as he mentions to the others let's go taste some of Margaret and Audra's fine cooking. They, meaning just about everyone at this event goes to the booth that was set up about twenty feet from everything else. Everyone could finally see what Earl was talking about. Audra and Margaret had five gallon buckets full of potato salad, homemade macaroni salad, beans and the best fried chicken that one could make all for the nice sum of ten cents. This was intermission time so everyone had ninety minutes before anything would be starting.

Normally, the house is a buzzing with everyone going in and out. This was the perfect time just to catch your breath. The front door opens but Esmira is lost in thought in her bedroom. Jeremy is looking for some cuff links that may be in the bedroom. As he opens the bedroom door he is startled to see his wife Esmira just looking at herself in the mirror. He sneaks up behind her and starts to rub her neck as Esmira looks in the mirror and says "there is only one man with thick hands that I will allow to touch me, but there are other areas that could use some attention". Jeremy speaks up and says "Oh, I am sure there is, but first let me brush your hair." As Jeremy reaches for the brush Esmira turns around, faces him and smiles. Esmira's hair is so long that when her five foot frame stands up her hair is below her butt. Jeremy holds her thick black hair in one hand and brushes backward in order to get all of her beautiful hair. Jeremy continues to brush Esmira hair because he realizes that doing this excites her. Esmira's eyes float down to Jeremy's belt as she reaches for his belt, Jeremy lowers his head and kisses her tenderly and then says "Oh, this is the perfect time, I would never want to leave you wanting the best experience in our life, but I have to get down to the gymkhana to announce the jumps". Esmira asks "promise me that we can take care of our feelings tonight! "Jeremy states "My beloved, you are prettier than beautiful, and I wouldn't miss a chance to fulfill your every desire!" As Jeremy puts on his cuff links and heads toward the gymkhana.

Victoria and her cousin are sitting in the bleachers waiting for the jumps, as her cousin points to the booth that house Kim, Margaret, Audra and Gala, who are busy passing out the food that took Audra and Margaret hours to prepare. A bystander states this is the best food I have tasted in a long time as he looks toward Audra. Audra says "thank-you, I would love to talk but as you can see we all are pretty busy." Just then a booming voice comes from atop the bleachers. "Ladies and Gentlemen if I can have your attention over here we will start the jumps." Victoria tells her cousin that this reminds her of the fox hunt that they have back in London, England. The way they have the jumps set up stretches the imagination. From the steeple chase to the water creek to the brick fence and then over the bushes, this is exciting. All this time people are listening to the music in the background that Ross and Byron are playing to put the audience at ease.

Since lunch is finishing up, Kim is excited about showing Gala some basics in sewing with the hopes of three months from now she will be able to say yes to Victoria and go overseas. Wow! She thinks of herself and her family in a different location for at least a year. Maybe this dream will come true but for now her main focus is to train Gala. So there is a tree stump nearby and Kim says to Gala "I want you to sit down here and lift your right heel up and down until I come back." Kim goes over to her booth and sells the sky blue dress for two hundred dollars and tells Audra and Margaret that she will be spending time with Gala for the rest of the afternoon. Kim comes back to Gala and asks "how are you doing". Gala replies "well my foot is a little tired but other than that I am great". Kim states "there is a reason why I had you do that, let's go up to my boutique and I will show you further." They go up to the boutique and Kim shows her the Singer treadle sewing machine and asks her to sit down and get comfortable. Kim hands her two pieces of cloth one grey and one black. Kim tells her to put one piece of cloth on top of another and pump the sewing machine with her foot until you are done sewing the cloth. Gala does so very successfully and makes Kim wonder if she might just be a natural at sewing. Gala shows the two pieces to Kim and is just as excited as Kim is when she sees a nice completed job. Kim asks Gala how comfortable she is and Gala says "fine". Kim goes on to say that since she did a great job of sewing a straight line she will show her the button hoops. Kim goes to her seat bench and pulls out button hoops. She tells Gala to sew the hoops on top of the grey and black practice slip and she does well. Kim tells Gala that the practice went well but they have to get back to the booth. They go back to the booth and Kim let's her talk to the customers as she sells the maroon dress for two hundred and fifty. Kim is impressed.

Chapter 21

Jeremy and Marc are back at the barn listening to Ross and Byron warming up with their instruments. As Jeremy listens he also talks to Marc on grooming the horses. However, the teacher that Jeremy is, he takes it to the next level. Jeremy gives him a parable and says, "There was a lady in the community that was despised by all, yet seeing this beggar beside the road she wondered what she could give. For the only thing she was carrying was an expensive bottle of cologne. She stopped by the beggar in the road and said, "Stop". "You have travelled a long way. Let me at least anoint your feet. "The beggar was shocked because no one had talked to him because he was a beggar. The lady anointed his feet and went on her way. When she had finally reached her destination with only half of what she started with, her neighbor was mad. The neighbor asked "why did you not bring me a full bottle just as I left it to you"? The despised lady said to her neighbor "I have always thought of you as a kind and generous lady and when I shared your cologne with this beggar an unusual feeling swept over me. Was I wrong? "The neighbor being wise beyond her years said "was it better to give than to receive? "The despised lady who no longer felt despised answered "Yes" and her neighbor said "well, then go and have a wonderful life" As the neighbor returned to her town she no longer felt despised and people came up to meet her. Jeremy asked Marc "was the lady wrong?" Marc answered with "it is always better to give than to receive". Jeremy said "you have surprised me with your answer, but I am glad that you learned". Marc and Jeremy stayed awhile listening to the music.

The day was drawing to a close and Jeremy had just finished his horse whispering. Some crowds were starting to come toward him as Ralph and Earl were pulling up the long wagon with the bed covered with hay. It was time for the hay ride. Ralph and Earl had to go up the road around a mile to catch the bon-fire that Audra and Jack have built so everyone on the wagon will be able to eat. The wagon pulls in around twenty minutes later and Jack and Audra have already got the branches tapered off for the sausage brats. The fire is hot and ready to go. Fifteen people climb out of the wagon and get their brats ready as Ralph tell all of them stories and jokes of the old country and why they should be thankful for where they are. One of the most memorable stories was about the older man crossing the prairie at night time and his favorite horse went lame. This meant that he had to put the horse down, to extinguish his life as he knew it. This horse had been with him for fifteen years. This horse had been closer than his best friend. To put him down? Crack came the noise from the woods, as a stranger came into this mans' camp. The man was startled and said who goes there? Everything about this intruder was dark in appearance. He couldn't make out his face. But the stranger asked the older man "are you going to continue to let the horse suffer or put him down"? "I can't! "So the quick wit of the stranger said to turn his head as the stranger put him down. He walked back into the forest and was gone. The older man waited for this strangers return. So he entered the forest to look for him, only to find a horse. Nowhere in sight was the stranger? If he told this story no one would believe him. Just when this story ended a stranger in the audience spoke up with excitement and said listen closely, Once upon a time out in the prairie were three boys ages twelve to fifteen. Although extremely tired the middle one spoke up and said, let me tell you about a story called swish-plop. The family had just gotten back from an outing and it was about four-thirty on a September day and the teenager asked his mother if he could go play and his mother said yes, but remember to stay away from the train tracks. So the three boys went off to the local hill to play hide and seek. A half hour had passed and the game was accelerating. In order to catch the new seeker, pushing came into play. Brian had pushed Felix who in turned pushed Larry. However, Larry was at the top of the hill and when he fell he rolled down the hill coming to a ravine just before the railroad tracks when the train was going thru. Larry looked up and saw a man sitting on the caboose steps looking down at him. However the site of this man was unusual. He had no legs below the knees. Now the only way this individual can get around is by dragging his lower body and plopping on his bottom. So the story goes swish-plop. Thank God the children listened to their mother when she said, stay away from the train tracks.

Chapter 22

It was five thirty in the morning and Jeremy is already reviewing what will happen today. However, the smell of coffee is carrying over to the barn. By six Jeremy is done with his share of the horses, it's time to get up to the house and relax. The smell of that great breakfast is even more inviting. Who could turn down all the fixings of hash browns, gravy, eggs, pancakes, bacon and sausage? Margaret and Audra were making it all. Soon they will have enough saved up for their dream café in town. It will be their mark in this western town. As breakfast is being served, Jeremy reviews the whole day, starting out with the bronco riding and ending up with the show casing of all the horses, then followed up by the dance at 7:30. Jeremy blesses the food and invites everyone to dig in.

Joe and Jack find their way over to the bronco chute, as they are both coming up next to ride. Jack likes the bay horse because he has ridden him before. However, he gets the sorrel. Jack gets into the chute and cinches his grip to a super tight one and away the chute opens. The horse is throwing his head down to the ground to cause mayhem. He throws his head to the right and to the left with no avail, as the buzzer rings and the rider make his eight seconds. Joe comes along with the white mare and helps Jack get away from the bronco. Now that Joe is up he is also hoping for the bay but gets the appaloosa instead. While Joe cinches up and is let out of his chute. Joe has never been on a horse that is so mean and cantankerous. Joe's grip becomes tighter and tighter and the horse acts as if he is going to roll. Suddenly, the buzzer goes off and Jack helps Joe off the horse. Jack congratulates him on a fine ride and Joe just shakes his head from side to side and says to himself Í don't understand". Jack says to Joe "what did you say" Joe replies with "nothing. I mean, the other day I did some horse whispering with this same animal and it was like the difference of night and day" Joe continues and says "from now on it is horse whispering for me. "Jack says to Joe "shake it off."

The booming voice comes thru the horn as he invites everybody for intermission time requesting that everyone go visit the food and dress booth. He also reminds them that a dance will be held at 7:30 tonight. As Jack and Joe go over to the booth, they see a lady different than Victoria and her cousin buying up the three dresses that Kim had showcased for six hundred dollars. Joe asked "Kim if she had ever met this lady before and Kim said "no. but, the word must of spread". Joe inquired "What do you mean?" Kim replies "well, I don't mean to sound conceited, but I think the public is starting to understand about my gift with the sewing machine. Many more people will come to buy my merchandise. "Just about this time an argument starts about a dress that Gala is about to sell. The young lady wants to buy the last dress for $250.00 but Elizabeth quickly bids $275.00 and this confuses Gala. Gala had never been in a bidding contest before and didn't know how to respond. Before Kim can say anything, Esmira happens to overhear and asks "ladies do we have a problem?" Elizabeth is just infuriated and speaks up "I believe that my higher bid should buy the dress!" Esmira says", well that is true but did this lady have a chance to top your bid?" The lady said "no and countered with $285.00." Kim spoke up and said "going once, going twice." and Elizabeth counters with $300.00. Kim whispers to this new lady and says "let her have this, and I will give you a private viewing of some fabulous dresses I have." Esmira says "going once going twice sold to Elizabeth." Kim says "I didn't catch your name." The lady says "my name is Sally". Kim motions for Gala as they show Sally the way to the boutique. Once there Sally looks at the burgundy, the crème, the forest green, and the sky blue dresses and says "I will take them all what's your price?" Kim speaks up "I would usually let them go for $1300.00 but since you had to miss out on the last dress, $1000.00 is my bottom offer." Sally says "sold". Kim gives direction to Gala on how to get the dresses wrapped up as Kim chats away with Sally.

Kim shows Gala the empty closet and says "now we have to get four dresses sewn by eleven o'clock tonight in order to meet the demand on tomorrow's public. Are you ready?" Gala says "as long as I can get ready for the dance tonight because Marc has asked me out." Kim states "sounds good to me". It's 5:30 in the evening and both Gala and Kim know that they have to move a mountain in order to get six dresses done by tomorrow and still go to the dance and be able to relax. Gala turns to Kim and says "what about this, I will make two dresses one with a smaller bust line around 5 foot ten or 6 foot and another around 5 foot 4 to 5foot six with a huge bust line, all in burgundy." Kim says "fine, I will take the 5 foot ten to six foot in a huge bust line and a 5 foot 4 with a small bust line all in an emerald green and I think I can get them done by eight. You need to get out of here by seven to make the dance." However, tell Prince Charming that you need to be back to work by 9:45. Gala smiles from ear to ear and says "thanks, I have a lot of work to do", Gala quickly puts the seam on the underneath side of the sleeves for both dresses and is busy putting the elastic thru the waist band for the taller dress. She flips the dress around and is quickly working on the bigger bust line. This is a bit of a chore, to make it firm but with a little give. There, she did it now with the forty two buttons from waist to the neckline and she will be done. It is approaching 7 o'clock and Gala will just be done with the half inch seam on the length, she proudly shows it off to Kim as she says "a job well done, but you best be getting ready for the dance" As Gala goes to get ready for the dance, she thinks to herself this is a lot better than roaming around. Gala remembers that living life without direction merely trying to survive from day to day was gone. Thank goodness! Life with direction was stimulating. Kim is half way done with her second dress and just has the sleeves to attach. Then she will make a 5 foot 4 dress with a huge bust line in yellow before going to the 5 foot 10 in purple with a small bust line. Kim is so in love with her work that the time flies and approaches nine o'clock. As she wraps up the purple dress she lays it aside and quickly puts on her crème colored dress to go to the dance. As she walks into the barn floor where the music is playing she has some on lookers. A few gentlemen have already asked her to dance as she politely tells them "if it is okay with my husband". That was enough for most of the men to look elsewhere. However, one gentlemen did ask her husband if it was okay and he said "sure, but just one". The gentlemen approached Kim and asked her again for one dance and she said "okay". Right now Gala's jaw drops wide open and is stricken by how much good can come from a sewing machine. Kim finally asks the loaded question "would you like to know how to sew on a full time basis?" Gala answers "are you kidding, sure, when do I start?" Kim is busy thinking to herself, now that I have a substitute; it's more like just waiting until the gymkhana is over with before I ask Esmira the question. She didn't hear Gala as she replied "Hum I am sorry, just thinking to myself. Well, and then let's get you started on some easy stuff. We will go up to the boutique and start making bonnets. The classic is the color white, but just for kicks let's make eight bonnets. Three will be white, one pink, one emerald green, one sky blue, one burgundy and one yellow. People will naturally buy white because it can go with everything. The reason why we are doing the bonnets is because it will bring another fifty dollars in a combined cost." The dance winds down and the crowd casually shuffles out.

The next morning Kim tells Margaret and Audra she will be gone for a couple of hours, she picks up a serving of chicken and potato salad for Gala and her. The husbands are busy eating at the booth. Kim tells her husband the same as he tells her that Jack and Joe will be doing the whispering with the horses. Jack and Joe go to the barn and get the most spirited horse, the appaloosa. As they bridle the horse, the stallion begins to stir, Jack slowly puts the burlap bag over his head. Joe begins to walk with the horse until they can get to the open field. Jack starts to speak to the audience about what Joe is doing. Right now to the audience it looks like Joe is just walking the horse. However, while Joe is walking the animal he is whispering to the animal this." **You are** the most strongest and beautiful of animals I have ever known. I want to thank you for allowing me to ride you. Every time I ride you it is my pleasure". Joe says this for ten minutes while walking at a leisurely pace. Joe tells the horse that he is going to stop and put the saddle on him. After Joe does this he mounts the horse and begins to walk with him. Jack points to the canal where on the other side is a two mile run. Joe spurs the horse a little and the horse is in a full gallop within seconds.

The crowd can't believe their eyes. This was the same horse that Jack had trouble with just yesterday when he was riding the broncos. When Joe returns he speaks through the mega phone insisting that the most important part of riding the horse is the brushing down afterwards. Kim returns back to the boutique with Gala's lunch as they go over the plan to make another seven dresses. Little does Gala know that Kim has already decided to make Gala a wedding dress for the day that she and Marc will walk the aisle. As they start on their dresses a knocking came at the door. Kim answered it and there was Jack and Marc. Gala asked if she could step out for an hour and Kim said "why don't Jack and I step out for an hour". Jack grabbed her hand and Kim knew immediately that he was looking for some special attention. Kim was up for it. They went over to the barn and climbed the ladder and got into the loft and began to kiss and cuddle. As Jack kissed her neckline Kim would kiss his forehead and then go down and squeeze his tight stomach area. This would get Jack ready. Jack would always ask Kim if this action was okay. Kim would get even more excited because of the respect he was showing her. Jack went for her huge breast and began to lick them. Jack knew she was ready. Jack was wise enough to take it slow making sure that Kim enjoyed everything. Kim loved using her hips especially at special moments like this. Since she was smaller in height she was able to kiss his chest as everything rhythmically fit together. The passion they showed each other was extremely heated. Now it was time to get their stuff together and get back to the boutique and gymkhana.

    Kim had just gotten the hay out of her hair when Gala returned. Kim was in the process of brushing her long hair as it renewed her spirit. Gala had some questions for Kim. Gala started to confess by saying "she had not been the best girl in the town but now she was feeling over joyed about everything. Marc would say, she could even complete his sentences." This struck Gala as kind of odd. "What do you think?" as she asks Kim, "Well, I am not a fortune teller, but it sounds to me like this is the person. Here's why. The thoughts that you are feeling are original. No one has caused you to have that shaking feeling. Something that you can't shake off but keep on thinking about. Even ways that you can be more considerate to his feelings. A feeling that you would do anything for him. That's love. Welcome to the exlirating feeling of love". "WOW! That does describe what I am feeling, how did you know?" Kim says "that could be explained in another day, but right now we have got a boatload of work to do." Kim starts on the wedding dress with a smaller bust line and a longer inseam for Gala. While Gala starts on one that is shiny purple almost satin with a huge bust line and an inseam that would fit a 5 foot ten to a 6 foot woman. Gala has never experienced so much feeling in her life. A strong young handsome man who cares what she thinks. A business experience that would topple most professionals, especially about the law of supply and demand. Then someone having enough trust in her to teach her. WOW! Gala guesses that no one promised her anything, but it is the joy of knowing about self-accomplishment. Kim's time management says that these dresses will be done on the day after tomorrow. Kim is already planning on the sales of today to surpass what she did on last year's gymkhana. Certainly this should be something to be proud of, but she is still thinking about the job that Victoria has offered her!

Marc seeks Jeremy's advice. He too has shaken feelings about Gala. He asks Jeremy. "I am not sure what to do. I want to hear everything she has to say. I can even finish her sentences. We think so much alike" Jeremy adds," so what is your question?" Marc says "am I in love?" Jeremy says,"…….. There's only two questions you have got to answer. First, are you having these feelings to cover up your being scolded earlier and second could you see yourself spending the rest of your life with her?" Amazing Marc thought, to have everything right in front of you and your destiny is only a decision away!

Much noise can be heard at the gymkhana; Kim thinks that she and Gala need to be out there. So Kim tells Gala to find a stopping point to pull seven dresses out of the closet to go sell to the crowd. Kim gathers four dresses and Gala grabs three and they are out of the boutique and on their way to the commotion. By the time Kim gets to their booth the noise has stopped but there are people lining up to see what Kim and Gala have brought. Before Kim can even hang the dresses up there are bidders. Victoria bids on the peach dress of $325.00 Kim says sold. The sky blue with the big bust line and short inseam takes $340.00. The burgundy dress with the huge bust line and tall inseam goes for $375.00. The orange dress with the average bust line and the average inseam goes for $300.00. The forest green with the huge bust line and small inseam goes for $290.00. The pink dress with the big bust line and an average inseam goes for $300.00. Then before anyone can say anything else Elizabeth bids $310.00 on the deep blue dress. Kim realizes that she needs to put forth a concentrated effort on producing a lot more dresses. The money that is coming in is good but she didn't expect this much business. She looks over to Gala and mentions to her that they will have to get the ten dresses up at the boutique for backup. They excuse themselves for ten minutes.

It is lunch time and Margaret and Audra have various lunches going on. Their booth is filled with German food such as Wiener schnitzel with Kraut included or Prime rib with beans or whipped potatoes. Audra and Margaret are having a thrilling day; they can't scoop up the food fast enough. They are waiting for the gymkhana to finish this year so they can start their café in town.

Margaret and Audra sat down and decided to make up a menu for their dream café. They decided the hours would be from six thirty to five thirty six days a week. Now they didn't want to give too much of a selection, just enough to keep them coming back for more. They had to have the best morning coffee. So they decided to have a rack of cups for the usual customers that came in knowing that their own cup would be waiting. Next they decided to have cobbler or pies depending on what part of the country you came from. Steak and eggs would be their normal breakfast along with ham and eggs and hash browns. Audra was more of the baker so she decided to take over the homemade bread and biscuit area. She asked Margaret if she would want to do both polenta and grits for breakfast and this is what Margaret had to say "you can usually tell a lot about a person on which they prefer, polenta is usually a more mushy meal, this type, which means a more relaxed person, where grits is usually thicker a toothsome meal in which the person shows more backbone." So she told Audra to list them both. Margaret was the brains behind the outfit. She handed Audra a piece of paper and on it was what she thought the menu should look like.

Flapjacks	05
Cornmeal biscuits	05
Biscuits	05

Oatmeal	05
Grits and polenta	05
Soups	
Catfish	05
Potato	05
Lunch and Dinner.	
Chicken, breast and leg	10
Quail, in season	10
Rabbit	10
Goose	10
Wiener schnitzel	10
Steak	10
Venison	10
Eggs any style	05
Cold meats with side of Beans	10
Kraut	05
Bacon or Ham	10
Vegetables	
Potatoes, Cabbage, Carrots	
Hominy, Rice, Fried onions	05
For the Gymkhana	
Peach preserves	05
Blackberry jam	05
Corn custard pudding	05

Margaret asked Audra to take a while and look the menu over. Audra had a sense that Margaret was right and almost immediately said she liked it. Now the only thing they had to wait on was time… time for the Gymkhana to be over.

As Gala and Kim are walking up to the boutique a rude man by the name of Buck gets in their way and tries to stop Gala by walking in their path. Gala is extremely polite and says excuse me. Buck says I don't think so. This is the perfect time for me to have my fun. Who would think of anybody getting harmed in mid-day? Buck chuckles. Kim realizes she needs to maneuver her way to his back side in a hurry. As Buck steps toward Gala, Buck doesn't realize that Kim has pulled a derringer from her garter. She reaches around Buck's neckline and says in her soft voice "if you don't leave us alone now my finger will slip and your life will be over." Buck is astonished and loosens Gala and runs to his horse and takes off. Gala is immensely surprised. She rapidly goes thru a thinking process such as, she saves me from my reckless behavior, and she teaches me about an occupation and now she literary saves my life. "Whoa this is way too much, we have to learn to take care of ourselves like that?" asks Gala. Kim responds "that's a question that I will answer later, but right now we have some dresses to get." Not only is Gala impressed but she believes she has found her calling in life. After she and Kim get the dresses and return to their booth Gala excuses herself momentarily to go tell Marc her thrilling day. Will he believe her? Back at the booth, Victoria and Elizabeth meet. This gentlemen buys the huge busted purple dress with the short inseam for his girl back east. Next was the Crimson dress with the small bust line but long inseam. The Emerald green was next with a huge bust line and long legs. The orange dress with a moderate bust size and a moderate inseam. The Ivory dress with the small bust line and long inseam was next. The lavender dress with a huge bust line and short inseam was bought for the young woman of Colorado. The pink dress with a moderate bust and long inseam went to the lady from Connecticut. Victoria and Elizabeth took the beige and the hunter green. The last one went to Marc who was buying the white dress for Gala with the huge bust line and the short inseam. However, Gala didn't know about it. Gala came back to the booth as soon as Marc left as she caught Kim's eye, knowing that for the next three days after the Gymkhana was done for the day, both Kim and her would be sewing.

 It was four thirty in the morning, Jeremy couldn't sleep. Not with an outstanding wife and partner with the stud farm just lying there peacefully. He kissed her forehead, then her lips, then her neckline and then finally her breasts. She opened up and received him knowing that it was her lover and partner. The rhythmic motion was heaven sent. She locked her heels around the back of his knees to allow him more access. Esmira knew that Jeremy would feel better. Jeremy thanked her and turned over to catch another half hour of sleep. It seems like time just flies by, before you know it the half hour had passed and Jeremy was up before the crack of dawn. He went directly to the barn as if by instinct to groom the horses. This was his time. Time to reflect. Time to set new goals but still appreciate all the beauty that was in his life. Well, the rest of the crew is up grooming the mares, time to go have that wonderful coffee with the wife.

As he sat at the table, he mentioned the successes that the stud farm has been having. He noticed the boutique had taken off especially with the new help of Gala. He was happy with the three mares to foal in early spring. All the crew's work was remarkable. It was times like this that Jeremy gave thanks to God for he knew that hard work would always be rewarded, meanwhile, there was three days left on the Gymkhana, before they could plan for next year. He looked into the beauty of his wife's eyes and pinched his wrist to make sure this wasn't a dream. Yes, he felt the pinch. This was real. Now it was time for those wonderful cooks, both Margaret and Audra were serving up a hearty breakfast. Jeremy always thought they were cooking for a small army, but never did he see a left over. Today, it was Flapjacks with eggs, bacon, sausages and biscuits. Everyone knew they had to fill up because lunchtime might not be there.

Chapter 23

Elizabeth and Victoria were walking the grounds just studying the layout as Victoria commented about the fox hunts and such that they had back in England. Victoria said "it was always calming when the men went out to hunt that gave us women time to reflect on our duties and such. Time to look at the new fashions of the day. Where our world was going and collect some peace. Do you miss that Elizabeth?" Elizabeth says "these commoners have more going for them than what I thought. Their freedom is outstanding. Yes, they work hard, but what they earn is what they keep. They don't have to give back 20 percent to their government. Imagine just for a minute Victoria that you were not in the position that you are, but a commoner and making really good money and able to keep it." Victoria states emphatically, "well how else is one suppose too run a country and all its provinces". Elizabeth states "I know it's a touchy subject for you so I am going to steer clear of this one. However, didn't I tell you she can turn out those dresses like no one else?" Victoria says "Yes you did, but I have to get a dress in sky blue, it makes me look so youthful". Elizabeth says "Yes it does."

The events of the Gymkhana have been going on like clockwork. It is lunch time and Margaret and Audra are doing their cooking magic. The three hundred pound hog has been slowly cooking over the spit for the last eight hours. The meat is now ready for what people say falling off the bone. Audra has a backup dish from the chickens she has prepared. She is ready with the ten gallon bucket of potato salad and beans. Audra and Margaret think to themselves as they serve these people, have they not seen great cooking before? The multitudes of people come thru this booth and Jeremy is amazed of how well the ladies are serving up the food. The line is coming to a close and a good thing too because they are nearly running out of potato salad. Both Audra and Margaret are pleased. They can't wait for the dance tonight.

The sky is just turning a midnight blue. Just in time for Ross and Byron to start their three hour performance. Kim, Margaret, Audra and Esmira are all dancing with their husbands. Marc asks Gala to dance, she is very happy he did. Victoria and Elizabeth have just been asked and have said yes. As Victoria and Elizabeth dance they are not accustomed to this western type of music but understand the steps are very similar. Victoria and Elizabeth are very curious of what the western people talk about, so they've put their listening skills to the test, and find that their interest lie in fashion for the women and farming business for the men. Victoria never gave it a second thought of how the calves are birthing or the weather that might force the animals inside the barn. This has been a rewarding experience for Victoria. Even though the dance is nearing to close there is part of Victoria that can't wait to be back at her country of England with Kim as her fashion designer. Marc and Gala wish the night would never end, but before the last song ends, Marc stops, gets down on one knee, and asks Gala "will you be my wife?" Everybody looks in her direction, and hears her answer, as Kim, Margaret and Audra rush to congratulate her.

Kim pulled aside the downtown attorney that she spotted in the crowd. Kim asked him if he could draw up some patents on some dress designs that she had invented. She gave him the patterns on the elastic waist, the wool ¾ sleeve and three different men suits. The attorney said it would take about six weeks for the process to occur, but to have no worry.

Kim sat down and wrote a letter to Victoria on some questions she had. She wrote, Victoria I have thought about your request. However, if this was to happen I would also have to bring my husband and my twins with me. I thought this thru, so if I was to fully accept this offer, it would have to be on a yearly trial at first. Sincerely Kim. She handed this letter to Victoria and mentioned to her to read this in her spare time.

As the rooster crows most everybody on the E&J stud farm are just finishing up their breakfast, ready for another day. Of course, the girls are still bubbling with excitement for Gala. Everyone but Gala knows that Marc has already bought her wedding gown the one that Kim just got thru with days before. Now Gala is waiting for the Gymkhana to end and start her married life with Marc. Gala is so in love that she hasn't even thought of what Marc would do to support her. All this time Kim is leaning more to a yes than no on to Victoria's proposition. She hasn't even confronted the idea with Esmira yet. That will be for another day. Right now Kim has got to get the dresses that Gala and she have spent every free minute on putting together. Yes, there is a sky blue dress that she made for Victoria and a soft lime green for Elizabeth. Kim has decided to put bonnets into all the new dresses that she will bring out. Kim and Gala have brought out ten dresses and bonnets in the following colors. The first is a soft brown followed by a sharp gold. The third and fourth are a cherry red and a crimson red. The fifth and six is a sky blue and a lime green. The seventh thru the tenth are Lavender, bright pink, yellow and silver. Gala is surprised at how fast the dresses sell out. Rather than complain because she has to sew more, she realizes that this is like people saying thanks for her work. Gala also stops and thinks of where she was just weeks ago. Gala was so absorbed in seeking attention that she didn't care what people thought of her as long as she could make a few men happy along the way. Thank goodness someone believed in her enough to give her a chance. Gala is very happy now. There are two more days left in the gymkhana. Margaret and Audra are expanding on their hopes for the café. Gala and Marc about marriage and Kim to make the bold move to ask Esmira about a year leave of absence on a once in a lifetime opportunity.

One more day has passed and Kim manages to get ahold of Jeremy to call a meeting with Esmira and Jeremy about her opportunity. Kim and her husband Jack have great respect for both Jeremy and Esmira and have to ask them this question. Kim steps forward and manages to get her question out. "Esmira and Jeremy, I have a lot to thank you for. I wish to ask for a leave of absence of a year for an opportunity that has come up." Esmira asks Kim "what could be that important that you would leave almost family behind?'" Kim states "my ability and talent have given me this opportunity. I have said that before I could take the position I would have to train someone as my substitute out of respect for my employer, and that I would have to be compensated enough because I would be taking my husband and my twins with me. Please, before you answer, I have both substitutes in place. Gala for me and Marc for Jack. If".... Esmira interrupts her and says "I think you have made a grand decision and I respect you for everything you have put in place and I would be foolish not to grant you this opportunity. Would there be anything else?" Kim is astonished and says "you are saying yes, yes. Oh thank you!"

Kim goes and tells her husband the good news. She realizes now that it is just setting up the arrangements with the booking company. Kim also wants to go tell Victoria and Elizabeth about the grand news. She will tell them after breakfast. Seeing that this is also the last day of the gymkhana she must also tell Gala. She had to thank Margaret and Audra for breakfast as well as breaking the news. Explaining in detail that it will only be for a year. It is only natural that the ladies shed tears and they say how much they are going to miss her and her family. Kim goes to the boutique and meets Gala over a cup of coffee and slowly begins to tell Gala the good news. That she has faith in her about carrying on in the boutique. Gala asks why and Kim tells her "that sometimes opportunity will come along once in a life time and one should take it". Gala understands. Kim excuses herself and goes to find Victoria and Elizabeth. As Elizabeth and Victoria meet Kim they have shared the good news and all are excited. As Kim goes to express herself about payment over to London England, Victoria assures her that her whole family passage has already been taken care of. Kim's mouth drops open and asks "how did you know?" Victoria says "call it a hunch. However, we will leave in five days. It will be a two day ride to where the boat will pick us up at the border of Montana. Then the boat will take another twelve days to get to England's harbor. Then we will be picked up by the courts escort, and taken to the Inn that everyone will stay at". As Kim tries to think all this through her husband Jack reassures her that everything will be okay.

Marc and Gala are busy talking about her new position as Marc wonders what he will do since the Gymkhana is over and Gala says "why don't you take Jack's position since he is leaving with his wife

Kim". Marc speaks up "great, I'll go ask Jeremy". After asking Jeremy and getting the job as cowhand Marc rushes over and tells Gala. Gala just twirls her hair with her finger saying, "I knew you could do it."

The five days flew by and Kim and her family were on their way. Jeremy and Esmira need to take a couple of days away from the stud farm so they volunteer to take Kim's family up to the drop off spot. It would be about a days ride. This would allow Esmira and Jeremy a chance to say a fabulous good-bye. All the horses were saddled and the buck board carrying Kim's belongings was ready. Kim and Victoria were following Esmira and Jeremy. Kim asked Victoria what to expect. Victoria responded with, there will be enough time to talk about those things on the twelve day cruise over there. I would put my efforts in saying good bye to the ones you are leaving. That way everything will fall into place. Kim wasn't prepared for that answer but accepted it. Jeremy was looking forward to looking in on the shack. Business is going on as usual back at the farm. All the Gymkhana stuff is being stored away for next year. Jeremy and Esmira finally reach the destination and say their good-byes to Kim and family. Jeremy reassures Jack and Kim that their positions will still be waiting for them. So have fun exploring in your next year, just keep in touch. Two big hands clasp each other in sincerity as they say good bye. As Kim and family board the boat, Kim mentions to her family that before they know it they will be docking at England's harbor, and let's make the best of it. As Esmira and Jeremy waved their final good byes, Jeremy said "I can't wait to check the shack out." as Elmira said "check the shack out or check out what I have to offer. "Jeremy says" now that you mention it, I could work it into my schedule". As Esmira says" let's hope you can." The shack was about a half day ride away. However, if Esmira was still in the mood Jeremy might accommodate her. The sun was beating down and it was getting rather warm in the saddle, or was that Jeremy's emotions being stirred up. Jeremy knew the shack was just over the hill. He looked back at his picturesque wife and thought this was no fair. How could he not touch his wife? Everyone made it to the top of the hill and the shack and boundary lines looked in place. As Jeremy was grooming down the horses, he thought of his wife was inside the shack. When suddenly, a small but firm hand reached around his waist from behind and startled him. As he turned around to see who it was Esmira ran around the front of the horse and got onto the back of the horse. As she lay on the back of the horse with her hair hanging down, Jeremy started to brush her long hair. As he kissed her relentlessly Esmira put her hands around his neck and then said. "Please can we take this inside" as Jeremy says, "not a bad idea?" They both scurry into the shack like scolded children. Once inside, Esmira knows her way around her man. However, it has to start off with a kiss and then down his neck to check his pulse and then to kiss his chest. When given half the chance Jeremy returned the favors, and made sure not to leave anything untouched or unkissed. Esmira told her husband Jeremy thank you for not leaving one stone untouched. Then said "I knew you were a man the first time I set my eyes on you. Now that I am exhausted let's get some shut eye." Jeremy says "I couldn't agree with you more."

Kim was worried if she had sea legs to make the trip. Jack knew that Kim was worried and told her politely not to even think about it. The first day Kim stayed with the twins as Jack looked over the seas and wondered about this new adventure that Kim got them into. Maybe it was better that he not think of it, just enjoy the ride. Jack went back to the room and suggested that Kim go on deck to catch some air. Kim jumped at the chance the twins were sleeping. Up on the deck she ran into Victoria without Elizabeth, this was unusual. Before Kim could say anything about it Victoria said "I know Elizabeth is not here, thank goodness. She chatters way too much." Kim starts to giggle and says "I thought it was just me. It's nice to know that I don't feel alone on that topic." Kim asks "so what is the next step". Victoria says "there will be plenty of time for business chat later, please let's go get some tea while Elizabeth is still sleeping and just relax." Kim agrees. As they sit in the chairs looking over the ocean, Kim commented on how calm the ocean can be. Victoria agreed but added a statement "it can be just like anything else given the chance to have a bad day." However, she had not seen too many a bad day with the ocean. Just when everything seem to fall in place, dinner was called. Kim said to Victoria that she would meet her after dinner if the opportunity arises. Dinner came and went and Kim decided to spend the evening with her family. Victoria made sure that she checked in on them every third day. Now the tug boat was coming up and pulling the boat in. They will be docking within the hour. At this time Victoria told Kim to make sure they were the last people off the boat. This would make it easier for the escorts to pick up the baggage so everyone would be on their way. The escorts knew they had to bring two coaches up for baggage alone. After everything was loaded and people boarded it took another fifteen minutes to reach the Inn. Then, Victoria instructed all the servants to put Kim's sewing machine and tools in a private boutique along Victoria's chamber.

It was four thirty in London time. Just in time for tea and crumpets. Kim and family were not used to this. Victoria tried to explain that the tea was soothing for the people that just finished work. The time to unwind. So Kim turned to Jack and said why not. When Jack took a bite out of the crumpets he did say it was better than the hard tack he was used to. So Kim and her family spent the next hour sipping on tea and nibbling on the crumpets. Victoria mentioned to Kim "please take about three days to walk the palace grounds just to get your bearing on everything. This will allow the servants to put everything in its place. Dinner will be served in an hour. Elizabeth and I will leave you alone. See you at dinner."

Dinner was on time at 6:00. This would be something that Kim would have to get used to because Victoria was a stickler about punctuality. Any way Kim and her family sat down at a table that looked like the League of Nations would sit at. The table was at least twenty feet long. So, how would you pass the food around? That was it, one didn't pass the food the servants would bring it to you. Kim made up her mind that this servant stuff has got to stop. So, the duck was neatly carved and served around as well as the stuffing and the corn and the yams. Kim was one that was taught to always clear the plate, but at this rate she would be bigger than she was being pregnant. Before everyone was excused Victoria mentioned that there would be a fox hunt around dawn and that Jack was invited to come. Jack replied, "I didn't bring my guns with me". Victoria said "no worry, I have a Brown Bess musket that is good for about eighty yards that you can use. If for some reason that one won't fit for you I have a Brunswick rifle that carries a .704 caliber muzzle loading percussion rifle. If your answer is yes I will see you in the a.m. bright and early. This will give Kim and me a chance to better familiarize the grounds on which she will be doing her sewing. Oh! I failed to mention that a week from now there will be a parade in Kim's honor. So is your answer yes Jack"? Jack immediately says "sure". "Great, the head master Henry will show you the way to the stables at 6:00 in the morning" says Victoria.

Knock, knock, and knock on the door as Henry awaits the answer. Kim opens the door in her robe as she kisses her husband good-bye and wishes him good luck. As Henry walks with Jack they make small talk about what Jack does. Jack answers with "I am a cowboy with the E. & J. Stud farm in Big Horn Montana. This means that I do everything farm related from a to z on the farm." So Henry says "you would know about horses in general?" Jack humbly says "from when I was about ten, when I broke my first horse." Henry realizes that the barn is getting closer and it's time to leave his company, so Henry mentions one more thing. "Have you ever heard of English riding?" Jack says "what?" Henry says "we'll talk later, good luck."

Victoria has said that she had rented the dogs out for the day from Mr. John Charworth Musters. He has allowed us until tomorrow to hunt with the dogs so if one does get tired, there will be others to take your place. So with no further ado, as she sounds the horn as someone else says "tally ho". The dogs are off on the scent. Barking can be heard everywhere. Jack raises the rifle and shoots killing one fox with eight more to go. Victoria is amazed at Jack's marksmanship. Victoria sends someone out to get the pelt as the hunt continues. Jack loads the rifle for the next round. Jack sees another fox round the tree and waits a split second then fires winging the fox in his left hind leg while an Englishman hits the fox dead in the chest. Now they only have six more to go. It seems like an hour has gone by and the hounds are on to a fresh scent, barking everywhere. Everyone see three foxes splitting up and muskets and rifles sounding off. The view is clouded by the smoke but this time Jack had put the round thru the fox's head and killed it at once. The Englishman that hit the last fox rode up to Jack and calmly says "you yanks know how to shoot. I was under the impression that yanks couldn't hit the side of the barn. I owe you my deepest apology." Jack says "great let's ride on, I think I know where two are hiding". The Englishman is impressed as Jack rides thirty yards and gets off his horse and motions for Earl the Englishmen to do the same. Earl does so with doubts. Jack shows him a tree that is down and shows Earl the entrance and the exit hole. Jack motions for Earl to get over to the exit hole and point the rifle down the hole. Thru sign language Jack says "when I speak, fire your rifle." Jack calls out to Earl and they both discharge their rifles as the two fox were coming out, killing them both. Earl is astonished, after he reloads his rifle he asks "Jack, where did you learn that trick. "Jack responds "have you ever been so hungry that you go after ground squirrels?" Earl says "good point, let's go see what everyone else is doing. "Both Jack and Earl have seen a cloud of smoke off in the distance so they wait for the dust to settle before moving on. As the smoke settled the horn blew again, a signal to bring everyone in. The time was approaching 8:00 and Jack's stomach was growling from hunger. Jack turned to Earl and says "what is going on?" Earl responds "it's either breakfast time or tea time. However, I wouldn't be surprised if the hunt is over, because you and I have bagged five of the fox. Surely the other hunters have gotten three between them." As they approach the barn they see some moisture coming off pans so it looks like it is breakfast time. Victoria looks at the pelts on the back of Jack's horse and Earl's and counts a total of seven that everyone has taken. Victoria asks if anyone needs to be excused to let others hunt. Jack and Earl look across from each other and say at the same time "let's give someone else a try. We have definitely proven ourselves." Earl says "I am impressed, I think we have a lot to talk about!" "I believe your right" says Jack. Earl says, "it is around 8:30, tea isn't around for another hour and a half, what do you say we go look at the sheep?" Jack gives Earl the weirdest glare and Earl acknowledges the stare and asks "did I say something wrong?" Jack says "let me explain, in the states, when we are driving cattle to market we expect the paths to have grazing land all the way. Now if sheep have gotten to the grazing land first they've cleaned up on our feed so to speak so that makes the cow leaner at market time which really cuts into our bottom line." Earl says, "Now I understand. Over here in London we do it way different. We usually raise the meat for ourselves or if we want to take it to market the locker usually comes up to us offers us so much per pound minus the cost for dressing it out and that's it. It sounds like in the states you have a few central locations that you have to go to. Is that correct?" Jack answers "yes". The hunters finally found the last fox so Henry will return the dogs back to the master, Victoria and Elizabeth have excused themselves so the people from the locker can have all this meat ready for dinner tonight.

Kim and the twins are walking around the palace grounds staring in awe at the big ceilings, the huge beds, the big rooms. Some of these rooms can fit the house they were used to back home. The two year olds have a lot of questions. Kim takes them up to the boutique to check out her new location. The movers have placed the sewing machine right where she requested. She checked out the spacious closet, all empty. She will have her work cut out for her. Mommy saw Janet the twin pointing to some crimson fabric on a roll. Kim answers "just material honey". Kim is satisfied with what she saw, she turns to her twins and says "I have a surprise for you, after you take your nap". Kim turns the twins around and puts them to sleep in their bedroom.

Earl has invited Jack to the nearby pub. Earl was inquisitive, he had to know where Jack had learned to shoot and hunt. Earl knew that when you get someone to drinking they usually open more than what they normally do. Earl ordered two draughts and asked "where did you learn to shoot that way?" Jack commented, "In the states it is a prerequisite to carry a firearm where ever you go for safety reasons. What I am trying to say here is a lot of practice needs to go into shooting the firearm because you might only have that one chance. Then you have to be careful because it is only a protection device. One should always practice on being the best in this situation because you want to live to see tomorrow." Earl asks "is it that bad in the states?" Jack states "one always needs to be prepared for the worst situation, so things don't get out of hand!" Jack tips his bottle toward Earl's bottle and says "show me some different cuisine, I will buy." Earl quickly spouts off "barkeep can we have some Shepard's pie for my Yankee friend?" Jack asks "what it is" and Earl says "taste it first and you tell me!" The barkeep gives the dish to Jack and requests a comment when he is done." Jack sees the potato and the meat and what looks like a crumbled biscuit. Jack consumes the pie with delight, as Earl asks, "How did you like it?" "Jack says very tasty, my compliments to the cook."

Meanwhile as Janet the twin is waking up, Kim her mother presents her with a lace dress. Janet says "to her mommy, wow! It looks so nice. "Kim replies "well, get used to it. This is the way you will represent the people in England." Janet says "Mommy, what does represent mean?" Kim says "to show". Kim was not worried about her sewing. She knew that was a gift and she knew she did it well. She was more concerned with the models she had to approve of tomorrow. It would be first time picking out the models, but she thought to herself, the models wouldn't know that. It was time for lunch, so she gathered the twins together and was meeting her husband Jack in the formal dining room. Lunch was serving up roasted duck sandwiches with a dark gravy to dip in if desired. She looked at the pan of caramelized peaches and had to taste them. She put a scoopful on her plate. As she tasted the peaches she was hooked as they melted in her mouth. This made her think of her sisters Audra and Margaret and how their venture of cooking was going back in the states. Lunch was wrapping up and it was time for the governess to pick up the twins as Kim headed off to her boutique, to sew.

The queen Victoria asked Kim "how she was doing" she replied with "just fantastic, ready to get on with business." That was just what the queen wanted to hear. She mentioned that the auditions would be held just after the morning tea. Kim couldn't wait. She excused herself to the queen and said "I have two dresses to fill for tomorrow, so the models will have some idea of what they will be wearing". The queen replied "I have all the confidence in the world that you will do just fine. I will see you tomorrow at the audition." Kim sat down to her sewing machine as she put together the back of the dress and the neckline. It was extremely important to get the high neckline just right. This would make all the women seem very desirable. As she put the back to the waist, Kim was inventing a different waistline together with a material called elastic. Kim knew the elastic would work. Kim was one of the few that would understand this marketing technique. Kim had heard so many complaints about how the ancient time of the corset had to go. The corset had to be laced in the back so any women needed a helper just to get dressed. Then after four hours one needed to be released of all the pressure just to be able to be comfortable. Kim felt so proud of herself. One size would fit from the waist size of 26 to the waist size of 34. The other size would be from the waist size of 34 to the waist size of 42. Kim was so excited, she knew the technique would work. Kim continued to sew the burgundy material with the elastic into the waistline. She had the high neckline done and it was off to the shoulders and into the three quarter sleeve. Kim did her best work when inventing new ways a women can be desirable without the pain of a corset. Now it was off to the bust line where she would make it big. With the help of elastic here in some places the women could be more comfortable. As she thought to herself, now that the bust line was taken care of she could move to the upper chest where it would be adorned with ten ivory buttons. Now it was off to the skirt part of the dress where bloomers would be sewn in as part of the skirt. This would make the waist line so improved and the women wouldn't have to worry about having an extra garment to fill up their closet. This dress would fit a smaller woman with a big bust line. Now that she was finished with this dress she would do the same with the next dress. However, this would be a soft lime green with a smaller bust line and a longer length in the skirt part. This would take about another hour and a half to get the dress completed. This would mean she is right on target as far as time is concerned. As soon as she was done with the dress she knew it would be time for afternoon tea. This was a good time for it allowed time to share your day with the people you cared about. Almost a time to refresh oneself. As soon as the tea was over Jack and Kim allowed themselves time for each other. Soon time would come for the twins when Jack would read certain stories to them letting them know how important reading was.

    Morning came and as soon as breakfast was over it was off to the auditions. Among the six women of various height and bust lines that had already been picked, it was important to say as little as possible about the dress. What needed to be done was have the women go to separate dressing rooms and try them on. Kim went with the first model and as she was thinking that Kim would be there for lacing the corset, when she saw that the bloomers were sewn in, she was distracted. She asked Kim "what is this"? Kim asked her just to put her legs in the bloomers and pull up the dress so she could button the back. The model said "okay". The model was surprised at how well the waist and the bust line felt so comfortable. She asked the model not to say a word but go show the other models. The model agreed. The model walked into the small ballroom and showed the other four because the other model was putting on the lime green dress. She too was distracted about the sewn in bloomers. Kim said "she understood, but to just slip into them anyway." This model also found out that the waistline and bust line fit extremely well. Kim also told her the same as the last model. Say nothing but show it off. Then send the bigger waist woman back. The model did as instructed. The bigger waist women as she was going back commented to Kim on how beautiful the dress looked. Kim said "thank –you". Kim told all the models to just put the dress on and that she would button them up. All the models were totally surprised of how well the dress felt to wear. After every model had a chance to put the dress on, they were instructed to wear them around for two hours and that to meet Kim back at the small ballroom. Kim went on over to grab some crumpets and tea. During this time she checked on the twins and talked to Jack. Jack had shared with Kim that he had been talking to Earl about meeting his cousin, who had some nobility rank over in Wales. Kim was intrigued but she was more concerned about the test period on the models. She looked at her husband's watch and she had about fifteen minutes to get back to the small ballroom to talk with the models. If everything goes as planned and the models are happy with the fit, this would revolutionize the garment industry. Who would have thought that a small town girl born in Nebraska could have done such a thing? Kim took a walk down the hall and met the models to get the final say on the fit of the dress. The first model said "I can finally keep on bathing, I don't have to look for my best friend to loosen my corset". The second model agreed and added to the statement "I even like how it fits in the chest area, being a big busted women I don't feel any unbearable back pain to wear and it is not hard to breathe". The third model with a smaller bust line but a tall lady was impressed with the length of the gown and the ability to move more freely around a dance floor. The fourth model who was a shorter lady with a big bust line had to agree with model number two. The fit in the waist and in the chest area was not only incredible but enjoyable. The fifth and the sixth model agreed with the others that not only was the dress enjoyable but comfortable. Kim thanked the ladies and told them for their time they would be paid by allowing them to keep the dresses. They were all so excited, to be the first to wear a new designer dress.

Kim met with Victoria and shared the good news about the dresses. Victoria who was known for not smiling much had broken out with a full smile. Kim knew she was in the right place for now. It was time for lunch and Kim couldn't be more ready she was starving. She wondered why everyone here was being directed to the back balcony where a full pig was being roasted over the barbecue pit. The whole pig, snout and all. Before Kim could say anything, Victoria spoke out "I would like to take this time to welcome again our neighbor from the states and London's prime seamstress by their style of cooking. Please enjoy yourself". Kim looked over the whole display and thought of her sister's back home and their fantastic dream of becoming world renowned cooks. Kim knew they could do it based on the backbone they have inherited directly from Charlie there father. The beverages flowed heavily, it wasn't like Jack to have this much beer available so early in the day. Jack knew that he would only be here a year so why not just enjoy. Lunch was excellent, the pig, the vegetables, the biscuits, the jam, everything was perfect. Kim knew that she had to get back sewing in order for this new apparel thing to get kicked off. She did the math and figured that it would take about four dresses a day to shock the designers in town about the comfort gowns being around to stay, at an affordable price. Kim knew that she can do it. Kim couldn't wait to get back to her boutique to prove it. Even though nobility surrounded her at these kind of parties, Kim wasn't much for mingling and rubbing elbows with the rich and proud. Kim always had an agenda that would make today's computers jealous. Kim had a sharp mind and filed everything alphabetically. It was easier to retrieve that way. These lunches could usually last 2-3 hours, as long as the twins and Jack were comfortable, Kim could relax and be productive. Elizabeth and Victoria had come by to chat. The first thing that Victoria asked "is everything up to your satisfaction?" before she could answer, Elizabeth chimed in "how do you like it over here?" Victoria cut into Elizabeth "please don't be so rude, give her a chance to answer one thing at a time". Elizabeth curtsy towards the queen has she fans herself and say "please excuse me your majesty" Victoria says "please don't continue that behavior, it's so NOT you". Elizabeth says "your right". Victoria says "where were we?" Kim says "thank you so much, everything is working out better than I dreamed! And to your question Elizabeth I am adjusting quite nicely". Victoria wraps up the conversation by stating to Kim "if there is anything you need, please ask. "Kim says

"I will!" Kim got a hold of Jack and says to him, "please make sure that the governess will have the twins. We need some private time." Jack says "oh my dear, I thought you would never ask. Let's go to the bedroom and think of different joyous ways to hook up". Kim sounds off "it sounds like heaven to me."

After hooking up Jack and Kim realize they have an hour before dinner. Jack says "let's steal away and go look at the big clock that is about three blocks away. I could have the stable boy put us a buck board together and within ten minutes we could be looking at one of the great monuments of all." The stable boy pulls up the buck board and asks Kim "would there be anything else?" Kim says "No, but thank you." Jack takes the reins and turns the horses onto the path of the big clock. As they were traveling Kim clutches his arm and proudly says, "I know I am going to be extremely busy in the coming weeks, but your love is more important than anything else." Jack stops the horses and leans over to give Kim a big kiss. Jack says "know and believe me if I think I am losing you to work, I will be the first to let you know". Now let's go see the clock. It was phenomenal, a clock that stood around twenty three feet high and just kept incredible time. What kept Kim's attention was the street lights that were set every sixty feet. Kim always saw them from the balcony, lighting up the whole city. Dinner time was getting close so they hurried back to the castle in time to get to the main dining room, just in time.

The feeding of all the different animals just stunned Kim. Having pig for lunch and a rack of lamb with mint julep and fixings for dinner was outstanding. Kim wanted to pinch herself to see if this was some kind of dream. Ouch, as she pinched herself, this was not a dream. Kim was famished, she sat right by her husband and watched him devour the lamb, the sweet potato the vegetables and the bread pudding. This was a whole lot better than chasing cattle around the range all day. Kim commented on the bread pudding and said "this is so good I will have to get a recipe on it, and probably send the recipe back to Audra and Margaret."

It was early a.m. around 5:45. Dog gone it. She could smell the coffee from the main kitchen from her suite. Kim couldn't see life without coffee. She believed it was heaven sent. She would have her cup of coffee and do her planning of the day. This planning was extremely important to her. She would always plan two weeks out, then do the plan, then review what she did and any mistakes that happened along the way so in the future, perfection would come. She would never give this secret away. Kim also knew that one had to have a passion for what one would do. Passion is the wind behind the sails. Kim stated in her plan to have eighteen dresses made within the week. One would be for the queen in a soft pink. Another would be a teal green for Elizabeth. The sixteen others in different sizes and shapes would be to sale at the show coming in two weeks. However, since it was coming into December, Kim wanted to try another material sewn in the sleeves only for warmth. Kim knew that she could do it, since the elastic fit worked. It was off to the boutique and passion time.

Jack was busy watching Billy spin his wool. His foot pumped the pedal faster as he watched the small strand or string is developed. Jack remembers back home in the states his thick jacket that kept him warm, and this is the way the fabric started out. Jack was amazed. Jack says "how long does this take?" Billy says, "I have noticed the time it takes, but I would guess around three hours. I just love doing it, kind of like a passion." Jack says "you do it well." Billy says "I am almost done here give me ten minutes, then we can go grab some tea and talk about what is next". Jack states "Do all New Englanders grab tea around this time?" Pretty much, it's a time to reflect on how much you have done and how much you want to do, knowing you can relax with your time. Some people might think that the tea time is a silly tradition. It's kind of like planning, doing and then looking at what you have done. However, I think people miss another message that goes on here." "Oh" says Jack "What would that be?" Billy says "Developing people skills. Having the ability to talk to strangers and leave them with the message that you want to deliver. Whether it be the selling of your product or the development of a new gun or rifle or what's happening in your world, just to see if others feel like you. Kind of like staying in touch with everything." Jack is amazed and says "one can get all that over a tea time?" Billy says "I am done now. Why don't you shadow me on the conversations that I have and learn?" Jack takes the offensive and says "are you calling me dumb? "Billy comes back with "not at all. Remember when you first learned to ride a horse?" Jack says "yes, but what does that have to do with anything?" Billy says "follow me on this; you developed a new skill when you learned to ride the horse, right?" Jack says "Sure" Billy says "Watch the people that I talk with. I am going to let you in on a big time secret. This is a secret that took me years to learn. Since you are my friend I will give this to you right now. God gave mankind two ears to listen with and one mouth to speak with. You will be surprised how many people get that mixed up. In other words they will speak twice as much as they listen. It's like they are NOT listening. So you have to deliver your message two or three times so the individual will take the message with him or her. People are not dumb, they just like to complicate everything. That's like their own private drama. Watch and learn." Billy and Jack go down to the market square where a few dozen people are having tea. Billy sees Thomas and asks "How are you doing? I was wondering if you know of anyone that I could sell my wool to at two schilling a pound." Thomas replies with "Have you seen the new fashion trend? Some lady believes that she can make a dress comfortable for a lass to fit into. Have you ever heard anything so ridiculous?" Jack takes the offensive and was ready to say something when Billy nudges him with his elbow and says "So you know of someone looking to buy wool at two schilling a pound?" Thomas speaks up and says "Oh, yes I do. Lawrence down at the pier was looking for some for his mates, you know." Billy says "thanks 'old boy, be seeing you around. Say hi to the Mrs." As Billy leaves he tugs on Jack's arm and says, "Do you see what I mean? That bloke wanted me to chat with him all day about some kind of fashion trend. My purpose was to get in and out of there as quick as possible. So I had to say my message twice. Ten to one he is probably taking his whole tea time on a fashion trend to someone who will listen. That's okay. However, he won't be doing it with me because I heard once, repeated my message, got what I needed and got out of there." Jack says "I understand now". Billy asks "How is you tea?" Jack says "Just dandy".

Kim hands Queen Victoria and Elizabeth their dresses. Kim instructs them both to let her know how they fit. They both go to the changing room and slip into their dress and come out. They have to walk the long hallway to get back to Kim. Both the Queen and Elizabeth were impressed with the waist area. They told each other that they could live without the corset. As they turned into the room that Kim was in they both echoed about the fit of the dress. That whatever she did, please continue. Kim said "thank you".

Kim was just finishing up the sixteen dresses. Each one was a different color. Kim started out with Violet then went to White, then onto a loud Pink. After the pink she went to a soft beige, then to a dark blue, then an orange. She continued with a sky blue, crimson and then a forest green, then others with a dark brown, black and then a maroon and finally with gold, royal blue and yellow and grey. Kim always had fun picking out the colors. This was her passion. All of these dresses were to be at the show at the end of the week. Kim hoped that they would just fly off the rack. She knew from experience that she would have to be buried in her boutique while doing another eighteen dresses. All of these would be a different color than what she had already made. She believed that her dresses were like a painter's canvas. Which made the women inside the dress an original. The show was on. Kim didn't expect the photographers but she let them stay. The dresses were going for a good price. This was just the beginning. The dresses caught on. The models were ecstatic. This was an easy show for them. They got to keep the dresses and Kim had a double for every color that was shown. The four dress shops had already purchased the dresses. Kim knew her next market would be Liverpool.

Queen Victoria and her assistant came into the long ballroom to congratulate Kim. Kim had hinted of the new things to come and Victoria asked "would that be wise". Kim answered back "Oh, no worry, I won't change the waist. It would have to do with the sleeve. Just wait and see, you will love it! "Victoria thinks of home and Kim says, "I have no doubt that everything you touch will turn to gold."

Kim decided to sit down and pen a letter to her sisters Audra and Margaret.

Dear Audra and Margaret;

How are things going back in the states? Any new happenings to the Gymkhana? How is everybody and all the twins doing? Let me tell you what I have been up to! I have never seen so much different cuisine in my whole life. Bread pudding in the morning with tea. Hog roasted for a barbecue, rack of lamb with mint

> julep for dinner. Buffalo steak with poached eggs for breakfast and Shepard's pie for lunch and chicken fricassee for dinner. It is like my taste buds have been overloaded with different food. I have put on a couple of dress shows for the public on the new dresses that I have sewn. I have had good luck so far. My twins are growing like weeds and enjoying the different games over here. Jack has already been in the hunting games here and bagged some foxes. They were impressed with his marksmanship. Well the dinner bell is ringing so enough for now.
>
> Love Kim and family.

Jack wakes early around five in the morning. He goes over to the balcony and stretches as he looks at the sunrise just coming on the horizon. He is excited about hunting antelope, caribou and bear, all in the same excursion. Jack kisses Kim good bye and says that he will see her in three days. Billy and Earl have invited him to the location they have always spotted at least bear. Earl has loaned him one of his rifles with ammo to boot. As they are ready to come out of the forest, Jack holds his arm back so Earl and Billy don't move. Jack points to a figure 200 yards away. The antelope is brushing against the tree. This is great because Jack wets down his scope and raises the rifle for wind direction as he slowly squeezes the trigger and hits the animal right between the shoulders as he falls to the ground. Before Jack set's his rifle down he sees a bear about twenty yards away coming toward the antelope. Jack doesn't have time to site him in, but takes a clean shot anyway and is a little high from the shoulder hitting the bear in the left eye, killing him immediately. Earl and Billy look at each other and say "is this luck or what?" Earl states well, that's it for the day. It will take the rest of the day to dress them out and get to the locker. Jack states "I want both their hides to be sent to the taxidermy". Billy turns to Earl and says "you weren't kidding about his marksmanship." They finally reach the animals in which some raccoons were just starting in for a feast as Jack shoes them away. Jack, Earl and Billy start to separate the hide from the meat. This will take 2-3 hours on an animal this big. The three hours have passed and they are ready to put the animals on the pack horse to get it to the locker. Within another hour they will be at the locker. Once at the locker the butcher tells them that the meat will be ready at weeks end at half a schilling a pound to have the meat completed. Jack tells Billy and Earl that he is ready for some tea and it is time to get back to the wife because he was bushed.

As soon as Jack gets back to the castle Elizabeth greets Jack and introduces him to Phillip the Prince of Wales. Jack shakes his hand like he would a normal individual. He politely excuses himself and asks for a rein check on the party that he was invited to. Phillip is taken back, does he realize who he shook hands with! Elizabeth holds Phillip back because she realized that he was getting excited and says "calm down, I don't think he remembers". Phillip says under his breath "who needs him anyway".

Jack goes to his bedroom and is ready for a nap. Kim says to him, please hurry up the party is starting in fifteen minutes. Jack says "what party?" Kim looks at him and says "it's our anniversary." Jack is horrified that he forgot and asks for forgiveness. Kim blows it off and says "no worry, I made a new shirt for you please wear it." They go down to the long ballroom where everyone is waiting. Phillip holds out his hand and says "welcome, to your party". Jack shakes his hand and says "I owe you an apology, I forgot what day it was". Phillip replies "it happens to the best of us, relax and enjoy the party." Jack couldn't believe his eyes, at least twelve feet of table adorned with bear meat and beef and caribou and mutton and fish. Then dessert a plenty followed by breads and rolls and vegetables. All of this for us……. Why? Kim catches up to Jack and grabs his hand and says" I love you." Jack tells Kim "I am speechless, why would they throw a party for us? We are just westerners trying to put our life together". Kim says "someday I will tell you all about it." Jack listens to the band playing music, a sweet noise that could be used for rest therapy. Something to relax with and forget everything else. Phillip catches up to Jack and asks "do they do this in the states?" Jack replies "usually at barn raisers where most of the community get together for a three day weekend, while they help build a barn. That's where in the evenings when the music starts for around three hours and people dance and the ladies chit-chat over their clothing and the children. While the men when not dancing talk their business and look toward the future. However, the food we share is usually cow or pig. I am impressed with the way the help has displayed all the food." Phillip says "Thank you". Jack excuses himself as he asks his wife for a dance. As they dance Jack asks "how are you doing?" Kim says "I am holding up, the Queen has asked if I am ready for the royal ball. Which means clothing everyone here in dresses and suits and charging three times as much so the Queen can give the proceeds to the poor. This will make her look good so if she does have to raise taxes in the future, people won't complain." Jack is impressed at how well she addressed this situation and says "does this usually happen?" Kim says "I can only assume, but the queen has impressed me with her business tactics. I can only believe that the Queen has asked me up for a year to revolutionize the garment district with my new innovations. Then after I leave she could take all the credit. However, before I left the states, I applied for a patent on this elastic girdle, just in case it would catch on. If it does my patent enables me to be the only one to use this type of girdle. Unless, they want to pay me royalties, for using the girdle. This is one item that will be our secret. If the Queen would find out, we would be sent to the states immediately. This would be a secret worth more than a million dollars. If you were the queen and found out about it what would you do?" Jack says "good point, but where did you learn about this business savvy?" Kim states "back home when Esmira would take us out for gun practice, she would always emphasize on being prepared for the worst. So I figured if I could come up with something better in a dress how would I protect myself. Then when I went to town one day I literally bumped into a lawyer named Joe. He needed a dress for his wife for a convention that was coming up. His wife was the school teacher and I had coffee with her so I could see what figure to make the dress." Joe said "he would apply for the patent and gave me the paper work on the acceptance of patent, when I gave him the dress." Jack is amazed of how well Kim has done her homework. The song was ending and Jack wanted to try that new ale or beer that Phillip was talking about. Right when he started to walk over to the refreshment table Phillip asked Kim to dance. Jack wasn't worried because he knew Kim could hold her own. Phillip was about a foot taller than Kim so it appeared that he was looking down her chest, that is why Kim always wore her dresses with a collar that went up to the neckline. Kim knew that temptation had to be avoided at all cost, unless it was selling dresses.

The song was nearing its end and Kim was getting hungry. With all this wonderful food being laid out she was going to sample most of it. Before the ball started she made sure the twins were okay. Besides sewing they were her love. Now it was time to get focused on who she had to meet, after she ate. Jack pulled up a chair and started to talk. This was a special time for him. Kim's busy schedule always put her in the fast lane to who knows where. Jack stated "that caribou looks like the one I got a few days ago, how do you like it?" Kim says, "I am not sure if the meat is usually this sweet, but it is good. Now I have to try that mutton and the antelope." As the band played on Jack was very impressed of how business was going, how his hunting was coming along and his family. He missed his brothers back home but that was only expected. Jack knew that Kim and he would be there for another hour and a half and he had to chat with some of his fellow hunters when he was done with Kim. Jack looked deep into Kim's eyes and she knew that loving look and responded by saying "I know that look and I promise after the ball and we take care of the twins, then it will be our turn." Jack says "sounds good to me. Anything else I can help with?" "Not unless you want to feed me" says Kim. "Okay, then you wouldn't mind if I go chat with my hunting buddies", states Jack. Kim says "you go right ahead". As Kim is eating Jack goes over to Earl and Phillip and begins to chat. Although, Jack's mindset is on hunting, Phillip is intrigued with Kim's dancing ability and says so. Jack quickly quips back with "Oh, that's nothing you should see her marksmanship". Phillip says "Oh, really. I would like to see that". Jack turns his head toward Phillip and says with an elevated tone "With her schedule, I don't think that is going to happen. Now let's get back to hunting." Phillip sees the anger in his face and leaves it alone. Earl says "There is an outstanding hunt for the Ram three hours north of here. This will bring a one hundred pound purse to whomever bags it. The contest will begin Saturday at high noon. Are you in?" Jack says "count me in." Phillip snidely remarks, "Even with your talent Jack this will be a challenge." Jack calmly replies to Phillip "maybe, this contest has never had a fierce competitor!" As the band plays on Jack asks Phillip and Earl "are you two in?" There is a long pause…….. After about a minute Phillip and Earl wringing their faces come up with a meek "yes". Jack was always taught by his dad a saying 'either put up or shut up'. Jack didn't feel out of place. He was usually in the leadership role that prompted people to go deep within themselves and pull the winner out. Jack looked at Phillip and thought to himself, he might be the Prince of Wales but I haven't seen the royalty come out yet. So Jack all excited asks "what time do we leave?" Earl speaks up, "how about eight o'clock, that will give us enough time?" Jack says "sure, I will be down at the barn at eight." Jack says "please excuse me, I have a WIFE to talk to." Jack walks back over to Kim and says "trust me, you don't want to have another dance with Phillip." Kim replies "okay." Jack starts to talk to Kim about her upcoming dress events, as Phillip interrupts and asks Kim for a dance. Kim turns to Phillip and says, "I am sure that you are a gentlemen and would understand that I politely decline, because I am tired." Phillip is enraged and says "do you understand that I am Prince of Wales? No one tells me no!" Kim replies "Do I need to get Victoria the Queen over here?" Phillip suddenly remembers his place in life and says" that wouldn't be necessary, please excuse me." Phillip exits and walks back over to Earl and says vehemently to him "who does she think she is saying no to me for a dance? I have a plan for Jack." Earl interrupts Phillip and says "well count me out, I don't want any part of it!" As the band plays on Kim realizes that she has one half hour before the party stops. She decides to go chat with the Queen. Phillip from across the way thinks that Kim is telling on him and was tempted to walk over there. Phillip thinks it thru and decides not to. Kim keeps on talking to Victoria on the events coming up and believes that everything will come out right. Kim compliments Queen Victoria on the whole banquet and says it's been a long night and she was going to retire. Kim does thank her for everything and says good night. As Jack and Kim go into their mansion suite, Jack holds one twin as he lays him comfortably in bed as Kim does the same. Then their eyes meet and Kim is ready for his embrace. Kim thinks to herself, things go so fast, too fast. She embraces Jack like only Jack knows and their private time begins.

 Queen Victoria and her assistant Elizabeth have breakfast in their private parlor as they discuss Kim's productivity. The Queen already knows the results before she asks Elizabeth. The Queen loves to test her assistant because she wants to know if her loyalty will get confused in telling the truth. Elizabeth says to the Queen "that everything is on the fast pace and Kim seems to be ahead of everything". The Queen says "yes you are right. Thank-you."

The day was Friday and to Kim that meant checking inventory of all the new dresses she made. She had nineteen and only needed fifteen. An event was going on right underneath the Eiffel tower. All the royalty of France and Wales and the United Kingdom were there. The models were taking their show walk. All the dignitaries were loving what they were seeing. The colors, the tight form of the dress and a wonderful high neckline. The dignitaries would get together with Kim on how to open a brand new market, with distribution and retail cost. Kim said that she would sit down with the Queen to hammer everything out. Kim knew this venture would be a success. She would double her sewing so only she would know her inventory. The key here is that she would keep the quality of her dress and she would only take qualified orders.

Meanwhile, it was Saturday and 8 a.m. was approaching. Jack headed for the barn to meet Earl and Phillip. This was the day for the three hour trip to bag the ram that would bring an extra one hundred pounds in wealth to the household. Everyone saddled their horses and the trip would begin. Phillip was being cocky towards Jack and said "what makes you think you can bag this ram". Jack calmly said "it's all in the tools one uses." Earl asked, "What do you mean?" Jack says "its better I show you. When we get to our destination, I will show you." This piqued their curiosity. An hour into the trip Jack pulls Earl to the side and says "when you get a chance look to your west and then to your south. Earl if you look over your shoulder, that man has been following us for half an hour. I'm not sure if he is following us because of Phillip or because of me, our plan is to get to our destination in order to get the hunt. What would you think if someone was following you?" Earl says "I understand, but what gives you the idea he is following us?" Jack responds "when we stopped twenty minutes ago to look at the horses' hoof he also stopped". Earl is intrigued now, and then says "well what are we to do?" Jack says "pretend like nothing has happened. However, we bolt once we are over the hill; you have to follow my lead!" The hill was coming up and there was a clump of trees to the east. Just over the hill and down about twenty feet Jack bolts to the trees. Once Phillip and Earl and Jack get to the woods, Phillip is angry and asks "what the heck are you doing?" Jack shows his superiority by saying "shut up Phillip if you had the slightest idea what was going on you would trade all your yesterdays for this day. Someone has been tracking us for forty minutes. Now I don't know if they want me for my hunting or you because of your nobility. Look west, you see how he is frantically looking for us. My question is why? Everyone knows how to get to the hunting destination, what would you say Phillip?" Phillip is temporarily speechless but he pushes out the words. "I have to thank you for saving our lives. I had not noticed our follower" Jack interrupts Phillip and says "How does it feel to be the hunted?" Earl says "well what do we do?" Jack says "we stay here for around ten minutes and let him panic. In that time he will be ahead of us and it will appear to him that we are tracking him." Phillip responds in a heated fury "Do you know who you are talking to". Jack quickly responds with a "if your dead do you really think people would care? I saved your life. How are people going to remember you, besides your title? In case you hadn't noticed we all bleed the same, title or not. Now do you want to get out of this mess or are you ready to go meet your killer and tell him you are Prince Phillip as he blows your head off?" Phillip says "good point but I do have one question, are most of you Yankees this outspoken?" Jack says "probably, but only when it comes to staying alive!" Jack laughs as he sees the tracker getting lost and looking around. Jack points to the lost tracker on how he is handling his horse. Both Phillip and Earl look on as they see the tracker get off his horse and scan the field with his binoculars. Jack quietly says "it's not like he wants to introduce himself. Wait until he looks the other way and we will get on the east side of the woods and get out of here. These woods will give us about an hour of protection. By that time the tracker will give up." Earl asks "how do you know these things?" Jack says "it's a common sense thing in the wilderness. Let me ask you, would you stay around for an additional hour if you lost your group you were tracking?" Earl takes offense and says "wait a minute are you saying I am stupid again?" Jack replies "only you can answer that question, but let's get moving". All three mount their horses quietly and are on their way. Jack leads the group, as he points out the level ground that was stopping him from seeing the bluff that Jack was working from. Jack had already figured on walking the horses for the first hour then running them hard for ten minutes to put the tracker completely lost. Then they would only have thirty minutes to the destination. As they continue on Prince Phillip is like a young child while he continues to ask questions, like the following. "Where did you learn to hunt? How long have you been tracking? How do you pick your rifles? Why do you pick certain rifles?" Then Jack interrupts, "before you start writing a book on me, let me suggest a thinking question. This question has many answers all of them right. Before I do anything, I ask myself what Jesus would do. If I hear nothing then that's an answer like 'no news is good news' and I can go ahead as planned. However, if I start to hear interferences like people questioning my judgment and I haven't looked at that particular view, I will delay until I can find the answer." "Every time" says Earl and Jack says "why not". "Wait a minute, Phillip says, what about hunting" Jack replies, "I am not going to preach to you but in the beginning of the bible God gives man 'dominion over the animals and beasts of the world', that's good enough for me. So do you read this book daily?" and Jack answers "yes, because I know that the more I learn the more I know how much more I need to know. If you want a quick laugh look over your shoulder and look at the person that was tracking us". Phillip looks over his shoulder and sees the tracker just sitting in his saddle looking for Jack and the crew. Earl says "well now that I know a little more about you, what do you need to know about us". Jack says "sometimes your silence will tell me more about you than one wants to know. But, we will get to that another day". An hour had passed and as Jack looked over his shoulder the stalker had given up but that was no reason to let the others know. So he said "let's ride", as he put the horses into a strong gallop. Just as he said earlier Jack took them into a hard ride for ten minutes. Jack knew that the destination wasn't too far off. As they were coming into camp Jack noticed a big crowd. Surely the ram wasn't worthy of this much attention. Jack knew that he had to position himself and crew to at least the third position. So Jack told Earl to go introduce himself to the judges. As Phillip and Jack sought out the competition. This took about another half an hour. Suddenly, the bell rang and the judges picked four groups. One to start in the west. One to start in the north. One to start in the south. Then, finally Jack's group to start in the east. Immediately, Earl begins to complain, as he says "everyone knows the ram likes to hug the western region." Jack understands and tells Earl to "shut up, that he will explain later". Earl is taken back, but shuts up. As they go to their positions, Jack tries to explain to Earl that the positions are not important as you think. Watch and learn. Phillip is on Earl's side and tries to defend him but Jack quickly silences him. Jack says "let's get into our positions and follow me." Jack immediately goes into a gallop so they follow. He does this gallop going into a semi-circle for around fifteen minutes. Earl and Phillip are totally confused. Jack tells them he doesn't have time to explain, that he will tell them later, let's ride. Jack got over the mountain side and could see the ram around six hundred yards off. Jack got about fifty yards closer and positioned himself on a branch on a nearby tree. Jack slowly took his 1865 Spencer rifle and told everybody to be quiet. He laid the barrel on the tree branch lifted up the scope frame and moisten it. He had to take the wind trajectory into account and his distance of 550 yards away. Jack had to hit between the front shoulders. The wind was traveling around five miles an hour from the west. So in order to hit the ram there he had first sight the animals shoulder, then go just four inches above his head and around nine inches west of the animals head as Jack slowly pulled the trigger. Phillip's mouth dropped in awe as the ram fell. Jack suggested that they quickly retrieve the animal before someone else tries to claim it. Sure enough Phillip and Earl get there with guns drawn and the western group is trying to claim the ram as Prince Phillip says to them "if I were you I would step away, because the same person that shot the ram has a bead on your head as we speak." The western group talks back and say, "Well that's only one shot". Earl rings out "I will guarantee you that I can take two of you with my colt revolver and Phillip will get the other. Now you have to answer the question are you prepared to never say hello to your love ones again?" The western group backs away and asks "was there only one shot?" As Jack was approaching he answered himself "yes". The western group says "this is the ninth year we have entered and we always get the primo location, how did you do it and so quickly." Jack says "a whole lot of practice and dedication". Jack and his crew go down to the judges as they are adorned with a hunting medal and with the 100 pound purse. As they go toward home, Phillip is full of questions about Jack's marksmanship. As they travel for the next three hours Jack answers them all.

This was one of the few weekends that Kim had off as she played with the twins. All though Kim's passion was sewing she remembered the rough time growing up and wanted to shield the twins from any neglect based on just trying to live. The laughter on the twins face was good enough for her. Kim knew that Jack would be there within the hour. She just figured giving quality time to the twins, then she could give quality time to Jack. She just finished a game of hop scotch with the twins and Kim knew it was nap time. As she laid down with the twins and they fell asleep, Kim drifted off to her dream state. As her dream developed, she is standing in front of Queen Victoria being offered an honorary duchess award for being an outstanding human and best innovative designer for her ideas and work in fashion. Kim gladly accepted the award because she did work hard. Then she heard a noise of a door shutting and she woke up to see her husband Jack. Before Kim could ask Jack about his venture, she guessed that he had a perfect day. Jack admitted that it was a wonderful hunt as he bagged the ram that had been teasing the countryside for the last nine years. Kim looked up at Jack with her beautiful eyes and told him to shhhhh and grabbed his hand and took him to quality time. Quality time was more than just sharing each other intimately. It was about relishing in the present, thankful for your blessings and willing to push the envelope into the future. Just being prepared was a gift itself.

Back in the states, Margaret and Audra had just got their license to open up their café in town. The menus had been thought thru with the cuisine, made simple. They didn't want to confuse their customers with too many choices. They centered the customer's appetite on eggs, hash browns, Flapjacks, toast, French toast and hash for the breakfast. Lunch was filled with different sandwiches and different pies for dessert. Dinner was filled with homemade breads, potatoes, meat of different kinds and vegetables to choose from. Audra was extremely excited to field her way thru this venture. Her dreams were to be invited to the White House based on her cooking skills. Margaret was always busy behind the scenes creating new dishes.

Gala and Marc were busy with the boutique and the horses. Marc was beginning to see that hard work can get one full of pride and accomplishment. This made him happy. He looked over at Gala and knew he had the best catch around. Now life was full of wishes and dreams. Marc knew that if it was God's will he would have his own homestead within three years. All he had to do was follow the leadership of Jeremy and Esmira and he would be safe. Gala was wondering how Kim was doing over in London. Gala knew that Kim would be proud of her accomplishment on the dresses.

Jack was being interviewed by the London press. Out of the nine years they have been hunting this ram, scores of people have tried and miserably failed. They were extremely curious of how a Yankee can come over here and accomplish the hunt with one shot. Jack began his reply "I thank you for all this attention. I knew the hunt was over if I could get a clean shot. With the ram being to the side of the tree I knew with years of practice, where I had to sight the animal and the rest was just slowly pulling the trigger". The press was intrigued, nothing like this has ever happened before, there had to be some other knowledge that Jack wasn't sharing. So the press pried deeper. One of the reporters said "now come on Jack admit to us, you just got lucky!" Jack knew how to face this adversity, this wasn't the first time. So he engaged the reporter with a challenge. Jack spoke "how long have you been in your business and have you yet to bag the 'one hit wonder' of stories?" Immediately the rest of the press turned and said to Craig "answer truthfully now". Craig said, "I haven't been that lucky yet". Jack retorted "if I can show you that luck has nothing to do with it, but being fully prepared does. Would you change your thinking?" Craig was absolutely astonished and momentarily speechless. Jack said, "Hello, did you understand what I said." Craig said, "oh, perfectly, and I accept your challenge. When do we start?" Jack said immediately. Suddenly all the press felt like they were also invited. Jack holds up his hand and says "this is for Craig only." The reporters feel outraged and voice their displeasure by saying together "what do you mean?" Jack says "I will let Craig answer that question by tomorrow" as Jack prods his horse into a gallop and Craig quickly follows. It was a half an hour ride before Jack felt comfortable to stop. Jack got off his horse and so did Craig. Jack said to Craig do you see that boulder over there about fifty yards away?" Craig says "yes". Jack says, "It would be stupid of me to ask you to hit that twenty foot boulder, but what if I asked you to hit that crow that is perched at one o'clock?" Craig immediately said "that's impossible"! Jack goes further and says "now, what if I asked you to shoot his foot off?" Craig says, "Do I look like an idiot to you? That can't be done! "Jack sights his rifle at about two o'clock and about a foot to the right of the bird. Jack is tempted to take the shot himself but restrains and says "what if I were to tell you that the rifle is sighted to take his left foot off." Craig tells Jack "no way, could you hit that bird!" Jack says you are right, because with my direction you will shoot this rifle and detail the bird, still leaving him alive." Before Craig could object, Jack had the rifle in Craig's hand teaching him how to scope the rifle. So Jack tells Craig to aim at two o'clock and aim almost a foot above the bird and to slowly squeeze the trigger. Craig is an excellent pupil, does what is told and he sees feathers flying everywhere. Craig is excited and says I got the bird. Jack understands and says "we kept the bird alive, you got his tail feathers." "But how could that be?" Jack says "how many shots were taken?" Craig says "say no more, I fully understand your point, and will do my best to convince my colleagues that marksmanship was involved."

Prince Phillip is talking to Earl and bragging about how Jack just got lucky and swore that Jack couldn't do it again. Earl knows better and chides Phillip with a goad by saying "would you bet your crown on it"? Phillip stares harshly at him and says "what!" Earl says "I have learned from that Yankee. What are you willing to put up? In other words put up or shut up." Phillip tries to change the subject and says "what are you saying?" Earl says "Just calling it like I see it are you willing to call his bluff by putting up your crown or are you willing to shut up?"....... Prince Phillip remains silent.

Craig is beginning to understand Jack's dilemma. Although Craig tries to convince his colleagues about Jack's marksmen ship, it goes nowhere. They are willing to keep their false pride and believe luck is Jack's middle name, then to admit to themselves that being prepared goes toward action.

Queen Victoria and Elizabeth are sitting down with Kim talking about the shows they have had. They remarked at how well everything is being received. Kim understands one thing, that she has her patent and that when she leaves, the queen will be hurting for a replacement. Kim has already thought this thru. That if the queen asks her to start training someone for her departure in six months that she will refuse to train them. No one taught Kim. It was making mistake after mistake until she learned. Kim stated to the Queen "that as long as she was here there would be no problem." The Queen agreed. As she asked Kim "if she ever thought of doing men's suits?" Now before Kim could answer she already knew that this opportunity would come up so she applied for another patent on the men's suit jacket, before she left the U.S. So Kim said "I could try". It was not enough for Kim to say she could do something. When you play with the professional people one has to protect oneself. So Kim had to communicate with her attorney back home on patents regarding men's attire. If one is to be extremely successful in the apparel business one has to have the cutting edge. In this case, it would be the cut in the back of the jacket. If a French cut is made this would make the person wearing it look slimmer. Would this sell? Could this be patented? Kim knew that to corner the market she would have to provide a choice. Kim had to get away from the sack look. Kim went to her boutique and quickly started three different pieces. She made a luxurious look with the front ending two inches below the waist, and the back being extended to about four inches above the knee and then cutting the back right in the middle. She called this piece, tails. This cut would be for the well to do. The second cut would be seven inches below the waist with tapered corners in the front, three buttons down the front and a pocket on each side right above the waist. Then to be risky she did a double breasted jacket with five buttons down the front, with the last button to be just below the waist, with a belt to wrap around in front. The front of the jacket would be right below the groin. Kim believed the double breasted jacket would be the one widely excepted, based on cost. So Kim made four samples of the tails in different colors. One would be black, the other brown, the other blue, and the last one would be maroon. She did the same with the second cut which we will call the front cut. Then the double breasted jacket was provided in three colors black, brown and blue. Kim didn't have any male models so she asked her husband Jack to get Earl and the butler, Henry down in the small parlor. Kim asked Earl to try the tails on. She asked Henry to try the front cut on and Jack to do the double breasted cut. Kim also had a photographer in place. The photographer took three shots of each, one in the front, one on the side look and the last a back look. Kim asked them to walk toward her which was about thirty feet. She liked what she saw.

The next day the Queen heard about this secret meeting and was furious. She called for Henry the butler to go get Kim immediately. Henry went to Kim's suite and was told that the Queen wishes to talk to her. Kim relayed the message back to Henry that she will be there in ten minutes. Henry went back and told the Queen. Kim arrived when she said she would. The Queen responded with "would you like some tea" Kim said "I will have some, thank you". With a scowl on her face the Queen asked "what's this I hear that you had a meeting behind my back?" Kim responded "I had a fitting of the three suits that I intend to introduce to the public real soon. I had to see what they looked like because we don't have any male models. If you have any questions about my integrity please let me know or should I pack my bags immediately?" The Queen is taken back, she is used to people groveling at her feet, not standing up to her. So the queen hesitates and thinks hard before she speaks. The Queen tries to lay a procedure down by saying "in the future, if you could keep me informed, it would be greatly appreciated". Kim knew she had control and was not going to mildly release it by saying okay. So Kim answers "being head seamstress, I need full use of tools to develop any fashion I desire before presenting that fashion to the public. I believe that the Queen will at least afford me that much". The Queen is astonished at her answer. The Queen could understand if Kim was educated with a college degree, but Kim isn't. How dare Kim challenge the throne! The Queen realizes that she has to be the one to give in this situation. However, the Queen feels the sting and she quietly tells herself that this will not happen again. So the Queen says, "I understand and to the best of my ability, you will have it". Kim is pleased with her new venture with the men's suits. She is also concerned about how she patented the design. This will take some time and correspondence with her attorney back in the states. Since the post office is right near the pub she will give all information to Jack to drop off. That way no suspicion would be brought to her. Since Jack was headed that way tomorrow anyway she would let him know. It was time for bed, what an exhausting day. As Kim reached her suite she noticed a paper that was stuck half way beneath the door. She picked it up. The note was from the queen. The queen was thanking Kim for all of her efforts and due to time constraints a rush dress showing had to be planned for this weekend. Both men models and female models would be available. This would be in the long ballroom starting at 10:00a.m. Signed Queen Victoria. Rather than be annoyed at the time crunch, Kim was pleased with herself, because she had mad an extra six different suits for the men. She was always ready with different dresses. In fact she had a new idea for the women dresses and would throw it in without anyone being the wiser. However, right now was time for bed and time to dream. Kim tucked the twins in and let Jack know to drop the papers off at the post office tomorrow and kissed him good night.

    As Kim drifted off to sleep she heard what she thought were gun shots. Instead of being gun shots they were fire crackers going off in celebration for her coming home. The whole crew of about forty people plus her attorney were there to greet her. The attorney was in a rush so he squeezed himself to the front of the crowd to hand deliver the patents that she applied for. Then the attorney was off to meet with the governor. Margaret and Audra were next, they had to hug Kim. Audra and Margaret missed her so much. Margaret and Audra were trying to pry all the news out of Kim before anyone else could say hello. Jack was pulling up the rear with all luggage beside him. Jeremy, Jim, Bill and Ralph decided to help with the luggage. Esmira in her picturesque form squeezed Kim extra hard to let her know she had been missed. Then let her know that all her good news could be left for when she settles back in.

    Suddenly, she awakes to the sound of her twins coughing. Kim hugs them both and gives them some syrup to get back to sleep, so Kim can get back to sleep and enjoy her dream. Kim went back to sleep but the dream didn't return and she woke again at the crack of dawn. She called for the governess by way of butler to see if she could come to the suite and watch the twins while Jack and her go to the short dining room for coffee. The governess was available and Kim could squeeze Jack's big hand in loving fashion all the way to the dining room. Once they got there Kim reminded Jack of the information to drop off at post office and let him know about her fashion meeting tomorrow at 10:00a.m. Jack looked deeply into Kim's eyes and said "are you missing home"? "Incredibly" said Kim, "how did you know"? Jack replied "call it instinct, we have much to talk about and no time to connect. So from now on let's have these mornings for chit chat and feelings and leave the business side for tea and crumpets at ten". Kim looked into Jack's eyes and with a loving squeeze of the hand said "I like the way you think. I knew I had a champion when we first met". Kim talked about the twins cough and the syrup she gave them. This syrup was to loosen all the congestion with a sleepy affect. Jack mentioned to Kim that this weekend was a relaxation weekend with nothing to do but play with the twins. The hunting for caribou will be next weekend which will probably start out with leaving on Friday right after tea.

Jack's weekend was here with the twins. It was his decision on which game to play. Jack had a choice of four games: Cat's cradle, a string game, Hopscotch, Dominoes or checkers. He chose two, Cat's cradle that would need at least four hands with a six foot cord and checkers. They never got to the checkers game they had way to much fun with Cat's cradle. What's a parent to do when having so much fun with your children? The governess had to interrupt their fun because tea and crumpets were being served down at the parlor. Jack saw the disappointing look on their faces but mentioned they would continue the game later.

Haw-haw Kim thought her new idea would be accepted without a hitch. As one of the bigger busted ladies came in, Kim made sure to grab her and a taller women with a small bust line. The models were very inquisitive. Kim silenced the questions with a question of her own. "How would you like to be the two women that revolutionized the fashion industry"? Both the women didn't understand so they asked "what do you mean?" Kim said "action speaks louder than words, go to the dressing room". As they went to the dressing room the models didn't know what to expect. Since these were brand new models they thought they were just trying on the regular dresses with the bulky corset. So what is the big deal? When they got in the dressing room they looked for the corset and looked confused. They both asked Kim "where is..." Kim immediately cut them off and said "step into the dress"! Both immediately did and looked amazed. As they were pulling it up to the waist they noticed they had to slip into the sleeves before they could zip up. They were looking to be zipped up in the back. As they slipped into the sleeves they noticed there was no back, and the zippers were on the side. As they zipped up the zippers they noticed a firm tightness in the belly. A nice snug fit. The smiles showed on their face as Kim put her finger to her mouth to show silence. Then Kim stepped forward and gave both of them shawls and told them, only after your complete walk do you want to put the shawl on. Both models were shocked so they asked about the zippers. Kim asked "does the fit explain everything?" The big busted model says" you are a genius, I can throw the corset away!" The smaller busted women states "this is like a tailor made fit!" Kim says "thank you" and shows the models the runway. As the judges see the smiles on all the models, they too were amazed. The models had three dress changes and were back on the runway in the quickest of time. This made the judges very inquisitive. Kim took the female judges aside and pulled them to the dressing room to show them the way the dress had to be put on quieting all their questions. The male models had the same reaction from the judges. The judges liked all of the three different coats or suits on the men and were impressed that a lady came up with the ideas.

The Queen and Elizabeth were gloating with each other about the success that Kim had. Everything was coming together. Just as the Queen planned. This was easier than taxing the peasants. Just thinking of all the money that would come in off the new fashions made the Queen excited. The Queen knew that she had six more months of Kim and she started to get greedy. She started to think of other fashion avenues that would help the crown.

It seemed like the weekend just flew by. Here it was Monday and 7:00a.m., as Kim squeezed Jack's big hand as they walked to the parlor. As they sat in the parlor drinking coffee, Jack pulled a chair behind Kim and started to massage her shoulders. This made Kim tingle all over. Only Jack her husband could make her feel this way. Jack could feel the tightness in her shoulders slowly begin to dissipate. Jack loved to please his wife. After another ten minutes of the wonderful massage, Kim turned around and pressed her body firmly against his and gave him a sweltering kiss. Then she said" thank you". Jack reminded her of the hunt this weekend and she acknowledged and said" great this is my free weekend for the twins".

It was Tuesday and that meant it was pub night. Jack went down to the pub and met Prince Phillip and Earl to plan for this weekend hunt. For some reason Phillip felt the need to be ornery and cocky.

He started off with the snide remark, "what is the great marksmen up to". Jack played it down and looked around for someone else and then pointing to himself and saying "you talking to me?" This made Phillip have to praise Jack one more time or leave it alone. Phillip decided not to voice his sarcasm again. Earl bought a round of ale for his two partners as he called them and asked "what's the plan for this weekend?" Jack surprised them both by saying "let's be total gentlemen about this hunt. Let's go dead last." "What?" said both Earl and Prince Phillip? They couldn't believe what they heard. They repeated themselves, "what, are you crazy, and let the other blokes have a shot first. You better think this thru". Jack said "precisely, I already have thought it thru. What would the blokes say if they all had a shot before us and we go out and bag the caribou"? This thought process blew both Earl and Phillip away. They began the objections by saying "what if the blokes get the hunt before us?" Jack replies "with, then it wasn't supposed to be. However, what if the opposite happens? That everyone had their shot and we bag it"? Jack heard everything go silent. Then Jack said "trust me on this!" Although Jack and the crew were around the first ones there and received their number he emphatically stated that he wanted to be the last crew out. The judges looked at him strangely and said "that's your decision". Three hours had passed and seven crews had already come and gone with no reward. It was Jack's crew time. Even though he had a beginning number Jack was trying to show his crew about faith. All the cards might seem that they were stacked against them, Jack knew better. Phillip started to go west and Jack stopped him and said "why would you take the same path as everyone else?" Phillip glared back at him and said "everyone else is doing it". "Precisely," said Jack "and what did they come back with...... nothing". Earl interrupted what Phillip was going to say and said "let's listen to him". Jack said "let's turn north and be down wind. The caribou have been smelling these hunters for hours now. If they can't smell us they will think the hunt over and not be in the alarmed state. We want them to relax and drop their guard." Phillip is upset with himself, why did this damn Yankee have to think of this. So they head uphill and north for twenty minutes. Once upon the hill they could see a reserve of caribou all grazing. Jack whispered in their ears "if we do this correctly and all squeeze the trigger on our rifles at the same time we could bag three of them, which would sound like one shot. Please take careful aim and slowly squeeze the trigger." Phillip propped his rifle on a tree branch and gave the okay sign. Earl propped his rifle on a boulder and Jack got off his horse and laid his rifle across the saddle. Jack moisten his guide to see if any wind was blowing. There was no wind, Jack told everyone he had the eight point. He looked at his directional near the scope and had the tip of the antler firmly in scope. Jack motioned on three to shoot. One, two, three. Crack went the sounds of the rifles all at the same time. Jack and Earl had hit the one they aimed at. Phillip had hit dirt next to the ten point. Jack's and Earl's hit immediately fell to the ground. Phillip was perplexed. Why had he missed? Jack saw the confusion on Phillips face and said "we'll talk about it later". After dressing out the caribou they had to go back to base camp and show their reward to the judges. Once back at camp the judges were amazed at two caribou being taken down. They only heard one shot. Jack looks over with a gleam in his eye at Phillip and Earl as they smiled back. The judges confer with one another and come out of their huddle with the decision that only one shot was heard the hunters were allowed to keep their hunt. One of the judges pulled Jack aside and asked "were you the same hunter that bagged that ram around three weeks ago?" Jack admitted "I was". The judge asked "may I see your rifle?" As he looks over the rifle he sees that it is a Henry rifle built between 1860 and 1866. This was a sixteen shot .44 caliber rim fire, lever action breech-loading rifle made famous during the civil war. The judge spoke and said "you have a keeper in this rifle, but what made you purchase this one?" Jack said "the fact it can hold sixteen ammo in one clip. I don't have to stop and reload after every shot. However, that's not my hunting rifle. I have two rifles that I carry. The one I hunt with is on the other side of my saddle. This is an 1861 Springfield model which is known for its distance. The flip-up leaf sight is good for 300-500 yards with both leaves down the sight is good for 100 yards. I get excited about the 500 yard range, which helped me bag the ram three weeks ago." The judge stated "I wish our blokes over here took to their hunting like you do. You are a name to remember". Jack says "thank you." Phillip is excited to get back to Jack. Phillip is feeling pretty worthless right now because of no reward in the hunt. Jack responds "before we get back home, you will have another chance of hunting". Phillips face lights up as if he is thinking there is still hope. The trip back home was beginning to wear on everyone, they were only half way thru, but up on the hill Jack spotted some antelope around four hundred yards away. Jack motioned for Phillip to come over as he pulled his Springfield rifle out. Jack points to the flip up sight one three hundred and one five hundred. Now look at your five hundred sight and remember where its sighting. Now look thru your three hundred sight and remember your sight. Now take note that you will have to be somewhere between the two sightings in order to be successful. Now moisten the sight. If it stays wet there is no wind deflection. Now take your time and hunt. Phillip does everything as told and says a silent prayer as he slowly squeezes the trigger. By the time the rifle let's off the crackling sound Phillip sees the animal go down. He looks to Jack with a smile similar to a child in a candy store. Phillip screams out "thanks, Jack." As Phillip races down to the site that the animal was felled he doesn't see that another party is moving in. Jack tells Earl to flank to the left as he will flank to the right. They both go into a full gallop reaching the five hundred yards in just under a minute. The intruding party is already trying to tell Phillip not to worry about dressing the animal, but if he knows what's good for him, he would take heed and go. Phillip speaks up, "I am afraid I can't do that". The intruding party asks "why not?" Phillip says "there is a gentleman fifty yards behind you, with an 1861 Henry repeating rifle with a sixteen shot clip. This would take care of the first three in the first ten seconds and then if you look to your west fifty yards we have another that would take out the other two". Before Phillip could say any more the riders bolted north bound as fast as possible. Jack reminded Phillip of the question he asked Jack "why do you know so much about hunting!" Phillip knows now, and is very thankful to his hunting party. Now let's dress this animal and get out of here.

    Phillip on the route returning home can't thank Jack enough on teaching him a better way to hunt. Jack acknowledges the compliment and says "thank you". Then he asks, "well, what got you into hunting?" Phillip responds "the thrill of bagging the animal, and having the ability to feed my family". Jack responds with "good answer, is there anything else?" Phillip says "having the ability to be the best there is and after seeing you hunt I have a lot to learn". Jack says "if you have a lot of patience and a lot of practice you will achieve that dream". Earl asks "what gave you the motivation?" "My uncle! As long as I could remember, I never saw him miss a shot. Right then and there at a young age of ten, I told myself if I could be half the hunter my uncle was then I would be satisfied". "Wow!" Earl says "at least you had a role model to look up to". Jack expresses himself "what exactly do you mean?" Earl says "my dad was killed when I was seven so I had no model to copy after". Jack interrupts "let me give you a scenario that few people could ever imagine. Let's imagine that your dad lived and made a good living. However, he was void of ever saying I love you, or teaching you the basics of life. So by outward appearances everything looked normal. But on the inside you almost wanted to beg for companionship. A father and son relationship that was basically okay. But that never happened instead just the opposite happened. He would always tell you how worthless you are. Now compare that to having no dad around. Which would be worse?" Earl replies "well naturally having no dad around would be better than one that makes you feel awful". So let me ask you "is your glass half empty or half full?" Earl and Phillip say "they don't understand". Jack breaks it down for them by saying "imagine you have two glasses on the table. Both of them filled up half way. One can see that if it is half empty, one can say woe is me, their whole life and be right. One can see that the other glass is half full. The same person can say I am happy, I can do anything I set my mind to, my whole life and be right. Now which one of those people would you choose to be?" Both Earl and Phillip say "well naturally, the one who chose the glass that was half full"! "So whatever you do in life, take that attitude with you and see what surprising results you come up with." Earl says "I don't know how you do it all, but if that's the ground work you go by and it has given you that much success, you can count me in." Phillip echoes "me too."

 Back at the castle Victoria has talked extensively to Elisabeth about throwing a dance in the main ballroom. Victoria had something else in mind and she knew if she leaked the information out everything would be ruined. Victoria always had a keen sense of timing about her. She knew that within the hour the gentlemen would be arriving. She called the butler aside and told him to get the sword and the pillow ready. All the servings of meat and vegetables were being brought in from the main kitchen. Victoria made sure that the band was all set up. Victoria was just wondering where Kim was. Just like clockwork Kim came around the corner with twins in tow. Naturally Kim asked "can I help", and Victoria surprised her with "just be with your family".

Kim heard the horses go into the main barn. So she knew that as soon as Jack had curried his horse down he would be coming in. It has always been important to Jack to show respect to his horse by currying the horse down. For some reason, respect was always number one in his mind. The currying would take a good ten minutes. Then he could meet his wife.

Jack changed his clothes and put some good dress jeans on, with a blue plaid flannel shirt. Jack was ready to meet his wife. He headed up to the main ballroom and before he could join his wife, Victoria, the queen had intercepted him. As Victoria raised her hand for the band to start playing, she motioned that the butler would come forward with pillow and sword. Victoria had her circle of the Queen's court at hand. Before Jack knew what was going on, Victoria had started her speech. "As everyone knows Jack has taken a back seat to his wife the head seamstress of our court. He has allowed her to bloom and quite well I might add thru all the public shows. Just recently Jack and his hunting ability has taken care of the ram that has just about terrorized our hunters for the last nine years. With one shot I might add. So with putting his marksmanship ability aside we are here today to knight this young man who will receive the title of "Sir" from here on out". So without further ado she lays the sword on his right shoulder and then his left shoulder and then laying softly upon his head she asks "do you honorably accept this title"? Jack says "I do". As the whole court breaks out in applause, Kim moves to her husband with tears coming down her face, and says "I love you". The band plays on and the party continues till midnight. As Jack leans into Kim and says "I need some extra attention" as Kim replies "I would be happy to oblige." As the hour closes in on the midnight hour, both Kim and Jack await their alone time. This is the time that they share their inner most secrets as it is Jack's turn. Kim can't wait. Jack reassures her that it is worth the wait. As the band starts to shut down, Jack grabs Kim's hand and at a brisk walk quickly leaves the large ballroom. Kim is walking just as fast as she states "whoa, big fellow, what's the rush?" Jack states "it is more than just alone time that I will share with you". As Jack comes to their door and opens the door, Kim sees balloons and streamers everywhere. Kim jokingly replies "I had no idea I excited you this much" Jack states "that will only be an understatement, because you do. However, if you saw this in the small ballroom or the indoor patio with firecrackers going off how would you react?" "Oh, you do have a way of getting a ladies attention. I would be flabbergasted." Kim replies. Jack says "fine, because this is what is going to happen a week from today. I have asked for a favor from Prince Phillip on decorating the indoor patio without permission from the Queen. If she asks what is going on I will say, this is how the westerners celebrate the fourth of July! I am sure she will be shocked, but that is the point. Prince Phillip will explain that he owed me a favor and that we both came up with the idea. Since we also leave in a month this is kind of like a thank you party." Kim grabs his hand and says "I like the way you think, now let me show you how I think…… in private time!"

A week later Prince Phillip had talked Earl and Billy and their spouses to get on over to the indoor patio and decorate. So it was only natural that Earl would ask questions on 'why'. Prince Phillip wasn't exactly honest and said "it was for the Queen." Then when the room was decorated he became honest and told everybody that it was Jack. Then both Earl and Billy spoke up and said "should we add more?" Within the hour Prince Phillip had told the Queen that there was a sense of emergency and that she and Elizabeth should come to the indoor patio as quick as possible. When she got there everybody was already on the inside. As the Queen opened the doors the balloons raised and firecrackers went off. This startled the Queen as she gave off a scream. Then as soon as she settled down Prince Phillip came over and explained, that this is the way our American folk celebrate the fourth of July. Prince Phillip then asked "how do you like?" Well you have definitely surprised me and you are lucky I am in a good mood, as long as you are here do I get the first dance? Phillip responds with a 'yes'. The firecrackers go off for the next half hour. Then Prince Phillip gets up and says "I understand that within the month Jack, Kim and the twins are due to return home. It has been an honor to have known them, both in the hunting circles and the fashion circle. This is our way of saying thank you in advance." The Queen sheds a few tears but for all the wrong reasons. If Kim is not going to be here, will the passion for the fashion stay as high? Who will replace her? The queen believes that the money from her patents will last until she can get someone else. But we are talking about Kim, and her replacement will be hard to find. As the party nears its end the Queen announces that the week before Kim will take off back to America there will be the hunt for the bear. This bear has been tormenting the countryside for the past three years. So immediately Jack feels his passion for hunting.

The three weeks have slowly passed; the hunt will begin within the hour. Kim wishes Jack good luck. The horn sounds and everybody split off and going their own direction. However, Earl, Prince Phillip and Jack stay back for twenty minutes. This confuses the judges. Just as when the judges were going to come over, Earl states to Jack "your teaching didn't fall on deaf ears. Everyone else went in different directions leaving the east direction open. Let's get downwind from the bear so she can't smell us". Jack smiles and says "you have become a knowledgeable pupil". They set off into the east for around thirty minutes. They have one last hill to climb. Jack motions to Earl and Prince Phillip to get off their horses and walk slowly up the hill and get into a prone position at the top of the hill. Earl can barely contain his excitement. Jack says "shhh." Then says" now you know how to take him down. But there is a catch here. Since you are such a giving individual, once you bag him, the meat goes to the Queen and the hide goes to Prince Phillip. As long as the Queen gives you full credit, would it matter?" Earl begins to object and Jack interrupts him and says" this is what giving is all about. You will receive all the blessings overflowing in time, just find it in your heart to do it!" Earl has the bear in his sights, he moistens the guide, there is no wind. The bear is about two hundred yards off. He is aiming at the bears' right ear to hit him in the chest. Since the bear is standing the bullet hits him square in the throat and he falls to the ground. Jack jumps on his horse and tells Earl and Prince Phillip to stay twenty yards behind. As Jack approaches the bear he sees another party coming in and trying to claim the kill. Jack hollers at the man to stay his distance, as he dismounts his horse putting himself behind the horse with rifle drawn. Jack states "what's your business?" The stranger from the west says "I have come to claim what is mine" Jack says "well, we have two options. We can go back to the judges and let them examine the caliber that came from my rifle and they will find out that it came from my rifle and then you will be disgraced the rest of your life, or the two other rifles that are set upon you could blow you right out of your saddle. It is completely your choice!" The stranger eyes the other rifles before he comes to a decision to ride off. Both Earl and Phillip rejoice as they come in to load the animal. They all head back to the judges to finalize the hunt. Earl says to the judges that he will donate the meat to the Queen as everybody's jaw just drops. As they near the castle Earl says to Prince Phillip, "would you like to have the hide?" Prince Phillip says, "Well thank you very much but I couldn't do that to you. Your kill, your hide". Earl says "thank you."

Now it was time for the trip back to America. Kim was overcome with feelings. The friends she made here were fantastic. This might be the last time she ever sees them. Sure she was hoping to get back to her family and friends. There was a lot to catch up on. Kim told herself that she would put it out of her mind, at least until she got well on her way on the ship. Jack was just thankful that the journey home was finally here. Yes, Jack did have a blast over in London, and yes he appreciated the opportunity to show off his hunting ability. But now was time to get back to his side of the world which was the E. &J. Stud farm and the happiness that exuded from Jeremy and the closeness of everybody involved. Well, the ship was shoving off. As everybody stood on the rail waving goodbye, it seemed like an hour had passed before everyone moved away from the rail and got back to business. Jack wanted to go take a nap and if he was lucky that would happen. The trip would take ten days and he had to tell himself that he could make it. Kim had the twins so Jack snuck off to bed. The nap must have gotten the best of him, he started his nap around three and now it was dark. Jack had to find his jacket because that was where his watch was. The time said seven, and it was dark? He had to find Kim. So he headed down to the eating lounge. There sure enough was Kim and the twins eating chicken and working on the brownies. Jack walked up and asked Kim what time it was. Kim said "seven ten." Jack said "I was a little surprised, I feel asleep around three and woke up a few minutes ago, and it was dark." Kim asked Jack "if he was hungry," and he said "yes." Kim had already checked her trunks to make sure the dresses were there. All seven of them. These were the winter ones with the lining of wool and the famous elastic waist. Kim was excited not only because of the dresses but because of the patents she secured. The seas looked choppy ahead as far as Kim was concerned the London chapter in her life was fulfilled. It was the sense of self accomplishment that made her feel so good. Thinking that millions of women would benefit from her designs. At least for now. Kim was wondering if she could just shut her eyes and she would be appearing at the American dock. Well it was time to go to her room and just relax.

A new day meets the dawn, it must be around five thirty in the morning. The sun is just coming up and it looks so beautiful. This reminds Jack of home. Jeremy would be in the barn currying the horses and coffee would be brewing. There are moments in life where you just have to let everything go. All those bombarding thoughts on what could have happened, really isn't important. As Jack looks across the ocean he takes a deep breath of the ocean's air and just remains motionless. A time to be serene. Then Kim's touch glides down his chest and stops at his belt. As Kim says "you look so peaceful, so relaxed, are you foreseeing the landing at the dock and the trip home?" Jack replies, "no, my thoughts were in the barn back home currying the horses and smelling that wonderful coffee. Look at this ocean and relax with all beautiful thoughts. Somehow someone could make money on this, it will come to me." Kim says "that's my darling always thinking". The two remain there for around ten more minutes, just relaxing.

Back in the states the white mares were beginning to foal. This meant they were laying down ready to give birth to the colt. Everyone had to act quickly in case there might be trouble. However, both the mares were blessed with giving birth on the same day. Prayers were being said that the births would go smoothly. So far so good. The first mare was getting restless, she was wanting to move. This meant Jeremy had to get in there and start stroking her neck to calm her down. As Jeremy was doing this Ralph just told him that the other colt was born with no trouble. Now if we can get thru this one, it will be a good day. The horse tried to get up and Jeremy kept her down forcing her to push the colt out. Here it comes. There that wasn't so bad, was it, as Jeremy talks to the horse? Jeremy let's out a yippee, as Esmira and the whole team rejoice. One came out in a painted design of a palomino, color mixed with a swirl of white on the belly and neck. The other came out with a pure white except for a palomino colored star on forehead. Everyone was happy; the colts were nursing so everyone departed.

Back on the ship, about a day from the dock. Kim, Jack and the twins were looking out at the ocean, when they saw dolphins jumping about one hundred yards away. It looked so peaceful. Both Jack and Kim were getting restless. They knew that their journey was about over, but they were terribly homesick. They realized the old saying 'time cures all things'. They also knew it was true. By mid-morning tomorrow they would be docking and enjoying their company. Lunch was being served and it was lamb with mint julep. Wow! The captain knew how to treat his passengers. The food was excellent.

Jeremy, Esmira, Ralph, Bill and Jim got the horses ready plus the buck board for Jack and family. It was a near days' ride up to the port. As the crew left the farm Esmira left instructions with Margaret and Audra about the hog to be roasted in time for when they arrived back. Ralph started to talk about how much he missed Jack and his family. Jim, and Bill agreed, Jack was more than just a hired hand. He was someone that a lot of people looked up to. Now he was coming home and the family would feel whole again. Since they were passing by the shack Jeremy took about a half hour to make sure that everything was okay. It was. Esmira was being extremely quiet and Jeremy asked "why?" Esmira stated "that she was in her quiet mood. However, she whispered in Jeremy's ear that she was feeling extremely well if he knew what she meant." Jeremy just nodded his head letting her know that he understood. It was getting time to make camp for the night. Jeremy had selected a wooded area in case it would rain. But also, they would have enough wood for the fire. Ralph securely tied the horses up while Jim took care of the buck board. It would be a jerky for meat accompanied with hard tack for biscuits kind of meal. Just enough to whet the appetite. Morning would come fast enough the two things Jeremy was concerned with was the fire for warmth and sleep for strength. It looked like a storm was coming in. Maybe Jeremy would get lucky and it would pass. He looked at the sky one more time before he laid his head down to sleep. CRACK was the next sound he heard as the lightning sounded. Jeremy woke up and saw that it was around 6a.m. This put him about a half hour behind. Everyone will have to ride hard for the next fifteen minutes. The buck board was a little shaky for the first five minutes, but it settled down. Now everyone could relax. They could see the dock from here and the tug boat was pulling the big ship into dock. Jeremy and team had made it on time. They could see Kim waving. As the boat was being unloaded, Esmira and Kim were talking like long lost sisters. It sure made the unloading go a lot quicker. Ralph, Bill and Jim were busy making camp so they could have a hearty breakfast before they set out again. Jeremy had bought two dozen eggs from the captain. Esmira and Kim couldn't wait to start cooking. This in when she started to share with Esmira about the servants in the castle and the different food they ate. This made the time fly by as breakfast was cooked and served. Now the only thing Esmira could think of was getting back to the farm in time to enjoy that roasted hog.

Now it was Jack's turn. Jim and Ralph had to hear about all of his expeditions. Ralph told Jack "don't try to down size it either. I want to know all the juicy parts". Jack said "which one the caribou or the grizzly bear or the long horn sheep. Oh! I forgot about the fox hunt". Both Ralph and Jim wanted to hear about the long horn sheep. So in detail Jack told them the whole story which led them right into the Stud farm. At last they were finally home and Kim could smell that delicious cooking. The hog just got finished. Now it was time to eat and share stories about London. Audra and Margaret were the first to ask about the cuisine. Kim and Jack tried to make it short when they volunteered the story about Jack getting knighted. This opened up another can of worms, Knighted? Jack tried to down play this immediately. Jack said "the caribou, the sheep, the bear and the foxes all tasted incredibly great". The hunting was a little bizarre because most of them weren't marksman. It was like they were happy enough just to be in the hunt. Now we had two instances of hunters trying to rob what you just took down. But other than that it was a very good time. Jack stated "That he didn't understand why the room they slept in was bigger than the farm's house. That Jack didn't understand why there was so many servants." Jeremy was concerned about the barns and was shocked when he heard that they were made out of brick. As Kim finished her first plate she went into the story about the big ballroom versus the small ballroom which was twice the size of our barn and house put together. But enough about the trip I am really interested in how

Audra's and Margaret café is working out. Margaret chimes in "with everything going on, we felt better to open our café from April first to September thirtieth. That allows us to keep the space year round and share that space with the ladies auxiliary, when not in use."

The next day has begun and Kim starts to ask how everything is with the boutique. Esmira says "that Gala has kept everything up, but in the last few days she's been acting kind of jittery. I believe she was getting anxious about your returning home. Other than that things have been smooth". Kim replies" I will be right back. I must see Gala and share my good news about some dresses that I brought back. Is she around?" Esmira says "yes, she's been helping Margaret and Audra with the hog; I will send her right up". Esmira goes to Gala and sends her to the boutique. Gala comes to the boutique in tears. Kim asks "what is wrong." Gala confesses her fears that she believes she will be out of a job because Kim is back. Kim looks fiercely at your face and says "don't be silly. Here I will show you why. Kim opens up the trunk and hands her a soft crème color dress, with a large bust line and a short inseam. Just perfect for her size. try it on." Gala steps into the dress looking for the corset to be tied. Kim encourages her just to pull the dress up. Gala does and slips her arms into the sleeves. Kim tells her to just wear it for two hours and tell me what you think. Kim goes on to tell Gala to dry her tears, and please help me unpack." As they start to unpack, Gala finds a letter and asks what it is? Kim says "oh, I knew I put that somewhere. This is my document securing the patents on the dress that you are wearing". Gala says "I don't understand." Kim says "this document tells me, that if anyone wants to copy my dresses without permission from me they could be severely punished! Say how does the dress feel?" Gala says "you are a genius. No corset, extremely comfortable and whatever you did to the sleeves feels very warm". Kim states "that's why I applied for the patents and secured them to protect myself. I am getting hungry after that ride let's eat."

Down at the roasting pit, Audra has started to serve up the helpings as the meat comes easily off the hog. The whole crew all twelve of them were there. Kim stands up and says "although my experiences were phenomenal over there, and I met some wonderful people my heart was still back home. It is so very good to be back home, and since I encountered many different things there, It would be too difficult to put it in one statement. As time goes on I will share my stories on an individual basis. Right now I am hungry." As Kim fills her plate she goes to sit with Jack but sees that he is off sharing his stories. Jack is over with Ralph and Joe sharing the story on the long horn sheep. Jack emphasizes on the direction that he had to take. Letting everyone pick first there direction, then going dead last. Everyone there started to complain. I stated it's better to be up wind from the sheep. That way he won't smell you. I then told them that everyone else came back empty and that should tell you something. Then a half hour later about six hundred yards out I spotted the long horn and took him down with one shot. Joe asks "what was the area like?" Jack says "the areas that we hunted in were very woody so we had to figure a way to flush him out in the open for a clean shot. That was the most challenging, I take that back. Prince Phillip wanted to go in with guns blaring. So to teach him patience and still be respectful to his title was a little unnerving." Ralph says "you were hunting with a prince, what was he like"? Jack says "that will take a whole other day to explain, however for now let's just say he always felt superior to everybody else regardless of the circumstances". Jack continues" let's eat I will have plenty of time in the future to let you know of him."

Back in London Queen Victoria had just sent her messenger off to the post office to apply for her patents on the dresses. Both the elastic waist band versus the corset and the inner sleeves made of wool and the three men suits. The Queen was just reveling with a smile from ear to ear on the money she will secure with the patents in hand. Oh happy were her thoughts. Elizabeth broke her thoughts by being loud. This perturbed the Queen and she voiced her opinion about how Elizabeth needs to learn people skills. That she needs to be aware of people's surroundings, and not think she is the only one in the room. The messenger came back to the Queen with the statement that it would be six weeks before the patents are finished. The Queen thanked him and wished him a good day.

Back at the E.&J. Stud Farm Kim was busy looking at the colts and admiring their beauty. When her husband Jack came behind her and said boo which startled her. Before Kim could say anything Jack said "a little out of your arena here?" and gave her a kiss. Kim replied with "wow! Are you my cowboy or what?" As Jack says "it is so good to be back on American soil". Kim agreed as she gave Jack a kiss. Now it was time to go up to the house grab some coffee and get started on the routine for the day.

Six weeks had passed and it was time to hear the news on the patents. The messenger had just came back from the courts with the news. The messenger bravely approached the Queen with the news. As the Queen opened the scroll, her face went into a deep red rage as she read the news DENIED. She threw the scroll across the room like a child and was immediately reprimanded by Elizabeth when she said "who needs to learn about people skills"? Victoria was extremely upset, she is the queen, and who do they think they are talking to. She grabbed her pen and started to scroll.

> Dear Kim:
>
> I opened up my kingdom to you. I offered you the elite, the very best at every corner. I introduced you to kings of other nations and ambassadors, and this is the way you repay me.
>
> Signed Queen Victoria.

Three weeks later the letter arrived at the E&J stud farm and Kim read it. Kim decided to give the Queen a reply. This is what it said.

> Queen Victoria,
>
> Before I left the United States I had applied for patents on the elastic girdle, the wool sleeves and the men's suits. No question was ever asked me if I had any patents or otherwise. I am sure to thank you for introducing me to everyone you did. My question I have to ask you is 'were you thinking that all the shows I put on that you were to gain handsomely from all my efforts'? Who was thinking of who?
>
> Signed Kimberly Davis.

THE END